Dear Reader:

We were all thinking about summer and what made
it sizzling when we were planning this sixth volume
of *Silhouette Summer Sizzlers*. Ideas were bouncing
around, and then somebody said, "Well, you
remember the great blackout in 1977? Did you
know there was a *significant* rise in the birthrate
exactly nine months after that dark night....?"
Well, that got us thinking!

This year, we hope you enjoy three authors'
versions of what happened when the lights went
out. Linda Howard, Carole Buck and Suzanne
Carey are all bestselling authors and reader
favorites. They have three steamy stories to tell that
should get your temperature rising.

Join us—some like it hot!

The Editors
Silhouette Books

SILHOUETTE

SUMMER Sizzlers '93

LINDA HOWARD
CAROLE BUCK
SUZANNE CAREY

Silhouette® Books

Published by Silhouette Books New York
America's Publisher of Contemporary Romance

SILHOUETTE BOOKS
300 East 42nd St., New York, N.Y. 10017

SILHOUETTE SUMMER SIZZLERS 1993
Copyright © 1993 by Harlequin Enterprises B.V.

ISBN: 0-373-48255-8

Overload
Copyright © 1993 by Linda Howington

Hot Copy
Copyright © 1993 by Carol Buckland

Steam Bath
Copyright © 1993 by Verna Carey

Printed in the U.S.A.

CONTENTS

OVERLOAD

Linda Howard

Chapter One

It was hot, even for Dallas.

The scorching heat of the pavement seared through the thin leather of Elizabeth Major's shoes, forcing her to hurry even though it was an effort to move at all in the suffocating heat. The sleek office building where she worked didn't have its own underground parking garage, the builders having thought it unnecessary, since a parking deck was situated right across the street. Every time Elizabeth crossed the street in the rain, and every time she had risked being broiled by crossing it since this heat wave had begun, she swore that she would start looking for other office space. She always changed her mind as soon as she got inside, but it made her feel better to know she had the option of relocating.

Except for the parking situation, the building was perfect. It was only two years old, and managed to be both charming and convenient. The color scheme in the lobby was a soothing mixture of gray, dark mauve and white, striking the precise balance between masculine and feminine, so both genders felt comfortable. The lush greenery so carefully tended by a professional service added to the sense of freshness and spaciousness. The elevators were both numerous and fast and, so far, reliable. Her office having previously been in an older building where the elevator service had been cramped and erratic, Elizabeth doubly appreciated that last quality.

A private guard service handled the security, with a man stationed at a desk in the lobby for two shifts, from six in the morning until ten at night, as none of the businesses located in the building currently worked a third shift. Anyone wanting to come in earlier than six or stay later than ten had to let the guard service know. There was a rumor that the data processing firm on the tenth floor was considering going to three full shifts, and if that happened there would be a guard on duty around the clock. Until then, the building was locked down tight at 10:00 p.m. on weekdays and at 6:00 p.m. on weekends.

She pushed open the first set of doors and sighed with relief as the cool air rushed to greet her, washing over her hot face, evaporating the uncomfortable sweat that had formed in the time it had taken her to park her car and cross the street. When she entered the lobby itself through the second set of heavy glass doors, the full benefit of air conditioning swirled around her, making her shiver uncontrollably for just a second. Her panty hose had been clinging uncomfortably to her damp legs, and now the clammy feel made her grimace. For all that, however, she was jubilant as she crossed the lobby to the bank of elevators.

A big, unkempt man, a biker from the looks of him, entered the elevator just ahead of her. Immediately alert and wary, Elizabeth shifted her shoulder bag to her left shoulder, leaving her right hand unencumbered, as she stepped in and immediately turned to punch the button for the fifth floor, only to see a big, callused hand already pressing it. She aimed a vague smile, the kind people give each other in elevators, at the big man, then resolutely kept her gaze on the doors in front of her as they were whisked silently and rapidly to the fifth floor. But she relaxed somewhat, for if he was going to the fifth floor, he was undoubtedly involved, in some way, with Quinlan Securities.

She stepped out, and he was right on her heels as she marched down the hallway. Her offices were on the left, the chic interior revealed by the huge windows, and she saw that her secretary, Chickie, was back from lunch on time. Not only that, Chickie looked up and watched her coming down the hall. Or rather, she watched the man behind her. Elizabeth could see Chickie's big dark eyes fasten on the big man and widen with fascination.

Elizabeth opened her office door. The biker, without pausing, opened the door to Quinlan Securities, directly across the hall from her. Quinlan Securities didn't have any windows into the hallway, only a discreet sign on a solid-looking door. She had been glad, on more than one occasion, that there were no windows for more than one reason. The people who went through that door were ... *interesting,* to say the least.

"Wow," Chickie said, her gaze now fastened on the closed door across the hall. "Did you see that?"

"I saw it," Elizabeth said dryly.

Chickie's taste in men, regrettably, tended toward the unpolished variety. "He wore an earring," she said dreamily. "And did you see his hair?"

"Yes. It was long and uncombed."

"What a *mane!* I wonder why he's going into Quinlan's." Chickie's eyes brightened. "Maybe he's a new staffer!"

Elizabeth shuddered at the thought, but it was possible. Unfortunately the "Securities" in Quinlan Securities didn't refer to the financial kind but the physical sort. Chickie, who didn't have a shy bone in her body, had investigated when they had first moved into the building and cheerfully reported that Quinlan handled security of all types, from security systems to bodyguards. To Elizabeth's way of thinking, that didn't explain the type of people they saw coming and going from the Quinlan offices. The clientele, or maybe it was the *staff,* had a decidedly rough edge. If they were the former, she couldn't imagine them having enough money to afford security services. If they were the latter, she likewise couldn't imagine a client feeling comfortable around bodyguards who looked like mass murderers.

She had dated Tom Quinlan, the owner, for a while last winter, but he had been very closemouthed about his business, and she had been wary about asking. In fact, everything about Tom had made her wary. He was a big, macho, take-charge type of man, effortlessly overwhelming in both personality and body. When she had realized how he was taking over her life, she had swiftly ended the relationship and since then gone out of her way to avoid him. She would *not* lose control of her life again, and Tom Quinlan had overstepped the bounds in a big way.

Chickie dragged her attention away from the closed door across the hall and looked expectantly at Elizabeth. "Well?"

Elizabeth couldn't hold back the grin that slowly widened as her triumph glowed through. "She loved it."

"She did? You *got* it?" Chickie shrieked, jumping up and sending her chair spinning.

"I got it. We'll start next month." Her lunch meeting had been with Sandra Eiland, possessor of one of the oldest fortunes in Dallas. Sandra had decided to renovate her lavish hacienda-style house, and Elizabeth had just landed the interior-design account. She had owned her own firm for five years now, and this was the biggest job she had gotten, as well as being the most visible one. Sandra Eiland loved parties and entertained often; Elizabeth couldn't have paid for better advertising. This one account lifted her onto a completely different level of success.

Chickie's enthusiasm was immediate and obvious; she danced around the reception area, her long black hair flying. "Look out, Dallas, we are cooking now!" she crowed. "Today the Eiland account, tomorrow—tomorrow you'll do something else. We are going to be *busy.*"

"I hope," Elizabeth said as she passed through into her office.

"No hoping to it." Chickie followed, still dancing. "It's guaranteed. The phone will be ringing so much I'll have to have an assistant. Yeah, I like the idea of that. Someone else can answer the phone, and I'll chase around town finding the stuff you'll need for all the jobs that will be pouring in."

"If you're chasing around town, you won't be able to watch the comings and goings across the hall," Elizabeth pointed out in a casual tone, hiding her amusement.

Chickie stopped dancing and looked thoughtful. She considered Quinlan's to be her own secret treasure trove of interesting, potential men, far more productive than a singles' bar.

"So maybe I'll have *two* assistants," she finally said. "One to answer the phone, and one to chase around town while I stay here and keep things organized."

Elizabeth laughed aloud. Chickie was such an exuberant person that it was a joy to be around her. Their styles complemented each other, Elizabeth's dry, sometimes acerbic wit balanced by Chickie's unwavering good nature. Where Elizabeth was tall and slim, Chickie was short and voluptuous. Chickie tended toward the dramatic in clothing, so Elizabeth toned down her own choices. Clients didn't like to be overwhelmed or restrained. It was subtle, but the contrast between Elizabeth and Chickie in some way relaxed her clients, reassured them that they wouldn't be pressured into a style they weren't comfortable with. Of course, sometimes Elizabeth wasn't comfortable with her own style of dress, such as today, when the heat was so miserable and she would have been much happier in shorts and a cotton T-shirt, but she had mentally, and perhaps literally, girded her loins with panty hose. If it hadn't been for the invention of air conditioning, she never would have made it; just crossing the street in this incredible heat was a feat of endurance.

Chickie's bangle bracelets made a tinkling noise as she seated herself across from Elizabeth's desk. "What time are you leaving?"

"Leaving?" Sometimes Chickie's conversational jumps were a little hard to follow. "I just got back."

"Don't you ever listen to the radio? The heat is *hazardous*. The health department, or maybe it's the weather bureau, is warning everyone to stay inside during the hottest part of the day, drink plenty of water, stuff like that. Most businesses are opening only in the mornings, then letting their people go home early so they won't get caught in traffic. I checked around. Just about everyone in the building is closing up by two this afternoon."

Elizabeth looked at the Eiland folder she had just placed on her desk. She could barely wait to get started. "You can go home anytime you want," she said. "I had some ideas about the Eiland house that I want to work on while they're still fresh in my mind."

"I don't have any plans," Chickie said immediately. "I'll stay."

Elizabeth settled down to work and, as usual, soon became lost in the job. She loved interior design, loved the challenge of making a home both beautiful and functional, as well as suited to the owner's character. For Sandra Eiland, she wanted something that kept the flavor of the old Southwest, with an air of light and spaciousness, but also conveyed Sandra's sleek sophistication.

The ringing of the telephone finally disrupted her concentration, and she glanced at the clock, surprised to find that it was already after three o'clock. Chickie answered the call, listened for a moment, then said, "I'll find out. Hold on." She swiveled in her chair to look through the open door into Elizabeth's office. "It's the guard downstairs. He's a substitute, not our regular guard, and he's checking the offices, since he doesn't know anyone's routine. He says that almost everyone else has already gone, and he wants to know how late we'll be here."

"Why don't you go on home now," Elizabeth suggested. "There's no point in your staying later. And tell the guard I'll leave within the hour. I want to finish this sketch, but it won't take long."

"I'll stay with you," Chickie said yet again.

"No, there's no need. Just switch on the answering machine. I promise I won't be here much longer."

"Well, all right." Chickie relayed the message to the guard, then hung up and retrieved her purse from the bottom desk drawer. "I dread going out there," she said. "It might be worth it to wait until after sundown, when it cools down to the nineties."

"It's over five hours until sundown. This is July, remember."

"On the other hand, I could spend those five hours beguiling the cute guy who moved in across the hall last week."

"Sounds more productive."

"And more fun." Chickie flashed her quick grin. "He won't have a chance. See you tomorrow."

"Yes. Good luck." By the time Chickie sashayed out of the office, scarlet skirt swinging, Elizabeth had already become engrossed in the sketch taking shape beneath her talented fingers. She always did the best she could with any design, but she particularly wanted this one to be perfect, not just for the benefit to her career, but because that wonderful old house deserved it.

Her fingers finally cramped, and she stopped for a moment, noticing at the same time how tight her shoulders were, though they usually got that way only when she had been sitting hunched over a sketch pad for several hours. Absently she flexed them and was reaching for the pencil again when she realized what that tightness meant. She made a sound of annoyance when a glance at the clock said that it was 5:20, far later than she had meant to stay. Now she would have to deal with the traffic she had wanted to avoid, with this murderous heat wave making everyone ill-tempered and aggressive.

She stood and stretched, then got her bag and turned off the lights. The searing afternoon sun was blocked by the tall building next door, but there was still plenty of light coming through the tinted windows, and the office was far from dark. As she stepped out into the hall and turned to lock her door, Tom Quinlan exited his office and did the same. Elizabeth carefully didn't look at him, but she felt his gaze on her and automatically tensed. Quinlan had that effect on her, always had. It was one of the reasons she had stopped dating him, though not the biggie.

She had the uncomfortable feeling that he'd been waiting for her, somehow, and she glanced around uneasily, but no one else was around. Usually the building was full of people at this hour, as the workday wound down, but she was acutely aware of the silence around them. Surely they weren't the only two people left! But common sense told her that they were, that everyone else had sensibly gone home early; she wouldn't have any buffer between herself and Quinlan.

He fell into step beside her as she strode down the hall to the elevators. "Don't I even rate a hello these days?"

"Hello," she said.

"You're working late. Everyone else left hours ago."

"You didn't."

"No." He changed the subject abruptly. "Have dinner with me." His tone made it more of an order than an invitation.

"No, thank you," she replied as they reached the elevators. She punched the Down button and silently prayed for the elevator to hurry. The sooner she was away from this man, the safer she would feel.

"Why not?"

"Because I don't want to."

A soft chime signaled the arrival of a car; the elevator doors slid open, and she stepped inside. Quinlan followed, and the doors closed, sealing her inside with him. She reached out to punch the ground-floor button, but he caught her hand, moving so that his big body was between her and the control panel.

"You do want to, you're just afraid."

Elizabeth considered that statement, then squared her shoulders and looked up at his grim face. "You're right. I'm afraid. And I don't go out with men who scare me."

He didn't like that at all, even though he had brought up the subject. "Are you afraid I'll hurt you?" he demanded in a disbelieving tone.

"Of course not!" she scoffed, and his expression relaxed. She knew she hadn't quite told the truth, but that was her business, not his, a concept he had trouble grasping. Deftly she tugged her hand free. "It's just that you'd be a big complication, and I don't have time for that. I'm afraid you'd really mess up my schedule."

His eyes widened incredulously, then he exploded. "Hellfire, woman!" he roared, the sound deafening in the small enclosure. "You've been giving me the cold shoulder for over six months because you don't want me to interfere with your *schedule?*"

She lifted one shoulder in a shrug. "What can I say? We all have our priorities." Deftly she leaned past him and punched the button, and the elevator began sliding smoothly downward.

Three seconds later it lurched to a violent stop. Hurled off balance, Elizabeth crashed into Quinlan; his hard arms wrapped around her as they fell, and he twisted his muscular body to cushion the impact for her. Simultaneously the lights went off, plunging them into complete darkness.

Chapter Two

The red emergency lights blinked on almost immediately, bathing them in a dim, unearthly glow. She didn't, couldn't move, not just yet; she was paralyzed by a strange mixture of alarm and pleasure. She lay sprawled on top of Quinlan, her arms instinctively latched around his neck while his own arms cradled her to him. She could feel the heat of his body even through the layers of their clothing, and the musky man-scent of his skin called up potent memories of a night when there had been no clothing to shield her from his heat. Her flesh quickened, but her spirit rebelled, and she pushed subtly against him in an effort to free herself. For a second his arms tightened, forcing her closer, flattening her breasts against the hard muscularity of his chest. The red half-light darkened his blue eyes to black, but even so, she could read the determination and desire revealed in them.

The desire tempted her to relax, to sink bonelessly into his embrace, but the determination had her pulling back. Almost immediately he released her, though she sensed his reluctance, and rolled to his feet with a lithe, powerful movement. He caught her arms and lifted her with ridiculous ease. "Are you all right? Any bruises?"

She smoothed down her skirt. "No, I'm fine. You?"

He grunted in reply, already opening the panel that hid the emergency phone. He lifted the receiver and punched the button that would alert Maintenance. Elizabeth waited, but he didn't say anything. His dark brows drew together, and finally he slammed the receiver down. "No answer. The maintenance crew must have gone home early, like everyone else."

She looked at the telephone. There was no dial on it, no buttons other than that one. It was connected only to Maintenance, meaning they couldn't call out on it.

Then she noticed something else, and her head lifted. "The air has stopped." She lifted her hand to check, but there was no cool air blowing from the vents. The lack of noise had alerted her.

"The power must be off," he said, turning his attention to the door.

The still air in the small enclosure was already becoming stuffy. She didn't like the feeling, but she refused to let herself get panicky. "It probably won't be long before it comes back on."

"Normally I'd agree with you, if we weren't having a heat wave, but the odds are too strong that it's a system overload, and if that's the case, it can take hours to repair. We have to get out. These lights are battery operated and won't stay on long. Not only that, the heat will build up, and we don't have water or enough oxygen in here." Even as he spoke, he was attacking the elevator doors with his strong fingers, forcing them open inch by inch. Elizabeth added her strength to his, though she was aware that he could handle it perfectly well by himself. It was just that she couldn't tolerate the way he had of taking over and making her feel so useless.

They were stuck between floors, with about three feet of the outer doors visible at the bottom of the elevator car. She helped him force open those doors, too. Before she could say anything, he had lowered himself through the opening and swung lithely to the floor below.

He turned around and reached up for her. "Just slide out. I'll catch you."

She sniffed, though she was a little apprehensive about what she was going to try. It had been a long time since she had done anything that athletic. "Thanks, but I don't need any help. I took gymnastics in college." She took a deep, preparatory breath, then swung out of the elevator every bit as gracefully as he had, even encumbered as she was with her shoulder bag and handicapped by her high heels. His dark brows arched, and he silently applauded. She bowed. One of the things that she had found most irresistible about Quinlan was the way she had been able to joke with him. Actually there was a lot about him that she'd found irresistible, so much so that she had ignored his forcefulness and penchant for control, at least until she had found that report in his apartment. She hadn't been able to ignore that.

"I'm impressed," he said.

Wryly she said, "So am I. It's been years."

"You were on the college gymnastics team, huh? You never told me that before."

"Nothing to tell, because I *wasn't* on the college team. I'm too tall to be really good. But I took classes, for conditioning and relaxation."

"From what I remember," he said lazily, "you're still in great shape."

Elizabeth wheeled away and began walking briskly to the stairs, turning her back on the intimacy of that remark. She could feel him right behind her, like a great beast stalking its prey. She pushed open the door and stopped in her tracks. "Uh-oh."

The stairwell was completely dark. It wasn't on an outside wall, but it would have been windowless in any case. The hallway was dim, with only one office on that floor having interior windows, but the stairwell was stygian. Stepping into it would be like stepping into a well, and she felt a sudden primal instinct against it.

"No problem," Quinlan said, so close that his breath stirred her hair and she could feel his chest brush against her back with each inhalation. "Unless you have claustrophobia?"

"No, but I might develop a case any minute now."

He chuckled. "It won't take that long to get down. We're on the third floor, so it's four short flights and out. I'll hold the door until you get your hand on the rail."

Since the only alternative was waiting there until the power came back on, Elizabeth shrugged, took a deep breath as if she were diving and stepped into the dark hole. Quinlan was so big that he blocked most of the light, but she grasped the rail and went down the first step. "Okay, stay right there until I'm with you," he said, and let the door close behind him as he stepped forward.

She had the immediate impression of being enclosed in a tomb, but in about one second he was beside her, his arm stretched behind her back with that hand holding the rail, while he held her other arm with his free hand. In the warm, airless darkness she felt utterly surrounded by his strength. "I'm not going to fall," she said, unable to keep the bite from her voice.

"You're sure as hell not," he replied calmly. He didn't release her.

"Quinlan—"

"Walk."

Because it was the fastest way to get out of his grasp, she walked. The complete darkness was disorienting at first, but she pictured the stairs in her mind, found the rhythm of their placement, and managed to go down at almost normal speed. Four short flights, as he had said. Two flights separated by a landing constituted one floor. At the end of the fourth flight he released her, stepped forward a few steps and found the door that opened onto the first floor. Gratefully Elizabeth hurried into the sunlit lobby. She knew it was all in her imagination, but she felt as if she could breathe easier with space around her.

Quinlan crossed rapidly to the guard's desk, which was unoccupied. Elizabeth frowned. The guard was always there—or rather, he had always been there before, because he certainly wasn't *now*.

When he reached the desk, Quinlan immediately began trying to open the drawers. They were all locked. He straightened and yelled, "Hello?" His deep voice echoed in the eerily silent lobby.

Elizabeth groaned as she realized what had happened. "The guard must have gone home early, too."

"He's supposed to stay until everyone is out."

"He was a substitute. When he called the office, Chickie told him that I would leave before four. If there were other stragglers, he must have assumed that I was among them. What about you?"

"Me?" Quinlan shrugged, his eyes hooded. "Same thing."

She didn't quite believe him, but she didn't pursue it. Instead she walked over to the inner set of doors that led to the outside and tugged at them. They didn't budge. Well, great. They were locked in. "There has to be some way out of here," she muttered.

"There isn't," he said flatly.

She stopped and stared at him. "What do you mean, 'there isn't'?"

"I mean the building is sealed. Security. Keeps looters out during a power outage. The glass is reinforced, shatterproof. Even if we called the guard service and they sent someone over, they couldn't unlock the doors until the electricity was restored. It's like the vault mechanisms in banks."

"Well, you're the security expert. Get us out. Override the system somehow."

"Can't be done."

"Of course it can. Or are you admitting there's something you can't do?"

He crossed his arms over his chest and smiled benignly. "I mean that I designed the security system in this building, and it can't be breached. At least, not until the power comes back on. Until then, I can't get into the system. No one can."

Elizabeth caught her breath on a surge of fury, more at his attitude than the circumstances. He just looked so damn *smug*.

"So we call 911," she said.

"Why?"

"What do you mean, why? We're stuck in this building!"

"Is either of us ill? Hurt? Are we in any danger? This isn't an emergency, it's an inconvenience, and believe me, they have their hands full with real emergencies right now. And they can't get into the building, either. The only possible way out is to climb to the roof and be lifted off by helicopter, but that's an awful lot of expense and trouble for someone who isn't in any danger. We have food and water in the building. The sensible thing is to stay right here."

Put that way, she grudgingly accepted that she had no choice. "I know," she said with a sigh. "It's just that I feel so... trapped." In more ways than one.

"It'll be fun. We'll get to raid the snack machines—"

"They operate on electricity, too."

"I didn't say we'd use money," he replied, and winked at her. "Under the circumstances, no one will mind."

She would mind. She dreaded every minute of this, and it could last for *hours*. The last thing she wanted to do was spend any time alone with Quinlan, but it looked as if she had no choice. If only she could relax in his company, she wouldn't mind, but that was beyond her ability. She felt acutely uncomfortable with him, her tension compounded of several different things: uppermost was anger that he had dared to pry into her life the way he had; a fair amount of guilt, for she knew she owed him at least an explanation, and the truth was still both painful and embarrassing; a sort of wistfulness, because she had enjoyed so much about him; and desire—God, yes, a frustrated desire that had been feeding for months on the memory of that one night they had spent together.

"We don't have to worry about the air," he said, looking around at the two-story lobby. "It'll get considerably warmer in here, but the insulation and thermal-glazed windows will keep it from getting critically hot. We'll be okay."

She forced herself to stop fretting and think sensibly. There was no way out of this situation, so she might as well make the best of it, and that meant staying as comfortable as they could. In this case, comfortable meant cool. She began looking around; as he'd said, they had food and water, though they would have to scrounge for it, and there was enough furniture here in the lobby to furnish several living rooms, so they had plenty of cushions to fashion beds. Her mind skittered away from that last thought. Her gaze fell on the stairway doors, and the old saying "hot air rises" came to mind. "If we open the bottom stairway doors, that'll create a chimney effect to carry the heat upward," she said.

"Good idea. I'm going to go back up to my office to get a flashlight and raid the snack machine. Is there anything you want from your office while I'm up there?"

Mentally she ransacked her office, coming up with several items that might prove handy. "Quite a bit, actually. I'll go with you."

"No point in both of us climbing the stairs in the dark," he said casually. "Just tell me what you want."

That was just like him, she thought irritably, wanting to do everything himself and not involve her. "It makes more sense if we both go. You can pilfer your office for survival stuff, and I'll pilfer mine. I think I have a flashlight, too, but I'm not certain where it is."

"It's eight flights, climbing, this time, instead of going down," he warned her, looking down at her high heels.

In answer, she stepped out of her shoes and lifted her eyebrows expectantly. He gave her a thoughtful look, then gave in without more argument, gesturing her ahead of him. He relocated a large potted tree to hold the stairway door propped open, handling it as casually as if the big pot didn't weigh over a hundred pounds. Elizabeth had a good idea how heavy it was, however, for she loved potted plants and her condo was always full of greenery. She wondered how it would feel to have such strength, to possess Quinlan's basic self-confidence that he could handle any situation or difficulty. With him, it was even more than mere confidence; there was a certain arrogance, subtle but unmistakably there, the quiet arrogance of a man who knew his own strengths and skills. Though he had adroitly sidestepped giving out any personal information about his past, she sensed that some of those skills were deadly.

She entered the stairwell with less uneasiness this time, for there was enough light coming in through the open door to make the first two flights perfectly visible. Above that, however, they proceeded in thick, all-encompassing darkness. As he had before, Quinlan passed an arm behind her back to grip the rail, and his free hand held her elbow. His hand had always been there whenever they had gone up or down steps, she remembered. At first it had been pleasurable, but soon she had felt a little smothered, and then downright alarmed. Quinlan's possessiveness had made her uneasy, rather than secure. She knew too well how such an attitude could get out of hand.

Just to break the silence she quipped, "If either of us smoked, we'd have a cigarette lighter to light our path."

"If either of us smoked," he came back dryly, "we wouldn't have the breath to climb the stairs."

She chuckled, then saved her energy to concentrate on the steps. Climbing five floors wasn't beyond her capabilities, but it was still an effort. She was breathing hard by the time they reached the fifth floor, and the darkness was becoming unnerving. Quinlan stepped forward and opened the door, letting in a sweet spill of light.

They parted ways at their respective offices, Quinlan disappearing into his while Elizabeth unlocked hers. The late-afternoon light was still spilling brightly through the windows, reminding her that, in actuality, very little time had passed since the elevator had lurched to a halt. A disbelieving glance at her wristwatch said that it had been less than half an hour.

The flashlight was the most important item, and she searched the file cabinets until she found it. Praying that the batteries weren't dead, she thumbed the switch and was rewarded by a beam of light. She switched it off and placed it on Chickie's desk. She and Chickie made their own coffee, as it was both more convenient and better tasting than the vending machine kind, so she got their cups and put them on the desk next to the flashlight. Drinking from them would be easier than splashing water into their mouths with their hands, and she knew Chickie wouldn't mind if Quinlan used her cup. Quite the contrary.

Knowing that her secretary had an active sweet tooth, Elizabeth began rifling the desk drawers, smiling in appreciation when she found a six-pack of chocolate bars with only one missing, a new pack of fig bars, chewing gum, a honey bun and a huge blueberry muffin. Granted, it was junk food, but at least they wouldn't be hungry. Finally she got two of the soft pillows that decorated the chairs in her office, thinking that they would be more comfortable for sleeping than the upholstered cushions downstairs.

Quinlan opened the door, and she glanced at him. He had removed his suit jacket and was carrying a small black leather bag. He looked at her loot and laughed softly. "Were you a scout, by any chance?"

"I can't take the credit for most of it. Chickie's the one with a sweet tooth."

"Remind me to give her a big hug the next time I see her."

"She'd rather have you set her up on a date with that biker who came in after lunch."

He laughed again. "Feeling adventurous, is she?"

"Chickie's *always* adventurous. Was he a client?"

"No."

She sensed that that was all the information he was going to give out about the "biker." As always, Quinlan was extremely closemouthed about his business, both clients and staff. On their dates, he had always wanted to talk about *her*, showing interest in every little detail of her life, while at the same time gently stonewalling her tentative efforts to find out more about him. It hadn't been long before that focused interest, coupled with his refusal to talk about himself, had begun making her extremely uncomfortable. She could understand not wanting to talk about certain things; there was a certain period that she couldn't bring herself to talk about, either, but Quinlan's secretiveness had been so absolute that she didn't even know if he had any family. On the other hand, he had noticed the gap in her own life and had already started asking probing little questions when she had broken off the relationship.

There was a silk paisley shawl draped across a chair, and Elizabeth spread it across the desk to use as an upscale version of a hobo's pouch. As she began piling her collection in the middle of the shawl, Quinlan casually flicked at the fringe with one finger. "Do people actually buy shawls just because they look good draped across chairs?"

"Of course. Why not?"

"It's kind of silly, isn't it?"

"I guess it depends on your viewpoint. Do you think it's silly when people spend hundreds of dollars on mag wheels for their cars or trucks, just because they look good?"

"Cars and trucks are useful."

"So are chairs," she said dryly. She gathered the four corners of the shawl together and tied them in a knot. "Ready."

"While we're up here, we need to raid the snack machines, rather than rely on what you have there. There's no point in making extra trips upstairs to get more food when we can get it now."

She gave him a dubious look. "Do you think we'll be here so long that we'll need that much food?"

"Probably not, but I'd rather have too much than too little. We can always return what we don't eat."

"Logical," she admitted.

He turned to open the door for her, and Elizabeth stared in shock at the lethal black pistol tucked into his waistband at the small of his back. "Good God," she blurted. "What are you going to do with that?"

Chapter Three

He raised his eyebrows. "Whatever needs doing," he said mildly.

"Thank you so much for the reassurance! Are you expecting any kind of trouble? I thought you said the building was sealed."

"The building *is* sealed, and no, I'm not expecting any trouble. That doesn't mean I'm going to be caught unprepared if I'm wrong. Don't worry about it. I'm always armed, in one way or another. It's just that this is the first time you've noticed."

She stared at him. "You don't usually carry a pistol."

"Yes, I do. You wouldn't have noticed it now if I hadn't taken my coat off."

"You didn't have one the night we—" She cut off the rest of the sentence.

"Made love?" He finished it for her. His blue eyes were steady, watchful. "Not that night, no. I knew I was going to make love to you, and I didn't want to scare you in any way, so I locked the pistol in the glove compartment before I picked you up. But I had a knife in my boot. Just like I do now."

It was difficult to breathe. She fought to suck in a deep breath as she bypassed the issue of the pistol and latched on to the most shocking part of what he'd just said. "You *knew* we were going to make love?"

He gave her another of those thoughtful looks. "You don't want to talk about that right now. Let's get finished here and get settled in the lobby before dark so we can save the batteries in the flashlights."

It was another logical suggestion, except for the fact that night wouldn't arrive until about nine o'clock, giving them plenty of time. She leaned back against the desk and crossed her arms. "Why don't I want to talk about it now?"

"Just an assumption I made. You've spent over half a year avoiding me, so I didn't think you would suddenly want to start an in-depth discussion. If I'm wrong, by all means let's talk." A sudden dangerous glitter lit his eyes. "Was I too rough? Was five times too many? I don't think so, because I could feel your climaxes squeezing me," he said bluntly. "Not to mention the way you had your legs locked around me so tight I could barely move. And I know damn good and well I don't snore or talk in my sleep, so just what in hell happened to send you running?"

His voice was low and hard, and he had moved closer so that he loomed over her. She had never seen him lose control, but as she saw the rage in his eyes she knew that he was closer to doing so now than she had ever imagined. It shook her a little. Not because she was afraid of him—at least, not in that way—but because she hadn't imagined it would have mattered so much to him.

Then she squared her shoulders, determined not to let him take charge of the conversation and turn it back on her the way he had so many times. "What do you mean, you *knew* we would make love that night?" she demanded, getting back to the original subject.

"Just what I said."

"How could you have been so sure? *I* certainly hadn't planned on it happening."

"No. But I knew you wouldn't turn me down."

"You know a damn lot, don't you?" she snapped, incensed by that unshakable self-confidence of his.

"Yeah. But I don't know why you ran afterward. So why don't you tell me? Then we can get the problem straightened out and pick up where we left off."

She glared at him, not budging. He ran his hand through his dark hair, which he kept in a short, almost military cut. He was so controlled, it was one of the few gestures of irritation she could ever remember him making. "All right," he muttered. "I knew you were hiding things from me, maybe because you didn't trust what was between us. I thought that once we'd made love, once you knew you belonged to me, you'd trust me and stop holding back."

She forgot to glare. Her arms dropped to her sides, and she gaped at him. "I *belong* to you? I beg your pardon! Do you have a bill of sale that I don't know about?"

"Yes, belong!" he barked. "I had planned on marriage, kids, the whole bit, but you kept edging away from me. And I didn't know why. I still don't."

"Marriage? Kids?" She could barely speak, she was so astounded. The words came out in a squeak. "I don't suppose it ever occurred to you to let me in on all of this planning you were doing, did it? No, don't bother to answer. You made up your mind, and that was it, regardless of how *I* felt."

"I knew how you felt. You were in love with me. You still are. That's why it doesn't make sense that you ran."

"Maybe not to you, but it's crystal clear to me." She looked away, her face burning. She hadn't realized her feelings had been so obvious to him, though she had known fairly early in their relationship that she loved him. The more uneasy she had become, however, the more she had tried to hide the intensity of her feelings.

"Then why don't you let me in on the secret? I'm tired of this. Whatever it is I did, I apologize for it. We've wasted enough time."

His arrogance was astonishing, even though she had recognized that part of his character from the beginning. Quinlan was generally a quiet man, but it was the quietness of someone who had nothing to prove, to himself or anyone else. He had decided to put an end to the situation, and that was that, at least from his viewpoint.

But not from hers.

"You listen to me, Tom Quinlan," she said furiously. "I don't care what plans you've made, you can just write me out of them. I don't want—"

"I can't do that," he interrupted.

"Why not?"

"Because of this."

She saw the glitter in his eyes and immediately bolted away from the desk, intent on escape. She was quick, but he was quicker. He seized her wrists and folded her arms behind her back, effectively wrapping her in his embrace at the same time. The pressure of his iron-muscled arms forced her against the hard planes of his body. Having seen him naked, she knew that his clothing disguised his true strength and muscularity, knew that she didn't have a prayer of escaping until he decided to release her. She declined to struggle, contenting herself with a furious glare.

"Cat eyes," he murmured. "The first time I saw you, I knew you were no lady. Your eyes give you away. And I was right, thank God. The night we spent together proved that you don't give a damn about what's proper or ladylike. You're wild and hot, and we wrecked my bed. You should have known there's no way in hell I'd let you go."

He was aroused. She could feel his hardness thrusting against her, his hips moving ever so slightly in a nestling motion, wordlessly trying to tempt her into opening her thighs to cradle him. It *was* tempting. Damn tempting. She couldn't deny wanting him, had never tried to, but he was right: she didn't trust him.

"It won't work," she said hoarsely.

"It already has." The words were soft, almost crooning, and his warm breath washed over her mouth a second before his lips were there, firm and hot, his head slanting to deepen the kiss and open her mouth to him. She hadn't meant to do so, but she found herself helpless to prevent it. Right from the beginning, his kisses had made her dizzy with delight. His self-confidence was manifested even in this; there was no hesitancy, no awkwardness. He simply took her mouth as if it were his right, his tongue probing deep, and a deep shudder of pleasure made her quake.

Held against him as she was, she could feel the tension in his body, feel his sex throbbing with arousal. He had never made any effort to disguise his response to her. Though it had been obvious even on their first date, he hadn't pressured her in any way. Maybe she had started falling in love with him then, because he had been both amused and matter-of-fact about his frequent arousal, his attitude being that it was a natural result of being in her company. She hadn't felt threatened in any way; in fact, looking back, she realized that Quinlan had gone out of his way to keep from alarming her. He had been remarkably unaggressive, sexually speaking, despite the persistent evidence of his attraction. She had never felt that she might have to face a wrestling match at the end of an evening. Even the night they had made love, she hadn't fully realized the seriousness of his kisses until she had somehow found herself naked in bed with him, her body on fire with need. Then she had discovered that he was very serious, indeed.

The memory made her panic, and she tore her mouth away from his. She had no doubt that if she didn't stop him now, within five minutes he would be making love to her. The hot sensuality of his kisses was deceptive, arousing her more and faster than she'd expected. It had been the same way that one night. He had just been kissing her; then, before she knew it, she had been wild for him. She hadn't known such intense heat and pleasure had existed, until then.

"What's wrong?" he murmured, reclaiming her mouth with a series of swift, light kisses that nevertheless burned. "Don't you like it? Or do you like it too much?"

His perceptiveness alarmed her even more, and despite herself she began to struggle. To her surprise, he released her immediately, though he didn't step back.

"Tell me what went wrong, babe." His tone was dark and gentle. "I can't make it right if I don't know what it is."

She put her hands on his chest to force him away and was instantly, achingly aware of his hard, warm flesh covered only by a thin layer of cotton. She could even feel the roughness of his hair, the strong, heavy beat of his heart pulsing beneath her fingers. "Quinlan—"

"Tell me," he cajoled, kissing her again.

Desperately she slipped sideways, away from him. Her body felt overheated and slightly achy. If she didn't tell him, he would persist in his seductive cajoling, and she didn't know how long she could resist him. "All right." She owed him that much. She didn't intend to change her mind about dating him, but at least he deserved an explanation. She should have told him before, but at the time all she had wanted was to stay as far away from him as possible. "But . . . later.

Not right now. We need to get everything gathered up and get settled in the lobby.''

He straightened, amusement in his eyes. ''Where have I heard that before?''

''It isn't polite to gloat.''

''Maybe not, but it's sure as hell satisfying.''

She was nervous. Quinlan was surprised at the depth of her uneasiness, because that wasn't a trait he associated with Elizabeth. He wondered at the cause of it, just as he had wondered for the past six months why she had run from him so abruptly after spending the night in his arms. She wasn't afraid of him; that was one of the things he liked best about her. For him to find women attractive, they had to be intelligent, but unfortunately that intelligence tended to go hand in glove with a perceptiveness that made them shy away from him.

He couldn't do anything about his aura of dangerousness, because he couldn't lose the characteristics, the habits or the instincts that made him dangerous. He didn't even want to. It was as much a part of him as his bones, and went as deep. He had made do with shallow relationships for the sake of physical gratification, but inside he had been waiting and watching. Though the life he had led sometimes made him feel as if only a few people in this world really *saw* what went on around them, that most people went through life wearing blinders, now that he was mostly out of the action he wanted the normalcy that the average person took for granted. He wanted a wife and fam-

ily, a secure, settled life; as soon as he had met Elizabeth, he had known that she was the one he wanted.

It wasn't just her looks, though God knew he broke
out in a sweat at the sight of her. She was a little over
average height, as slim as a reed, with sleek dark hair
usually pulled back in a classic chignon. She had the
fast lines of a thoroughbred, and until he had met her,
he hadn't known how sexy that was. But it was her
eyes that had gotten him. Cat eyes, he'd told her, and
it was true, but though they were green, it was more
the expression in them than the color that made them
look so feline. Elizabeth's nature shone in her eyes.
She had given him a warning look that had said she
wasn't intimidated by him at all, underlaid by a cool
disdain that was certainly catlike.

Excitement and arousal had raced through him. The
more he'd learned about her, the more determined he
had been to have her. She was sharply intelligent,
witty, sarcastic at times and had a robust sense of humor that sometimes caught him off guard, though it
always delighted him. And she burned with an inner
intensity that drew him as inexorably as a magnet
draws steel.

The intensity of his attraction had caught him off
guard. He wanted to know everything there was to
know about her, even her childhood memories, because that was a time in her life that would be forever
closed to him. He wanted to have children with her
and was fascinated by the possibility of a daughter in
Elizabeth's image, a small, strong-willed, sharp-
tongued, dimpled cherub. Talking about Elizabeth's

own childhood made that possibility seem tantalizingly real.

At first Elizabeth had talked openly, with that faint arrogance of hers that said she had nothing to hide and he could like it or lump it. But then he had begun to sense that she *was* hiding something. It wasn't anything he could put his finger on; it was more of a withdrawal from him, as if she had built an inner wall and had no intention of letting him progress past that point.

Both his training and his nature made it impossible for him just to let it pass. Her withdrawal didn't make sense, because he *knew,* knew with every animal instinct in him that she felt the same way he did. She wanted him. She loved him. If she were truly hiding something, he wanted to know about it, and he had both the skill and the resources to find out just about anything in a person's life. His inquiries had turned up the fact that she had been married before, but the marriage had seemed to be fairly typical, and fairly brief, the sort of thing a lot of college graduates drifted into, quickly finding out they didn't suit. He'd had his own short fling with marriage at that age, so he knew how it happened. But the more he'd thought about it, the more he'd noticed that the period of her marriage was the one period she didn't talk about, not even mentioning that she'd ever been married at all. He was too good at what he did not to realize the significance of that, and he had begun to probe for answers about those two missing years. At the same time, feeling her slipping away from him, he had made a bold move to cement their relationship and taken her to bed, trusting in the bonds of the flesh to both break down the barriers and hold her to him until she learned to trust him completely.

It hadn't worked.

She had fled the next morning while he was still in the shower, and this was the first time he'd gotten her alone since then.

Over half a year wasted. Almost seven long damn months, endless nights spent in burning frustration, both physical and mental.

But he had her now, all alone, and before they left this building he intended to know just what the hell happened and have her back where she belonged, with him.

Chapter Four

"Let's get those snack machines raided," she muttered, grabbing up her ditty bag of goodies and heading for the door. Quinlan had been standing there, staring at her for what seemed like several minutes but had probably been less than thirty seconds. There was a hooded, predatory expression in his gleaming blue eyes, and she just couldn't stand there, like a tethered goat, for another second.

He sauntered out in her wake, and she relocked the office door, then looked up and down the dim hallway. "Just where *are* these snack machines?" she finally asked. "I'm not a junk food junkie, so I've never used them."

"There's a soft drink machine at this end of the hallway," he said, pointing, "but there are snack machines in the insurance offices. They have a break room for their employees, but they let us use them." He set off down the long hallway, away from the bank of elevators, and Elizabeth trailed after him.

"How are we going to get in?" she asked caustically. "Shoot the lock off?"

"If I have to," he replied, lazy good humor in his voice. "But I don't think it will come to that."

She hoped not. From what she could tell, insurance companies tended to be rather humorless about such things. She could well imagine receiving a bill for damages, which she could certainly do without.

Quinlan knelt in front of the insurance company's locked door and unzipped the leather bag, taking from it a small case resembling the one in which she kept her makeup brushes. He flipped it open, though, and the resemblance ended. Instead of plush brushes, there was an assortment of oddly shaped metal tools. He took two of them out, inserted the long, thin, bent one into the keyhole, then slid the other instrument in beside it and jiggled it with small, delicate movements.

Elizabeth sidled closer, bending down to get a better look. "Can you teach me how to do that?" she asked in an absent tone, fascinated with the process.

The corners of his mouth twitched as he continued to gingerly work at the lock. "Why? Have you just discovered a larcenous streak?"

"Do *you* have one?" she shot back. "It just seems like a handy skill to have, since you never know when you'll accidentally lock yourself out."

"And you're going to start carrying a set of locksmith's tools in your purse?"

"Why not?" She nudged the black leather bag with her toe. "Evidently you carry one in yours."

"That isn't a purse. Ah," he said with satisfaction, as he felt the lock open. He withdrew the slender tools, stored them in their proper places in the case and replaced the case in the bag. Then he calmly opened the door.

"Explain the difference between my purse and yours," she said as she entered the dim, silent insurance office.

"It isn't a purse. The difference is the things that are in them."

"I see. So if I emptied the contents of my purse into your leather bag, it would then become a purse?"

"I give up," he said mildly. "Okay, it's a purse. Only men don't call them purses. We call them satchels or just plain leather bags."

"A rose by any other name," she murmured with gentle triumph.

He chuckled. "That's one of the things I like best about you. You're such a gracious winner. You never hesitate at all to gloat."

"Some people just ask for it more than others." She looked around, seeing nothing but empty desks and blank computer screens. "Where's the break room?"

"This way." He led her down a dark interior hallway and opened the last door on the right.

The room had two windows, so it wasn't dark. A variety of vending machines lined one wall, offering soft drinks, coffee, juice and snacks. A microwave oven sat on a counter, and a silent refrigerator stood at another wall. There was a vinyl sofa with splits in the cushions that allowed the stuffing to show, and a number of folding chairs shoved haphazardly around two cafeteria tables.

"Check the refrigerator while I open the machines," Quinlan said. "See if there's any ice. We don't need it now, but it would be nice to know that it's there just in case. Do it as fast as you can, to keep the cold air in."

"I do know about refrigerators and power failures," she said pointedly. Swiftly she opened the freezer compartment, and vapor poured out as cold air met warm. There were six ice trays there, all of them full. She shut the door just as fast as she had opened it. "We have ice."

"Good." He had the snack machine open and was removing packs of crackers.

Elizabeth opened the main refrigerator door but was disappointed with the contents. A brown paper bag sat in lone splendor, with several translucent greasy spots decorating it. She had no interest in investigating its contents. There was an apple, though, and she took it. The shelves in the door were lined with various condiments, nothing that tempted her. The thought of putting ketchup on the honey bun was revolting.

"Just an apple here," she said.

He finished loading his booty into the leather bag. "Okay, we have cakes, crackers and candy bars, plus the stuff you got from Chickie's desk. My best guess is we'll get out of here sometime tomorrow morning, so this should be more than enough. Do you want a soft drink, or juice? There's water downstairs, so we don't need to raid the drink machines. It's strictly a matter of preference."

She thought about it, then shook her head. "Water will be enough."

He zipped the bag. "That's it, then. Let's make ourselves comfy downstairs."

"Should we leave a note?" she asked.

"No need. I'll take care of things when the power comes on and everything gets back to normal."

The trip downstairs was considerably easier with the aid of one of the flashlights, and soon they reentered the lobby, which was noticeably cooler because of the two-story ceiling. She looked out through the dark glass of the double entrance; the street was oddly deserted, with only the occasional car passing by. A patrol car crawled past as she watched. "It looks weird," she murmured. "As if everyone has been evacuated."

"If the power doesn't come back on," Quinlan said in a grim tone, "it will probably get a lot busier once the sun goes down and things cool off a little. By the way, I tried to call out from my office, just to see what was going on and let someone know where we were, but I couldn't get a call to go through. If there's a citywide blackout, which I suspect, the circuits will be jammed with calls. But I did find a battery-operated radio, so we'll be able to listen to the news."

"Turn it on now," she suggested, walking over to a sofa to dump her load on it. "Let's find out what's going on."

He opened the leather bag and took out a small radio, not even as big as her hand. After switching it on and getting only static, he began running through the frequencies, looking for a station. Abruptly a voice jumped out at them, astonishingly clear for such a small radio. "—the National Guard has been called out in several states to help prevent looting—"

"Damn," Quinlan muttered. "This sounds bad."

"Information is sketchy," the announcer continued, "but more reports are coming in, and it looks as if there has been a massive loss of electrical power across the Southeast and most of Texas."

"I'm not an expert," a second voice said, "but the southern tier of the country has been suffering under this heat wave for two weeks, and I imagine the demands for electricity overloaded the system. Have we had any word yet from the governor?"

"Nothing yet, but the phone lines are tied up. Please, people, don't use the telephones unless it's an emergency. Folks can't get through to 911 if you're on the phone to your friends telling them that your power's out, too. Believe me, they *know.*"

The second announcer chimed in, "Remember the safety precautions the Health Department has been telling us for two weeks. It's especially critical without electricity for air conditioning and fans. Stay out of the sun if possible. With the power off, open your windows for ventilation, and drink plenty of liquids. Don't move around any more than you have to. Conserve your energy."

"We'll be on the air all night long," said the first announcer, "operating on emergency power. If anything happens you'll hear it first here on—"

Quinlan switched off the radio. "Well, now we know what happened," he said calmly. "We'll save the batteries as much as we can."

She gave him a mock incredulous look. "What? You mean you don't have replacement batteries?"

"It isn't my radio."

It wasn't necessary for him to add that if it had been, of course he would have had extra batteries. She wished it *were* his radio. And while she was wishing, she wished she had left the building on time, though she wasn't certain she wouldn't be in a worse situation at her condo. Certainly she was safer here, inside a sealed building.

The magnitude of the problem was stunning. This wasn't something that was going to be corrected in a couple of hours. It was possible they would still be locked in at this time tomorrow.

She looked at Quinlan. "Are you *sure* it won't get dangerously hot in here?"

"Not absolutely positive, but reasonably sure. We'll be okay. We have water, and that's the most important thing. Actually, we're probably as comfortable as anyone in this city is, except for those places that have emergency generators. If we start getting too warm, we'll just take off some clothes."

Her heart literally jumped, sending her pulse rate soaring, and immediately she began to feel uncomfortably warm. Her stomach muscles clenched at the thought of lying naked in the darkness with him, but it was the tightness of desire. While her mind was wary, her body remembered the intense pleasure of his lovemaking. She turned back to the windows to keep him from reading her expression. Staring at the glass made her think of something else, and gratefully she seized on it.

"When it gets dark, will anyone on the outside be able to see us in here when we turn on a flashlight? Does the privacy glazing work at night?"

"Anyone who looked closely would be able to tell that there's a light in here, I suppose," he said thoughtfully. "But no one will be able to actually *see* us."

Just the possibility was enough. She had been about to arrange their supplies in the seating area closest to the entrance, but now she moved farther away. The lobby had several comfortable seating areas, and she chose one that was close to the middle. It was at least semiprivate, with a long, waist-high planter that created the sense of a small alcove. It was also closer to the bathrooms, making it a better choice all the way around.

She arranged their food supplies on a low table, while Quinlan shoved the chairs around to make more room. Then he collected cushions from the other chairs and stacked them close to hand, ready to make into beds when they decided to sleep. Elizabeth gave the cushions a sidelong glance. She wasn't sure she would be able to close her eyes with Quinlan so close by, or that it would be smart to sleep, even if she could.

She looked at him and started when she found him watching her. He didn't look away as he unknotted his tie and stripped it off, then unbuttoned his shirt down to his waist and rolled up his sleeves. His actions were practical, but the sight of his muscled, hairy chest and hard belly aroused a reaction in her that had nothing to do with common sense.

"Why don't you take off those panty hose?" he suggested in a low, silky voice. "They have to be damn hot."

They were. She hesitated, then decided wryly that it wasn't the thin nylon that would protect her from him. Only *she* could do that. Quinlan wasn't a rapist; if she said no, he wouldn't force himself on her. She had never been afraid of that; her only fear was that she wouldn't be able to say no. That was one reason why she had avoided him for the past six months. So leaving her panty hose on wouldn't keep him from making love to her if she couldn't say no, and taking them off wouldn't put her at risk if she did keep herself under control. It was, simply, a matter of comfort.

She got a flashlight and carried it into the public rest room, where she propped it on one of the basins. The small room felt stuffy and airless, so she hurriedly removed her panty hose and immediately felt much cooler. She turned on the cold water and held her wrists under the stream, using the time-proven method of cooling down, then dampened one of the paper towels and blotted her face. There. That was much better.

A few deep breaths, a silent pep talk and she felt ready to hold Tom Quinlan at arm's length for the duration. With her panty hose in one hand and the flashlight in the other, she returned to the lobby.

He was waiting for her, sprawled negligently in one of the chairs, but those blue eyes watched her as intently as a tiger watches its chosen prey. "Now," he said, "let's have our little talk."

Chapter Five

Her heart lurched in her chest. It strained her composure to walk over to the chairs and sit down, but she did it, even crossed her legs and leaned back as negligently as he. "All right," she said calmly.

He gave her that considering look again, as if he were trying to decide how to handle her. Mentally she bristled at the idea of being "handled," but she forced down her irritation. She knew how relentless Quinlan could be when crossed; she would need to keep her thoughts ordered, not let him trip her up with anger.

He remained silent, watching her, and she knew what he wanted. He had already asked the question; he was simply waiting for the answer.

Despite herself, Elizabeth felt a spurt of anger, even after all these months. She faced him and went straight to the heart of the matter. "I found the file you had on me," she said, every word clipped short. "You had me investigated."

"Ah." He steepled his fingers and studied her over them. "So that's it." He paused a few seconds, then said mildly, "Of course I did."

"There's no 'of course' to it. You invaded my privacy—"

"As you invaded mine," he interrupted smoothly. "That file wasn't lying out in the open."

"No, it wasn't. I looked in your desk," she admitted without hesitation.

"Why?"

"I felt uneasy about you. I was looking for some answers."

"So why didn't you ask *me?*" The words were as sharp as a stiletto.

She gave him a wry, humorless smile. "I did. Many times. You're a master at evasion, though. I've been to bed with you, but I don't know much more about you right now than I did the day we met."

He neatly sidestepped the charge by asking, "What made you feel uneasy? I never threatened you, never pushed you. You know I own and run my company, that I'm solvent and not on the run."

"You just did it again," she pointed out. "Your ability to evade is very good. It took me a while to catch on, but then I noticed that you didn't answer my questions. You always responded, so it wasn't obvious, but you'd just ask your own question and ignore mine."

He surveyed her silently for a moment before saying, "I'm not interested in talking about myself. I already know all the details."

"I'd say that the same holds true for me, wouldn't you?" she asked sweetly. "I wanted to know about *you,* and got nowhere. But I didn't have you investigated."

"I wouldn't have minded if you had." Not that she would have been able to find out much, he thought.

Great chunks of his life after high school graduation weren't to be found in public records.

"Bully for you. *I* minded."

"And that's it? You walked out on me and broke off our relationship because you were angry that I had you investigated? Why didn't you just yell at me? Throw things at me? For God's sake, Elizabeth, don't you think you took it a little far?"

His tone was both angry and incredulous, making it plain that he considered her reaction to be nothing short of hysteric, far out of proportion to the cause.

She froze inside, momentarily paralyzed by the familiar ploy of being made to feel that she was in the wrong, that no matter what happened it was her fault for not being good enough. But then she fought the memories back; she would never let anyone make her feel that way again. She had gotten herself back, and she knew her own worth. She knew she hadn't handled the matter well, but only in the way she had done it; the outcome itself had never been in question.

Her voice was cool when she replied. "No, I don't think I took it too far. I'd been feeling uneasy about you for quite a while. Finding that you had investigated me was the final factor, but certainly not all of it."

"Because I hadn't answered a few questions?" That incredulous note was still there.

"Among other things."

"Such as?"

In for a penny, in for a pound. "Such as your habit of taking over, of ignoring my objections or suggestions as if I hadn't even said anything."

"Objections to what?" Now the words were as sharp as a lash. His blue eyes were narrowed and vivid. A bit surprised, she realized that he was angry again.

She waved her hand in a vague gesture. "Any little thing. I didn't catalog them—"

"Surprises the hell out of me," he muttered.

"But you were constantly overriding me. If I told you I was going shopping, you insisted that I wait until you could go with me. If I wanted to wear a sweater when we were going out, you insisted that I wear a coat. Damn it, Quinlan, you even tried to make me change where I bank!"

His eyebrows rose. "The bank you use now is too far away. The one I suggested is much more convenient."

"For whom? If I'm perfectly happy with my bank, then it isn't inconvenient for me, is it?"

"So don't change your bank. What's the big deal?"

"The big deal," she said slowly, choosing her words, "is that you want to make all the decisions, handle everything yourself. You don't want a relationship, you want a dictatorship."

One moment he was lounging comfortably, long legs sprawled out in front of him; the next he was in front of her, bending over to plant his hands on the arms of her chair and trap her in place. Elizabeth stared up at him, blinking at the barely controlled rage in his face, but she refused to let herself shrink from him. Instead she lifted her chin and met him glare for glare.

"I don't believe it!" he half shouted. "You walked out on me because I wanted you to change banks? God in heaven." He shoved himself away from the chair and stalked several paces away, running his hand through his hair.

"No," she shouted back, "I walked out because I refuse to let you take over my life!" She was unable to sit still, either, and surged out of the chair. Instantly Quinlan whirled with those lightning-quick reactions of his, catching her arms and hauling her close to him, so close that she could see the white flecks in the deep blue of his irises and smell the hot, male scent of his body. Her nostrils flared delicately as she instinctively drank in the primal signal, even though she stiffened against his touch.

"Why didn't you tell me you were married before?"

The question was soft, and not even unexpected, but still she flinched. Of course he knew; it had been in that damn investigative report.

"It isn't on my list of conversational topics," she snapped. "But neither is it a state secret. *If* our relationship had ever progressed far enough, I would have told you then. What was I supposed to do, trot out my past life the minute we met?"

Quinlan watched her attentively. As close as they were, he could see every flicker of expression on her face, and he had noticed the telltale flinch even though she had replied readily enough. Ah, so there *was* something there.

"Just how far did our relationship have to go?" he asked, still keeping his voice soft. "We weren't seeing anyone else. We didn't actually have sex until that last night together, but things got pretty hot between us several times before that."

"And I was having doubts about you even then," she replied just as softly.

"Maybe so, but that didn't stop you from wanting me, just like now." He bent his head and settled his mouth on hers, the pressure light and persuasive. She tried to pull away and found herself powerless against his strength, even though he was taking care not to hurt her. "Be still," he said against her lips.

Desperately she wrenched her head away. He forced it back, but instead of kissing her again, he paused with his mouth only a fraction of an inch above hers. "Why didn't you tell me about it?" he murmured, his warm breath caressing her lips and making them tingle. With his typical relentlessness, he had fastened on an idea and wouldn't let it go until he was satisfied with the answer. The old blind fear rose in her, black wings beating, and in panic she started to struggle. He subdued her without effort, wrapping her in a warm, solid embrace from which there was no escape.

"What happened?" he asked, brushing light kisses across her mouth between words. "What made you flinch when I mentioned it? Tell me about it now. I need to know. Did he run around on you?''

''No.'' She hadn't meant to answer him, but somehow, caught in those steely arms and cradled against his enticing heat, the word slipped out in a whisper. She heard it and shuddered. ''No!'' she said more forcefully, fighting for control. ''He didn't cheat.'' If only he had, if only his destructive attention had been diluted in that way, it wouldn't have been so bad. ''Stop it, Quinlan. Let me go.''

''Why did you start calling me Quinlan?'' His voice remained low and soothing, and his warm mouth kept pressing against hers with quick, gentle touches. ''You called me Tom before, and when we made love.''

She had started calling him Quinlan in an effort to distance herself from him. She didn't want to think of him as Tom, because the name was forever linked in her mind with that night when she had clung to his naked shoulders, her body lifting feverishly to his forceful thrusts as she cried out his name over and over, in ecstasy, in need, in completion. Tom was the name of her lover; Quinlan was the man she had fled.

And Quinlan was the one she had to deal with now, the man who never gave up. He held her helpless in his grasp, taking kiss after kiss from her until she stopped trying to evade his mouth and opened her lips to him with a tiny, greedy sound. Instantly he took her with his tongue, and the sheer pleasure of it made them both shudder.

His warm hand closed over her breast, gently kneading. She groaned, the sound captured by his mouth, and desperately tried to marshal her resistance. He was seducing her just as effortlessly as he had the first time, but even though she realized what was happening she couldn't find the willpower to push him away. She loved him too much, savored his kisses too much, desired him too strongly, found too much pleasure in the stroke of those hard hands.

The pressure of his fingers had hardened her nipple into a tight nub that stabbed his palm even through the layers of fabric protecting her. He deepened the kiss as he roughly opened the buttons of her blouse and shoved a hand inside the opening, then under the lacy cup of her bra to find the bare flesh he craved. She whimpered as his fingers found her sensitive nipple and lightly pinched at it, sending sharp waves of sensation down to her tightening loins. The sound she made was soft, more of a vibration than an actual noise, but he was so attuned to her that he felt it as sharply as an electrical shock.

She was limp as he bent her back over his arm and freed her breast from the lace that confined it, cupping the warm mound and lifting it up to his hungry mouth. He bent over her, sucking fiercely at her tender flesh, wild with the taste and scent and feel of her. He stabbed at her nipple with his tongue, excited and triumphant at the way she arched responsively at every lash of sensation. She wanted him. He had told himself that there had been no mistaking her fiery response that night, but the six months since then had weakened his assurance. Now he knew he hadn't been wrong. He barely had to touch her and she trembled with excitement, already needing him, ready for him.

He left her breast for more deeply voracious kisses taken from her sweetly swollen lips. God, he wanted her! No other woman had ever made him feel as Elizabeth did, so completely attuned with and lost within her.

He wanted to make love to her, *now,* but there were still too many unanswered questions. If he didn't get things settled while he had her marooned here, unable to get away from him, it might be another six months before he could corner her again. No, by God, it wouldn't be; he couldn't stand it again.

Reluctantly he left her mouth, every instinct in him wanting to take this to completion, knowing that he could if only he didn't give her a chance to surface from the drugging physical delight, but he still wanted answers and couldn't wait, didn't dare wait, to get them. "Tell me," he cajoled as he trailed his mouth down the side of her neck, nibbling on the taut tendon and feeling the response ripple through her. Finally—*finally*—he was on the right track. "Tell me what *he* did that made you run from *me.*"

Chapter Six

Frantically Elizabeth tried to jerk away, but he controlled her so easily that her efforts were laughable. Nevertheless, she lodged her hands against his heavy shoulders and pushed as hard as she could. "Let me go!"

"No." His refusal was flat and calm. "Stop fighting and answer me."

She couldn't do either one, and she began to panic, not because she feared Quinlan, but because she didn't want to talk about her marriage to Eric Landers, didn't want to think about it, didn't want to revive that hell even in memory. But Quinlan, damn his stubborn temperament, had fastened on the subject and wouldn't drop it until he got what he wanted. She knew him, knew that he intended to drag every detail out of her, and she simply couldn't face it.

Sheer survival instinct made her suddenly relax in his arms, sinking against him, clutching his shoulders instead of pushing against them. She felt his entire body tighten convulsively at her abrupt capitulation; her own muscles quivered with acute relief, as if she had been forcing them to an unnatural action. Her breath caught jerkily as her hips settled against his and she felt the thick ridge of his sex. His arousal was so familiar, and unbearably seductive. The lure of his sexuality pulled her even closer, her loins growing heavy and taut with desire.

He felt the change in her, saw it mirrored almost instantly in her face. One moment she had been struggling against him, and the next she was shivering in carnal excitement, her body tense as she moved against him in a subtle demand. He cursed, his voice thick, as he tried to fight his own response. It was a losing battle; he had wanted her too intensely, for too long. Talking would have to wait; for now, she had won. All he could think about was that she was finally in his arms again, every small movement signaling eager compliance. He didn't know what had changed her mind, and at this moment he didn't particularly care. It was enough that she was once again clinging to him, as she had the one night they had spent together, the night that was burned into his memory. He had tossed restlessly through a lot of dark, sleepless hours since then, remembering how it had been and aching for the same release, needing her beneath him, bewildered by and angry at her sudden coldness.

There was nothing cold about her now. He could feel her heat, feel her vibrating under his hands. Her hips moved in an ancient search, and a low moan hummed in her throat as she found what she had sought, her legs parting slightly to nestle his hard sex between them.

Fiercely he thrust his hand into her hair and pulled her head back. "Do you want this?" he asked hoarsely, hanging on to his control with grim concentration. It had happened so abruptly that he wanted to make sure before another second had passed, before she moved again and launched him past the point of no return. He hadn't felt like this since he'd been a teenager, the tide of desire rising like floodwaters in his veins, drowning thought. God, he didn't care what had caused her to change; right now, all he wanted was to thrust into her.

For a second she didn't answer, and his teeth were already clenching against a curse when she dug her nails into his shoulder and said, "Yes."

Her senses whirled dizzily as he lowered her to the floor, right where they stood. "The sofa..." she murmured, but then his weight came down on top of her and she didn't care anymore. Her initial tactic had been a panicked effort to distract him, but her own desire had blindsided her, welling up and overwhelming her senses so swiftly that she had no defense against it. She had hungered for him for so long, lying awake during the long, dark nights with silent tears seeping from beneath her lids because she missed him so much, almost as much as she feared him—and herself. The relief of being in his arms again was almost painful, and she pushed away all the reasons why this shouldn't happen. She would face the inevitable later; for now, all she wanted was Tom Quinlan.

He was rough, his own hunger too intense, too long denied, for him to control it. He shoved her skirt up to her waist and dragged her panties down, and Elizabeth willingly opened her thighs to receive him. He dealt just as swiftly with his pants, then brought his

loins to hers. His penetration was hard and stabbing,
and she cried out at the force of it. Her hips arched,
accepting, taking him deeper. A guttural sound vi-
brated in his wide chest; then he caught the backs of
her thighs, pulling her legs higher, and he began
thrusting hard and fast.

She loved it. She reveled in it. She sobbed aloud at
the strong release that pulsed through her almost immediately, the staggering physical response that she
had known only with this man and had thought she
would never experience again. She had been willing to
give up this physical ecstasy in order to protect her inner self from his dominance, but oh, how she had
longed for it, and bitterly wondered why the most
dangerous traps had the sweetest bait.

Blinded by the ferocity of his own need, he an-
chored her writhing hips with his big hands and
pounded into her. Dazedly she became aware of the
hard floor beneath her, bruising her shoulders, but
even as her senses were recovering from their sensual
battering and allowing her to take stock of her surroundings, he gripped her even harder and con-
vulsed. Instinctively she held him, cradling him with
arms and legs, and the gentle clasp of her inner
warmth. His harsh, strained cries subsided to low,
rhythmic moans, then finally to fast and uneven
breathing as he relaxed on top of her, his heavy weight
pressing her to the floor.

The silence in the huge, dim lobby was broken only
by the erratic intake and release of their breathing. His
slowing heartbeat thudded heavily against her breasts,

and their heated bodies melded together everywhere that bare flesh touched bare flesh. She felt the moisture of sweat, and the inner wetness that forcibly awakened her to the realization that their frantic mating had been done without any means of protection.

Her own heart lurched in panic; then logic reasserted itself and she calmed down. She had just finished her monthly cycle; it was highly unlikely that she could conceive. Perversely, no sooner had she had that reassuring thought than she was seized by a sense of loss, even of mourning, as if that panicked moment had been truth rather than very remote possibility.

"Elizabeth?"

She didn't open her eyes. She didn't want to face reality just yet, didn't want to have to let him go, and that was something reality would force her to do.

He lifted himself on his elbows, and she could feel the penetrating blue gaze on her face, but still she clung to the safety of her closed eyes.

She felt his muscles gathering, and briefly she tried to hold him, but he lifted himself away from her, and she caught her breath at the slow withdrawal that separated his body from hers. Despite herself, the friction set off a lingering thrill of sensation, and her hips lifted in a small, uncontrollable, telltale movement. Because there was no sanctuary any longer, she opened her eyes and silently met his gaze. That curious, sleepy blankness of sexual satisfaction was on his face, as she knew it must also be on hers, but in his eyes was a predatory watchfulness, as if he knew his prey had been caught but not vanquished.

His astuteness was disturbing, as it had always been. Her own gaze dared him to try to make anything more of what had just happened than an unadorned act of sex, without cause or future.

His mouth twisted wryly as he knelt away from her and pulled his pants up, zipping them with a faint, raspy sound. Then he got to his feet and effortlessly lifted her to hers. Her skirt, which had been bunched around her waist, dropped to the correct position. Elizabeth instinctively clenched her thighs to hold the wetness between them.

Quinlan shrugged out of his shirt and handed it to her, then leaned down and retrieved her panties from the floor. Thrusting them into her hands, too, he said, "Take off those clothes and put on my shirt. It's getting warmer in here, and you'll be more comfortable in something loose."

Silently she turned, picked up the flashlight and went into the ladies' rest room. Her knees were shaking slightly in reaction, and her loins throbbed from the violence of his possession. He hadn't hurt her, but it was as if she could still feel him inside.

She stared at her reflection in the mirror, the image ghostly with only the flashlight for illumination, making her eyes look huge and dark. Her hair had come loose and tumbled around her shoulders; she pushed it back distractedly, still staring at herself, then buried her face in her hands.

How could she go back out there? God, how could she have been so *stupid?* Alone with him for little more than an hour, and she had had sex with him on the floor like an uncontrolled animal. She couldn't even blame it on him; no, *she* had made the big move, grabbing at him, pushing her hips at him, because she had panicked when he had tried to pull back and begin asking questions again. She had gotten exactly what she had asked for.

She felt confused, both ashamed and elated. She was ashamed that she had used sex as an evasion tactic...or maybe she was ashamed that she had used it as an *excuse* to do what she had been longing to do anyway. The physical desire she felt for him was sharp and strong, so urgently demanding that stopping felt unnatural, all of her instincts pushing her toward him.

Her body felt warm and weak with satiation, faintly trembling in the aftermath. But now that he was no longer touching her, the old wariness was creeping back, pulling her in two directions. She had thought the decision simple, though it had never been easy, but now she was finding that nothing about it, either Quinlan or her own emotions, was simple.

Dazedly she stripped off her disheveled clothing and used some wet paper towels to wash; the cool moisture was momentarily refreshing, but then the close heat of the rest room made sweat form almost as fast as she could wash it off. Ironically she admitted that, no matter how reluctant she was, she had no real choice but to face him again. If she remained in here, she would have heat stroke. It was a sad day when a woman couldn't even count on a rest room for sanctuary. Ah, well, she hadn't yet found any place that was truly safe from him, for her own memories worked against her.

Just as she pulled on her panties, the door was thrust open and Quinlan loomed in the opening, his big body blotting out most of the light from the lobby but allowing the welcome entrance of relatively cooler air. The subtle breeze washed around her body, making her nipples pucker slightly. Or was that an instinctive female reaction to the closeness of her mate? She didn't want to think of him in such primitive, possessive terms, but her body had different priorities.

He noticed, of course. His gaze became smoky with both desire and possessiveness as he openly admired her breasts. But he didn't move toward her, holding himself very still as if he sensed her confusion. "Hiding?" he asked mildly.

"Delaying," she admitted, her tone soft. She didn't try to shield her body from him; such an action would seem silly, after what they had just done. It wasn't as if he hadn't seen her completely naked before, as if they hadn't made love before. Moreover, he had decided to remove his pants and stood before her wearing only a pair of short, dark boxers. Barefoot and mostly naked, his dark hair tousled and wet with both sweat and the water he had splashed on his face, he was stripped of most of the trappings of civilization. Despite the heat, a shiver ran up her spine in yet another feminine response to the primitiveness of his masculinity, and she looked away to keep him from seeing it in her face.

He came to her and took up his shirt, holding it for her to slip into; then, when she had done so, he turned her and began buttoning the garment as if she were a child being dressed. "You can't stay in here," he said. "Too damn hot."

"I know. I was coming out."

He shepherded her toward the door, his hand on her back. She wondered if the action was just his usual take-charge attitude, or if he was acting on some primitive instinct of his own, to keep the female from bolting. Probably a mixture of the two, she thought, and sighed.

He had been busy while she had been in the rest room, and she realized she had delayed in there much longer than she had intended. He had arranged the extra cushions on the floor—in the shape of a double bed, she noticed—and gotten some cool water from the fountain, the cups ready for them to drink. The water was welcome, but if he thought she was going to docilely stretch out on those cushions, he would shortly be disillusioned. She sat down in a chair and reached for a cup, sipping it without enthusiasm at first, then more eagerly as she rediscovered how good plain water was for quenching thirst. It was a delight of childhood that tended to be forgotten in the adult world of coffee, tea and wine spritzers.

"Are you hungry?" he asked.

"No." How could she be hungry? Her nerves were so tightly drawn that she didn't think she would be able to eat until they got out of here.

"Well, I am." He tore open the wrapping on the big blueberry muffin and began eating. "Tell me about your marriage."

She stiffened and glared at him. "It wasn't a good marriage," she said tightly. "It also isn't any of your business."

He glanced pointedly at the floor where they had so recently made love. "That's debatable. Okay, let's try it this way. I'll tell you about my marriage if you'll tell me about yours. No evasion tactics. I'll answer any question you ask."

She stared at him in shock. "*Your* marriage?"

He shrugged. "Sure. Hell, I'm thirty-seven years old. I haven't lived my entire life in a vacuum."

"You have your nerve!" she flared. "You jumped down my throat for not talking about my past marriage when you've only now mentioned your own?"

He rubbed the side of his nose and gave her a faintly sheepish look. "That occurred to me," he admitted.

"Well, let me put another thought in your dim Neanderthal brain! The time for heart-to-heart confidences was over a long time ago. We aren't involved any longer, so there's no point in 'sharing.'"

He took another bite of the muffin. "Don't kid yourself. What we just did felt pretty damn involved to me."

"That was just sex," she said dismissively. "It had been a while, and I needed it."

"I know exactly how long it had been." His blue gaze sharpened, and she knew he hadn't liked her comment. "You haven't gone out with anyone else since you walked out on me."

She was enraged all over again. "Have you had me followed?"

He had, but he wasn't about to tell her that now. Instead he said, "Chickie worries because your social life, in her words, resembles Death Valley—nothing of interest moving around."

Elizabeth snorted, but she was mollified, because she had heard Chickie make that exact comment on a couple of occasions. Still, she would have to have a word with her about discretion.

"I've been busy," she said, not caring if he believed her or not, though it happened to be the truth. She had deliberately been as busy as she could manage in order to give herself less free time to think about him.

"I know. You've found a lot of lilies to gild."

Her teeth closed with a snap. "That's so people will have a reason to install your fancy security systems. I gild the lilies, and you protect them."

"I protect *people,*" he clarified.

"Uh-huh. That's why you set up so many security systems for people who live in rough neighborhoods, where their lives are really in danger."

"I can see we aren't going to agree on this."

"You brought it up."

"My mistake. Let's get back to the original subject, namely our respective failed marriages. Go ahead, ask me anything you want."

The perfect response, of course, was that she wasn't interested. It would also be a lie, because she was not only interested, she was suddenly, violently jealous of that unknown, hitherto unsuspected woman who had been his wife, who had shared his name and his bed for a time, and who had been, in the eyes of the world, his mate. Elizabeth firmly kept her mouth closed, but she couldn't stop herself from glaring at him.

Quinlan sighed. "All right, I'll tell you the boring facts without making you ask. Her name was Amy. We dated during college. Then, when college was finished, it seemed like we should do adult things, so we got married. But I was away on my job a lot, and Amy found someone in the office where she worked who she liked a lot better. Within six months of getting married we knew it had been a mistake, but we held out for another year, trying to make it 'work,' before we both realized we were just wasting time. The divorce was a relief for both of us. End of story."

She was still glaring at him. "I don't even know where you went to college."

He sighed again. She was getting damn tired of that sigh, as if he were being so noble in his dealings with an irrational woman. "Cal Tech."

"Ah." Well, that explained his expertise with electronics and computers and things.

"No children," he added.

"I should hope not!" It was bad enough that he had, for some reason, concealed all the rest of the details of his life. "If you'd kept *children* hidden, I would never have forgiven you."

His eyes gleamed. "Does this mean you *have?*"

"No."

He gave a startled shout of laughter. "God, I've missed you. You don't dissemble at all. If you're grouchy, you don't feel any need at all to make nice and pretend to be sweetness and light, do you?"

She gave him a haughty look. "I'm not sweetness and light."

"Thank God," he said fervently. He leaned back and spread his hands, then stretched his long, muscular legs out before him in a posture of complete relaxation. "Okay, it's your turn. Tell me all the deep, dark secrets about *your* marriage."

Chapter Seven

"Show-and-tell was your idea, not mine." Her throat tightened at the idea of rehashing the details, reliving the nightmare even in thought. She just couldn't do it.

"You asked questions."

"I asked where you went to college, hardly the same as prying into your private life." Agitated, she stood up and longingly looked through the huge windows to the world outside. Only two thin sheets of transparent material kept her prisoner here with him, but it would take a car ramming into the glass at respectable speed to break it. The glass looked fragile but wasn't, whereas she was the opposite. She looked calm and capable, but inside she hid a weakness that terrified her.

"Don't run away," Quinlan warned softly.

She barely glanced at him as she edged out of the semicircle of sofa and chairs. "I'm not running," she denied, knowing that it wasn't the truth. "It's cooler moving around."

Silently Quinlan got to his feet and paced after her, big and virtually naked, the dark boxer shorts nothing more than the modern version of the loincloth. His muscled chest was hairy, the thick curls almost hiding his small nipples, and a silky line of hair ran down the center of his abdomen to his groin. His long legs were also covered with hair, finer and straighter, but he was undoubtedly a dominating male animal in his prime. Elizabeth gave him a distracted, vaguely alarmed look that suddenly focused on his loins, and her eyes widened.

He looked down at himself and shrugged, not pausing in his slow, relentless pursuit. "I know, at my age I shouldn't have recovered this fast. I usually don't," he said thoughtfully. "It's just my reaction to you. Come here, sweetheart." His voice had turned soft and cajoling.

Wildly Elizabeth wondered if this was going to degenerate into the stereotypical chase around the furniture. On the heels of that thought came the certain knowledge that if she ran, Quinlan would definitely chase her, instinctively, the marauding male subduing the reluctant female. She could prevent that farce by not running, thereby giving him nothing to chase. On the other hand, if she stood still things would only reach the same conclusion at a faster pace. Evidently the only real choice she had was whether or not to hold on to her dignity. If she had felt differently about him she could have said "no," but she had already faced that weakness in herself. For right now, in these circumstances, she couldn't resist him—and they both knew it.

He drew closer, his eyes gleaming. "For tonight, you're mine," he murmured. "Let me at least have that. You can't get away from me here. You don't even want to get away, not really. The circumstances aren't normal. When we get out of here you'll have options, but right now you're forced to be with me. Whatever happens won't be your fault. Just let go and forget about it."

She drew a deep, shuddering breath. "Pretty good psychologist, aren't you? But I'm not a coward. I'm responsible for whatever decisions I make, period."

He had reached her now, one arm sliding around her back. Elizabeth looked up at him, at the tousled dark hair and intense blue eyes, and her heart squeezed. "All right," she whispered. "For tonight. For as long as we're locked in here." She closed her eyes, shivering with sensual anticipation. She would let herself have this, just for now; she would feast on him, drown herself in sensation, let the darkness of the night wrap protectively around them and hold off thought. The time would come all too soon when she would have to push him away again; why waste even one precious minute by fighting both him and herself?

"Anything," she heard herself say as he lifted her. Her voice sounded strange to her, thick, drugged with desire. "For tonight."

His low, rough laugh wasn't quite steady as he lowered her to the cushions. "Anything?" he asked. "You could be letting yourself in for an interesting night."

She put out her hand and touched his bare chest. "Yes," she purred. "I could be."

"Cat." His breathing was fast and unsteady as he swiftly stripped her panties down her legs and tossed them to the side. "You won't be needing those again tonight."

She pulled at the waistband of his shorts. "And you won't be needing these."

"Hell, I only kept them on because I figured you'd fight like a wildcat if I came after you stark naked." He dealt with his shorts as rapidly as he had her underwear.

She was already excited by the anticipation of his slow, thorough loveplay. Quinlan was a man who enjoyed the preliminaries and prolonged them, as she had learned during the one night she had spent with him. It didn't happen this time, though. He pushed her legs open, knelt between them and entered her with a heavy thrust that jarred her. The shock of it reverberated through her body; then her inner muscles clamped down in an effort to slow that inexorable invasion.

He pushed deeper, groaning at the tightness of her, until he was in her to the hilt. She writhed, reaching down to grasp his thighs and hold him there, but he slowly withdrew, then just as slowly pushed back into her.

"Did your husband make you feel like this?" he whispered.

Her head rolled on the cushions at the speed and intensity of the sensations. It was an effort to concentrate on his words. "N-no," she finally sighed.

"Good." He couldn't keep the savage satisfaction out of his voice. He didn't like the thought of anyone else pleasing her. This was something she had known only with him; he had realized it immediately when they had first made love, but he had needed to hear her say it, admit that she had given her response to no one else.

He teased her with another slow withdrawal and thrust. "What did he do to you?" he murmured, and pulled completely away from her.

Her eyes opened in protest and she reached for him, moaning low in her throat as she tried to reestablish that delicious contact. Then comprehension made her eyes flare wider, and she jerked backward, away from him, trying to sit up. "You bastard!" she said in a strangled tone.

Quinlan caught her hips and dragged her back, slipping into her once again. "Tell me," he said relentlessly. "Did he mistreat you? Hurt you in any way? What in hell did he do that you're making me pay for?"

Elizabeth wrenched away from him again. She felt ill, all desire gone. How could he have done that to her? She fought to cover herself with his shirt, all the while calling herself several harsh names for her stupidity in thinking they could have this night, that she could give herself a block of time unattached to either past or present. She should have remembered that Quinlan never gave up.

No, he never gave up. So why didn't she tell him? It wouldn't be easy for her to relive it, but at least then he would know why she refused to allow him any authority in her life, why she had denied herself the love she so desperately wanted to give him.

She curled away from him, letting her head fall forward onto her knees so her hair hid her face. He tried to pull her back into his arms, into his lovemaking, but she resisted him, her body stiff in reaction to the memories already swamping her.

"Don't touch me!" she said hoarsely. "You wanted to know, so sit there and listen, but don't—don't touch me."

Quinlan frowned, feeling vaguely uneasy. He had deliberately pushed her, though he hadn't intended to push so hard that she withdrew from him, but that was what had happened. His body was still tight with desire, demanding release. He ground his teeth together, grimly reaching for control; if Elizabeth was ready to talk, after all these months, then he was damn well going to listen.

She didn't lift her head from her knees, but in the silent, darkening lobby, he could plainly hear every soft word.

"I met him when I was a senior in college. Eric. Eric Landers. But you already know his name, don't you? It was in your damn report. He owned an upscale decorating firm, and getting a part-time job there was a real plum."

She sighed. The little sound was sad, and a bit tired. "He was thirty-five. I was twenty-one. And he was handsome, sophisticated, self-assured, worldly, with quite a reputation as both a ladies' man and a well-known professional. I was more than flattered when he asked me out, I was absolutely giddy. Chickie would seem grim compared to the way I felt.

"We dated for about three months before he asked me to marry him, and for three months I felt like a princess. He took me everywhere, wined and dined me at the best places. He was interested in every minute of my day, in everything I did. A real princess couldn't have been more coddled. I was a virgin—a bit unusual, to stay that way through college, but I'd been studying hard and working part-time jobs, too, and I hadn't had time for much socializing. Eric didn't push me for sex. He said he could wait until our wedding night, that since I had remained a virgin that long, he wanted to give me all the traditional trappings."

"Let me guess," Quinlan said grimly. "He was gay."

She shook her head. "No. His ladies' man reputation was for real. Eric was very gentle with me on our wedding night. I'll give him that. He never mistreated me that way."

"If you don't mind," Quinlan interrupted, his teeth coming together with an audible snap, "I'd rather not hear about your sex life with him, if that wasn't the problem."

Elizabeth was surprised into lifting her head. "Are you jealous?" she asked warily.

He rubbed his hand over his jaw; as late in the day as it was, his five-o'clock shadow had become more substantial and made a rasping sound as his hand passed over it. "Not jealous, exactly," he muttered. "I just don't want to hear it, if you enjoyed making love with him. Hell, *yes,* I'm jealous!"

She gave a spurt of laughter, startling herself. She had never expected to be able to laugh while discussing Eric Landers, but Quinlan's frustration was so obvious that she couldn't help it.

"I don't mind giving the devil his due," she said in a generous tone. "You can pat yourself on the back, because you know you were the first to—umm—"

"Satisfy you," he supplied. A sheepish expression crossed his face.

"I'm not very experienced. You're the only man I've gone to bed with since my divorce. After Eric, I just didn't want to let anyone close to me."

She didn't continue, and the silence stretched between them. It was growing darker by the minute as the sun set completely, and she was comforted by the shield of night. "Why?" Quinlan finally asked.

It was easier to talk now, after that little bit of laughter and with the growing darkness concealing both their expressions. She felt herself relaxing, uncurling from her protective knot.

"It was odd," she said, "but I don't think he wanted me to be sensual. He wanted me to be his perfect princess, his living, breathing Barbie doll. I had gotten used to his protectiveness while we were dating, so at first I didn't think anything of it when he wanted to be with me every time I set foot outside the door. Somehow he always came up with a reason why I shouldn't put in for this job, or that one, and why I couldn't continue working with him. He went shopping with me, picked out my clothes . . . at first, it all seemed so flattering. My friends were so impressed by the way he treated me.

"Then he began to find reasons why I shouldn't see my friends, why first this one and then that one wasn't 'good' for me. I couldn't invite them over, and he didn't want me visiting them, or meeting them anywhere for lunch. He began vetting my phone calls. It was all so gradual," she said in a faintly bewildered tone. "And he was so gentle. He seemed to have a good reason for everything he did, and he was always focused on me, giving me the kind of attention all women think they want. He only wanted what was best for me, he said."

Quinlan was beginning to feel uneasy. He shifted position, leaning his back against one of the chairs and stretching out in a relaxed position that belied his inner tension. "A control freak," he growled.

"I think we'd been married about six months before I really noticed how completely he'd cut me off from everyone and everything except him," she continued. "I began trying to shift the balance of power, to make a few decisions for myself, if only in minor things, such as where I got my hair cut."

"Let me make another guess. All of a sudden he wasn't so gentle, right?"

"He was furious that I'd gone to a different place. He took the car keys away from me. That was when I really became angry, for the first time. Until then, I'd made excuses, because he'd been so gentle and loving with me. I'd never defied him until then, but when he took the keys out of my purse I lost my temper and yelled at him. He knocked me down," she said briefly.

Quinlan surged to his feet, raw fury running through him so powerfully that he couldn't sit there any longer. To hell with trying to look relaxed. He paced the lobby like a tiger, naked and primitive, the powerful muscles in his body flexing with every movement.

Elizabeth kept on talking. Now that she had started, she wanted to tell it all. Funny, but reliving it wasn't as traumatic as she had expected, not as bad as it had been in her memories and nightmares. Maybe it was having someone else with her that blunted the pain, because always before she had been alone with it.

"I literally became his prisoner. Whenever I tried to assert myself in any way, he'd punish me. There was no pattern to it. Most of the time he would slap me, or even whip me, but sometimes he would just yell, and I never knew what to expect. It was as if he knew that yelling instead of hitting me made it even worse, because then the next time I *knew* he'd hit me, and I'd try, oh, I'd try so hard, not to do anything that would cause the next time. But I always did. I was so nervous that I always did something. Or he'd make up a reason.

"Looking back," she said slowly, "it's hard to believe I was so stupid. By the time I realized what he had done and started trying to fight back, he had me so isolated, so brainwashed, that I literally felt powerless. I had no money, no friends, no car. I was ashamed for anyone to know what was happening.

That was what was so sick, that he could convince me it was my fault. I did try to run away once, but he'd paid the doorman to call him if I left, and he found me within half an hour. He didn't hit me that time. He just tied me to the bed and left me. The terror of waiting, helpless, for him to come back and punish me was so bad that hitting me would have been a relief, because that would have meant it was over. Instead he kept me tied for two days, and I nearly became hysterical every time he came into the room."

Quinlan had stopped pacing. He was standing motionless, but she could feel the tension radiating from him.

"He put locks on the phone so I couldn't call out, or even answer it," she said. "But one day he blacked my eye. I don't even remember why. It didn't take much to set him off. When I looked in the mirror the next morning, all of a sudden something clicked in my brain and I knew I had to either get away from him or kill him. I couldn't live like that another day, another hour."

"I'd have opted for killing him," Quinlan said tonelessly. "I may yet."

"After that, it was all so easy," she murmured, ignoring him. "I just packed my suitcases and walked out. The doorman saw me and reached for the phone . . . and then stopped. He looked at my eye and let the phone drop back into the cradle, and then he opened the door for me and asked if he could call a cab for me. When I told him I didn't have any money, he pulled out his wallet and gave me forty dollars.

"I went to a shelter for abused women. It was the hardest, most humiliating thing I've ever done. It's strange how the women are the ones who are so embarrassed," she said reflectively. "Never the men who have beaten them, terrorized them. *They* seem to think it was their right, or that the women deserved it. But I understand how the women feel, because I was one of them. Its like standing up in public and letting everyone see how utterly stupid you are, what bad judgment you have, what horrible mistakes you've made. The women I met there could barely look anyone in the eye, and they were the victims!

"I got a divorce. It was that simple. With the photographs taken at the shelter, I had evidence of abuse, and Eric would have done anything to preserve his reputation. Oh, he tried to talk me into coming back, he made all sorts of promises, he swore things would be different. I was even tempted," she admitted. "But I couldn't trust my own judgment any longer, so the safest thing, the only thing to do was stay away from romantic relationships in general and Eric Landers in particular."

God, it was so plain now. Quinlan could barely breathe with the realization of the mistakes he'd made in dealing with her. No wonder she had pulled away from him. Because he'd wanted her so much, he had tried to take over, tried to coddle and protect her. It was a normal male instinct, but nothing else could have been more calculated to set off her inner alarms. When she had needed space, he had crowded her, so determined to have her that he hadn't let anything stand in his way. Instead of binding her to him, he had made her run.

"I'm not like Landers," he said hoarsely. "I'll never abuse you, Elizabeth, I swear."

She was silent, and he could sense the sadness in her. "How can I trust you?" she finally asked. "How can I trust *myself*? What if I make the wrong decision about you, too? You're a much stronger man than Eric could ever hope to be, both physically and mentally. What if you *did* try to hurt me? How could I protect myself? You want to be in charge. You admit it. You're dominating and secretive. God, Quinlan, I love you, but you scare me to death."

His heart surged wildly in his chest at her words. He had known it, but this was the first time she had actually said so. She loved him! At the same time he was suddenly terrified, because he didn't see any way he could convince her to trust him. And that was what it was: a matter of trust. She had lost confidence in her own ability to read character.

He didn't know what to do; for the first time in his life he had no plan of action, no viable option. All he had were his instincts, and he was afraid they were all wrong, at least as far as Elizabeth was concerned. He had certainly bungled it so far. He tried to think what his life would be like without her, if he never again could hold her, and the bleakness of the prospect shook him. Even during these past hellish months, when she had avoided him so totally, even refusing to speak to him on the phone, he hadn't felt this way, because he had still thought he would eventually be able to get her back.

He had to have her. No other woman would do. And he wanted her just as she was: elegant, acerbic, independent, wildly passionate in bed. That, at last, he had done right. She had burned bright and hot in his arms.

He suspected that if he asked for an affair, and only that, she would agree. It was the thought of a legal, binding relationship that had sent her running. She had acted outraged when he had mentioned marriage and kids, getting all huffy because he hadn't included her in the decision-making, but in truth it was that very thing that had so terrified her. Had she sensed he had been about to propose? Finding the file had made her furious, but what had sent her fleeing out the door had been the prospect that he wanted more than just a sexual relationship with her. She could handle being intimate with him; it was the thought of giving him legal rights that gave her nightmares.

He cleared his throat. He felt as if he were walking blindfolded through a mine field, but he couldn't just give up. "I have a reason for not talking about myself," he said hesitantly.

Her reply was an ironic, "I'm sure you do."

He stopped, shrugging helplessly. There was nothing he could tell her that wouldn't sound like an outrageous lie. Okay, that had been a dead end.

"I love you."

The words shook him. He'd admitted the truth of it to himself months ago, not long after meeting her, in fact, but it had been so long since he'd said them aloud that he was startled. Oh, he'd said them during his marriage, at first. It had been so easy, and so expected. Now he realized that the words had been easy because he hadn't meant them. When something really mattered, it was a lot harder to get out.

Elizabeth nodded her head. It had gotten so dark that all he could see was the movement, not her expression. "I believe you do," she replied.

"But you still can't trust me with your life."

"If I needed someone to protect me from true danger, I can't think of anyone I would trust more. But for the other times, the day-to-day normal times that make up a true lifetime, I'm terrified of letting someone close enough to ever have that kind of influence on me again."

Quinlan took another mental sidestep. "We could still see each other," he suggested cautiously. "I know I came on too strong. I'll hold it down. I won't pressure you to make any kind of commitment."

"That wouldn't be fair to you. Marriage is what you want."

"I want *you*," he said bluntly. "With or without the legal trappings. We're great in bed together, and we enjoy each other's company. We have fun together. We can do that without being married, if that's all that's making you shy away from me."

"You want to have an affair?" she asked, needing to pin him down on his exact meaning.

"Hell, no. I want everything. The ring, the kids, all of it. But if an affair is all I can have, I'll take it. What do you say?"

She was silent a long time, thinking it over. At last she sighed and said, "I think I'd be a fool to make any decision right now. These aren't normal circumstances. When the power is back on and our lives are back to normal, then I'll decide."

Quinlan had always had the knack of cutting his losses. He took a step toward her. "But I still have tonight," he said in a low tone. "And I don't intend to waste a minute of it."

Chapter Eight

It was much as it had been that other night, and yet it was much more intense. Quinlan made love to her until she literally screamed with pleasure, and then loved her past her embarrassment. The darkness wrapped around them like a heated cocoon, suspending time and restrictions, allowing anything to be possible. The hours seemed endless, unmarked as they were by any clock or other means that civilized man had developed. The streets outside remained dark and mostly empty; he didn't turn on the radio again, because he didn't want the outside world to intrude, and neither did she.

It was too hot to sleep, despite the high ceiling in the lobby that carried the heat upward. They lay on the cushions and talked, their voices not much more than slow murmurs in the sultry heat. Quinlan's big hands never left her bare body, and Elizabeth suspended her thoughts for this one magic night. She became drowsy, but all inclination to sleep fled when he turned to her in the thick, heated darkness, pressing down on her, his callused hands stroking and probing until she writhed on the cushions. His lovemaking was as steamy as the night, as enveloping. In the darkness she had no inhibitions. She not only let him do as he wanted with her, she reveled in it. There wasn't an inch of her body that he didn't explore.

Daylight brought sunlight and steadily increasing temperatures, but the power remained off. Even though she knew it was impossible to see inside through the glazed windows, she was glad that they could remain snugly hidden in their own little lair. They drank water and ate, and Elizabeth insisted on washing off again in the smothering heat of the rest room, though she knew it wouldn't do any good to clean up with Quinlan waiting impatiently for her outside. Did the man never get tired?

She heard other voices and froze, panicking at the thought of being caught naked in the rest room. Had the power come back on? Impossible, because it was dark in the bathroom. Or had the guard cut off the lights in here before he'd left the day before? She hadn't even thought to check the switch.

Then she heard a familiar call sign and relaxed. The radio, of course. A bit irritated, with herself for being scared and with him because he'd caused it, she strode out of the rest room. "I nearly had a heart attack," she snapped. "I thought someone had come in and I was caught in the rest room."

Quinlan grinned. "What about me? I'm as naked as you are."

He was still sprawled on the cushions, but somehow he looked absolutely at home in his natural state. She looked down at herself and laughed. "I can't believe this is happening."

He stared to say, *It'll be something to tell our grandkids,* but bit the words back. She wouldn't want to hear it, and he'd promised he wouldn't push her. He held out his hand to her, and she crawled onto the cushions with him, sinking into his arms.

"What was on the news?"

"A relatively quiet night in Dallas, though there was some sporadic looting. The same elsewhere. It was just too damn hot to do anything very strenuous."

"Oh, yeah?" she asked, giving him a sidelong glance.

He laughed and deftly rolled her onto her back, mounting her with a total lack of haste that demonstrated how many times during the night he'd done the same thing. "The news?" she prompted.

He nuzzled her neck, breathing in the sweet woman scent. "Oh, that. The national guard has been mobilized from Texas to the East Coast. There were riots in Miami, but they're under control now."

"I thought you said things were relatively quiet?"

"That *is* quiet. With electricity off in almost a quarter of the country, that's amazingly quiet." He didn't want to talk about the blackout. Having Elizabeth naked under him went to his head faster than the most potent whiskey. He kissed her, acutely savoring her instant response, even as he positioned her for his penetration and smoothly slid within. He felt the delicious tightening of her inner muscles as she adjusted to him, the way her fingers dug into his shoulders as she tried to arch even closer to him. His feelings for her swamped him, and he found himself wishing the electricity would never come back on.

Afterward, she yawned and nestled down on his shoulder. "Did the radio announcers say when the power company officials thought the power would be back on?"

"Maybe by this afternoon," he said.

So soon? She felt a bit indignant, as if she had been promised a vacation and now it had been cut short. But this wasn't a vacation; for a lot of people, it was a crisis. Electricity could mean the difference between life and death for someone who was ill. If all they had was a few more hours, she meant to make the best of them.

It seemed that he did, too. Except for insisting that they regularly drink water, he kept her in his arms. Even when he finally tired and had to take a break from lovemaking, he remained nestled within her body. Elizabeth was too tired to think; all she could do was feel. Quinlan had so completely dominated her senses that she would have been alarmed, if she hadn't seen the same drugged expression in his eyes that she knew was in hers. This wasn't something he was doing to her; it was something they were sharing.

They dozed, their sweaty bodies pressed tightly together despite the heat.

It was the wash of cool air over her skin that woke her, shivering.

Quinlan sat up. "The power's back on," he said, squinting up at the overhead lights that seemed to be glaring after the long hours without them. He looked at his watch. "It's eleven o'clock."

"That's too soon," Elizabeth said grumpily. "They said it would be this afternoon."

"They probably gave themselves some extra time in case something went wrong."

Feeling incredibly exposed in the artificial light, Elizabeth scrambled into her clothing. She looked at her discarded panty hose in distaste and crumpled them up, then threw them into the trash.

"What do we do now?" she asked, pushing her hair back.

Quinlan zipped his pants. "Now we go home."

"How? Do we call the guard service?"

"Oh, I'll call them all right. Later. I have a few things to say. But now that the power's on, I can get us out of here."

While he tapped into the security system, Elizabeth hastily straightened the furniture, shoving it back into place and restoring all the cushions to their original sites. A blush was already heating her face at the possibility of anyone finding out about their love nest, literally in the middle of the lobby. She didn't know if she would ever be able to walk into this building again without blushing.

Quinlan grunted with satisfaction as he entered a manual override into the system that would allow him to open the side door. "Come on," he said, grabbing Elizabeth's hand.

She barely had time to snatch up her purse before he was hustling her out of there. She blinked in the blinding sunshine. The heat rising off the sidewalk was punishing. "We can't just leave the building un-locked," she protested.

"I didn't. It locked again as soon as the door closed." Taking her arm, he steered her around the corner and across the street to the parking deck.

Before she could react, he was practically stuffing her into his car. "I have my own car!" she said indignantly.

"I know. Don't worry, it isn't going anywhere. But we don't know that the electricity is on all over the city, and we don't know what kind of situation you'll find at your place. Until I know you're safe, I'm keeping you with me."

It was the sort of high-handed action that had always made her uneasy in the past, but now it didn't bother her. Maybe it was because she was so sleepy. Maybe it was because he was right. For whatever reason, she relaxed in the seat and let her eyes close.

He had to detour a couple of times to reach her apartment, but the traffic was surprisingly light, and it didn't take long, not even as long as normal. She didn't protest when he went inside with her. The electricity was on there, too, the central air conditioning humming as it tried to overcome the built-up heat.

"Into the shower," Quinlan commanded.

She blinked at him. "What?"

He put his arm around her, turning her toward her bedroom. "The shower. We're both going to take a nice, cool shower. We're in good shape, but this will make us feel better. Believe me, we're a little dehydrated.''

Their bargain had been only for the night, but since it had already extended into the day, she supposed it wouldn't hurt to carry it a little further. She allowed him to strip her and wasn't at all surprised when he undressed and climbed in with her. The shower spray was cool enough to raise a chill, and it felt wonderful. She turned around to let it wash over her spine and tilted her head back so the water soaked through her sweat-matted hair.

"Feel good?" he murmured, running his hands over her. She would have thought that he was washing her, except that he wasn't using soap.

"Mmm." He bent his head and Elizabeth lifted hers. If only she could stay this way, she thought. Kissing him, being kissed by him. His hard arms locked around her. Feeling him so close, all worries pushed aside...

The cool shower was revitalizing in more ways than one. Abruptly he lifted her and braced her against the wall, and she gasped as he drove deep into her. There was nothing slow about it this time; he took her fiercely, as wild as he had been the day before on the floor of the lobby, as if all those times in between had never been.

Later they went to bed. She could barely hold her eyes open while he dried her hair, then carried her to the bed and placed her between the cool, smooth sheets. She sighed, every muscle relaxing, and imme-

diately went to sleep, not knowing that he slipped into
bed beside her.

Still, she wasn't surprised when she woke during the
afternoon and he was there. Lazily she let her gaze
drift over his strong-boned features. He needed to
shave; the black beard lay on his skin like a dark
shadow. His hair was tousled, and his closed eyelids
looked as delicate as a child's. Odd, for she had never
thought of Quinlan as delicate in any way, never associated any sort of softness with him. Yet he had been
tender with her, even in his passion. It wasn't the same
type of gentleness Eric had displayed; Eric had been
gentle, she realized now, because he hadn't *wanted* any
responding passion from her. He had wanted her to be
nothing more than a doll, to be dressed and positioned and shown off for his own ego. Quinlan, on the
other hand, had been as helpless in his passion as she
had been in hers.

Her body quivered at his nearness. Still half asleep,
she pushed at him. His eyes opened immediately, and
he rolled onto his back. "What's wrong?"

"Plenty," she said, slithering on top of him and
feeling the immediate response between his legs. "It's
been at least—" She paused to look at the clock, but
it was blinking stupidly at her, not having been reset
since the power had come back on. "It's been too
damn long since I've had this." She reached between
his legs, and he sucked in his breath, his back arching
as she guided him into place.

"God, I'm sorry," he apologized fervently, and bit
back a moan as she moved on him. This was the way

he had always known his Elizabeth could be, hot with uncomplicated passion, a little bawdy, intriguingly earthy. She made him dizzy with delight.

Her eyes were sultry, her lips swollen and pouty from his kisses, her dark hair tumbling over her shoulders. He watched her expression tighten with desire as she moved slowly up and down on him, her eyes closing even more. "Just for that," she murmured, "I get to be on top."

He reached overhead and caught the headboard, his powerful biceps flexing as his fists locked around the brass bars. "No matter how I beg and plead?"

"No matter what you say," she assured him, and gasped herself as her movements wrenched another spasm of pleasure from her nerve endings.

"Good." Quinlan arched, almost lifting her off the bed. "Then I won't accidentally say something that will make you quit."

He didn't. When she collapsed, exhausted, on his chest, they were both numb with pleasure. He thrust his hand into her tangled hair and held her almost desperately close. She inhaled the hot, musky scent of his skin, and with the slightest of motions rubbed her cheek against the curly hair on his chest. She could feel his heart thudding under her ear, and the strong rhythm was reassuring. They slept again, and woke in the afternoon with the sun going down in a blaze of red and gold, to drowsily make love again.

He got up to turn on the television sitting on her dresser, then returned to bed to hold her while they watched the news, which was, predictably, all about the blackout. Elizabeth felt a little bemused, as if a national crisis had passed without her knowing about it, even though she had been intimately embroiled in this one. Intimately, she thought, in more ways than one. Perhaps that was why she felt so out of touch with reality. She hadn't spent the past twenty-four hours concentrating on the lack of electricity, she had been concentrating on Quinlan.

The Great Blackout, as the Dallas newscasters were calling it, had disrupted electrical services all over the Sun Belt. The heat wave, peak usage and solar flares had all combined to overload and blow circuits, wiping out entire power grids. Elizabeth felt as if her own circuits had been seriously damaged by Quinlan's high-voltage lovemaking.

He spent the night with her. He didn't ask if he could, and she didn't tell him that he couldn't. She knew that she was only postponing the inevitable, but she wanted this time with him. Telling him about Eric hadn't changed her mind, any more than knowing about Eric had changed Quinlan's basic character.

When morning came, they both knew that the time-out had ended. Reality couldn't be held at bay any longer.

"So what happens now?" he asked quietly.

She looked out the window as she sipped her coffee. It was Saturday; neither of them had to work, though Quinlan had already talked to a couple of his staffers, placing the calls almost as soon as he'd gotten out of bed. She knew that all she had to say was one word, "Stay," and they would spend the weekend in bed, too. It would be wonderful, but come Monday, it would make it just that much more difficult to handle.

"I don't see that the situation has changed," she finally said.

"Damn it, Elizabeth!" He got up, his big body coiled with tension. "Can you honestly say that I'm anything like Landers?"

"You're very dominating," she pointed out.

"You love me."

"At the time, I thought I loved him, too. What if I'm wrong again?" Her eyes were huge and stark as she stared at him. "There's no way you can know how bad it was without having lived through it yourself. I would rather die than go through anything like that again. I don't know how I can afford to take the chance on you. I still don't know *you*, not the way you know me. You're so secretive that I can't tell who you really are. How can I trust you when I don't know you?"

"And if you did?" he asked in a harsh tone. "If you knew all there is to know about me?"

"I don't know," she said; then they looked at each other and broke into snickering laughter. "There's a lot of knowing and not knowing in a few short sentences."

"At least we know what we mean," he said, and she groaned; then they started laughing again. When he sobered, he reached out and slid his hand underneath her heavy curtain of hair, clasping the back of her neck. "Let me give something a try," he urged. "Let me have another shot at changing your mind."

"Does this mean that if it doesn't work, you'll stop trying?" she asked wryly, and had to laugh at the expression on his face. "Oh, Tom, you don't even have a clue about how to give up, do you?"

He shrugged. "I've never wanted anyone the way I want you," he said, smiling back just as wryly. "But at least I've made some progress. You've started calling me Tom again."

He dressed and roughly kissed her as he started out the door. "I'll be back as soon as I can. It may not be today. But there's something I want to show you before you make a final decision."

Elizabeth leaned against the door after she had closed it behind him. Final decision? She didn't know whether to laugh or cry. To her, the decision had been final for the past six months. So why did she feel that, unless she gave him the answer he wanted, she would still be explaining her reasons to him five years from now?

Chapter Nine

The doorbell rang just before five on Sunday morning. Elizabeth stumbled groggily out of bed, staring at the clock in bewilderment. She had finally set the thing, but surely she had gotten it wrong. Who would be leaning on her doorbell at 4:54 in the morning?

"Quinlan," she muttered, moving unsteadily down the hall.

She looked through the peephole to make certain, though she really hadn't doubted it. Yawning, she released the chain and locks and opened the door. "Couldn't it have waited another few hours?" she asked grouchily, heading toward the kitchen to put on a pot of coffee. If she had to deal with him at this hour, she needed to be more alert than she was right now.

"No," he said. "I haven't slept, and I want to get this over with."

She hadn't slept all that much herself; after he'd left the morning before, she had wandered around the apartment, feeling restless and unable to settle on anything to do. It had taken her a while to identify it, but at last she had realized that she was lonely. He had been with her for thirty-six hours straight, holding her while they slept, making love, talking, arguing, laughing. The blackout had forced them into a hot-house intimacy, leading her to explore old nightmares and maybe even come to terms with them.

The bed had seemed too big, too cold, too empty. For the first time she began to question whether or not she had been right in breaking off with him. Quinlan definitely was *not* Eric Landers. Physically, she felt infinitely safe and cherished with him; on that level, at least, she didn't think he would ever hurt her.

It was the other facet of his personality that worried her the most, his secrecy and insistence on being in control. She had some sympathy with the control thing; after all, she was a bit fanatic on the subject herself. The problem was that she had had to fight so hard to get herself back, how could she risk her identity again? Quinlan was as relentless as the tides; lesser personalities crumbled before him. She didn't know anything about huge chunks of his life, what had made him the man he was. What if he were hiding something from her that she absolutely couldn't live with? What if there was a darkness to his soul that he could keep under control until it was too late for her to protect herself?

She was under no illusions about marriage. Even in this day and age, it gave a man a certain autonomy over his wife. People weren't inclined to get involved in domestic "disputes," even when the dispute involved a man beating the hell out of his smaller, weaker wife. Some police departments were starting to view it more seriously, but they were so inundated with street crime, drug and highway carnage that, objectively, she could see how a woman's swollen face or broken arm didn't seem as critical when weighed in that balance.

And marriage was what Quinlan wanted. If she resumed a relationship with him, he might not mention it for a while—she gave him a week, at the outside—but he would be as relentless in his pursuit of that goal as he was in everything else. She loved him so much that she knew he would eventually wear her down, which was why she had to make a final decision now. And she *could* do it now—if the answer was no. She still had enough strength to walk away from him, in her own best interests. If she waited, every day would weaken that resolve a little more.

He had been silent while she moved around the kitchen, preparing the coffeemaker and turning it on. Hisses and gurgles filled the air as the water heated; then came the soft tinkle of water into the pot and the delicious aroma of fresh coffee filled the room.

"Let's sit down," he said, and placed his briefcase on the table. It was the first time she had noticed it.

She shook her head. "If this requires thinking, at least wait until I've had a cup of coffee."

His mouth quirked. "I don't know. Somehow I think I'd stand a better chance if your brain stayed in neutral and you just went with your instincts."

"Hormones, you mean."

"I have nothing against those, either." He rubbed his beard and sighed wearily. "But I guess I could use a cup of coffee, too."

He had taken the time to change clothes, she saw; he was wearing jeans that looked to be at least ten years old, and a soft, white, cotton shirt. But his eyes were circled with dark rings and were bloodshot from lack of sleep, and he obviously hadn't shaved since the morning before the blackout. The blackness of his heavy beard made him look like a ruffian; actually, he looked exactly like the type of people he hired.

When the coffee stopped dripping, she filled two mugs and slid one in front of him as she took a seat at the table. Cautiously sipping the hot brew, she wondered how long it would take to hit the bloodstream.

He opened the briefcase and took out two files, one very thin and the other over an inch thick. He slid the thin one toward her. "Okay, read this one first."

She opened it and lifted her eyebrows when she saw that it was basically the same type of file that he'd had on her, though this one was on himself. Only it seemed to be rather sketchy. *Bare bones* was more like it, and even then, part of the skeleton was missing. It gave his name, birthdate, birthplace, social security number, physical description, education and present employment, as well as the sketchy facts of his brief marriage, so many years ago. Other than that, he seemed not to have existed between the years of his divorce and when he had started his security business.

"Were you in cold storage for about fifteen years?" she finally asked, shoving the file back toward him. "I appreciate the gesture, but if this was supposed to tell me about you, it lacks a little something."

He eyed her warily, then grinned. "Not many people can manage to be sarcastic at five o'clock in the morning."

"At five o'clock, that's about all I *can* manage."

"I'll remember that," he murmured, and slid the second file, the thick one, toward her. "This is the information you wouldn't have gotten if you investigated me."

Her interest level immediately soared, and she flipped the manila folder open. The documents before her weren't originals, but were a mixture of photostats and faxes. She looked at the top of one and then gave him a startled look. "Government, huh?"

"I had to get a buddy to pull up my file and send it to me. Nothing in there is going to reveal state secrets, but the information is protected, for my sake. I could have hacked into the computer, but I'd just as soon not face a jail term, so it took some time to get it all put together."

"Just exactly what did you do?" she asked, not at all certain that she wanted to know. After being so frustrated by his lack of openness, now that his life lay open before her, she wasn't all that eager to know the details. If he had been shot at, if he had been in danger in any way... that could give her a different set of nightmares.

"No Hollywood stuff," he assured her, grinning.

"I'm disappointed. You mean you weren't a secret agent?" Relieved was more like it.

"That's a Hollywood term. In the business, it's called a field operative. And no, that isn't what I did. I gathered information, set up surveillance and security systems, worked with antiterrorist squads. It wasn't the kind of job that you talk over with your buddies in the bar after work.''

"I can understand that. You got in the habit of not talking about yourself or what you did.''

"It was more than just a habit, it could have meant people's lives. I still don't talk about it, because I still know people in the business. Information is the greatest asset a government can have, and the most dangerous.''

She tapped the file. "So why are you showing me this?''

"Because I trust you," he said simply; then another grin spread across his face. "And because I didn't think you'd believe me if I just said, 'I can't talk about myself, government stuff, very hush-hush.' You would have laughed in my face. It's the kind of crap you hear in singles bars, hot-shot studs trying to impress the airheads. You aren't an airhead.''

After flipping a few pages and scanning them, she said, "You're right. I wouldn't have believed this. Most people don't do this type of work.''

He shrugged. "Like I said, I went to Cal Tech, and I was very good at what I did.''

"Did?" she asked incredulously. "It's what you still do. It's just that now you do it for yourself instead of the government.'' An idea struck her. "The people you hire. Are they—?''

"Some of them," he admitted.

"Like the biker?''

He laughed. "Like the biker. Hell, do you think I'd hire anyone who looked like that if I didn't personally know him? He really was an operative, one mean son of a bitch.''

''They come to you for jobs when they retire?''

''No, nothing like that. I'm not a halfway house for burned-out government employees. I keep track of people, contact them to see if they're interested in working for me. Most of them are very normal, and it's just a matter of moving from one computer job to another.''

She closed the file and pushed it away from her. Quinlan eyed her with alarm. ''Aren't you going to read it?''

''No. I don't need to know every detail of everything you've done. A brief overview is enough.''

He drew a deep breath and sat back. ''Okay. That's it, then. I've done all I can. I can't convince you, prove it to you in any way, that I'll never treat you the way Landers did. *I* know I won't, but you're the one who has to believe it. Elizabeth, sweetheart, will you marry me?''

She couldn't help it. She knew it wasn't the way a woman was supposed to respond to a marriage proposal, but the relentlessness of it was so typical of Tom Quinlan that she couldn't stop the sharp crack of laughter from exploding into sound. She would probably hear that question every day until she either gave him the answer he wanted or went mad under the pressure. Instead of making her feel pressured, as it would have before, there was a certain amount of comfort in knowing she could depend on him to that extent. Seeing that file had meant more to her than he could know. It wasn't just that it filled in the gaps of his life, but that he trusted her to know about him.

She managed to regain her composure and stared seriously at him. Somehow, what had happened during the blackout had lessened the grip that Eric Landers had still had on her, even after so many years. During the long hours of that hot night she had been forced to truly look at what had happened, to deal with it, and for the first time she'd realized that Eric had still held her captive. Because of him, she had been afraid to truly let herself live. She was still afraid, but all of a sudden she was more afraid of losing what she had. If it were possible to lose Quinlan, she thought, looking at him with wry fondness. But, yes, she could lose him, if she didn't start appreciating the value of what he was offering her. It was sink or swim time.

He had begun to fidget under her silent regard. She inhaled deeply. "Marriage, huh? No living together, seeing how it works?"

"Nope. Marriage. The love and honor vows. Until death."

She scowled a little at him. He was as yielding as rock when he made up his mind about something. "Yours could come sooner than you think," she muttered.

"That's okay, if you're the one who does me in. I have an idea of the method you'd use," he replied, and a look of startlingly intense carnal hunger crossed his face. He shivered a little, then gathered himself and raised his right hand. "I swear I'll be an absolute pussycat of a husband. A woman like you needs room."

She had taken a sip of coffee, and at his words she swallowed wrong, choking on the liquid. She coughed and wheezed, then stared at him incredulously. "Then why haven't you been giving me any?" she yelled.

"Because I was afraid to give you enough room to push me away," he said. He gave her a little half smile that acknowledged his own vulnerability and held out his hand to her. "You scare me, too, babe. I'm scared to death you'll decide you can get along without me."

She crossed her arms and glared at him, refusing to take his outstretched hand. "If you think you'll get a little slave, you'll be disappointed. I won't pick up after you, I don't like cooking and I won't tolerate dirty clothes strewn all over the place."

A grin began to spread across his face as she talked, a look of almost blinding elation, but he only said mildly, "I'm fairly neat, for a man."

"Not good enough. I heard that qualification."

He sighed. "All right. We'll write it into our wedding vows. I'll keep my clothes picked up, wash the whiskers out of the sink and put the lid back down on the toilet. I'll get up with the kids—"

"Kids?" she asked delicately.

He lifted his brows at her. She stifled a smile. God, dealing with him was exhilarating! "Okay," she said, relenting. "Kids. But not more than two."

"Two sounds about right. Deal?"

She pretended to consider, then said, "Deal," and they solemnly shook hands.

Quinlan sighed with satisfaction, then hauled her
into his arms, literally dragging her across the table
and knocking her mug of coffee to the floor. Oblivious to the spreading brown puddle, he held her on his
lap and kissed her until her knees were weak. When he
lifted his head, a big grin creased his face and he said,
"By the way, I always know how to bypass my own
systems."

She put her hand on his rough jaw and kissed him
again. "I know," she said smugly.

Over an hour later, he lifted his head from the pillow and scowled at her. "There's no way you could
have known."

"Not for certain, but I suspected." She stretched,
feeling lazy and replete. Her entire body throbbed with
a pleasant, lingering heat.

He gathered her close and pressed a kiss to the top
of her head. "Six months," he grumbled. "And it
took a damn blackout to get you to talk to me."

"I feel rather fond of the blackout," she murmured. "Without it, I wouldn't have been forced to
spend so much time with you."

"Are you saying we never would have worked it out
if it hadn't been for that?"

"I wouldn't have given you the chance to get that
close to me," she said, her voice quiet with sincerity.
"I wasn't playing games, Tom. I was scared to death
of you, and of losing myself again. You never would

have had the chance to convince me, if it hadn't been for the blackout."

"Then God bless overloaded power grids," he muttered. "But I'd have gotten to you, one way or another."

"Other than kidnapping, I can't think how," she replied caustically.

He went very still, and the silence made her lift her head to give him a suspicious glare. He tried to look innocent, then gave it up when he saw she wasn't buying it.

"That was what I had planned for the weekend, if you refused to have dinner with me Thursday night," he admitted a bit sheepishly.

"Ah-ha. I *thought* you waylaid me that afternoon."

"A man has to do something when his woman won't give him the time of day," he muttered. "I was desperate."

She said, "It's six-thirty."

A brief flicker of confusion crossed his face; then he glanced at the clock and grinned. "So it is," he said with satisfaction. She had just given him the time of day—and a lot more. With a lithe twist of his powerful body he tumbled her back into the twisted sheets and came down on top of her.

"I love you," he rumbled. "And I still haven't heard the 'yes' I've been waiting for."

"I agreed. We made a deal."

"I know, but I'm a little more traditional than that. Elizabeth Major, will you marry me?"

She hesitated for a second. Eric Landers had lost the power to keep her a victim. "Yes, Tom Quinlan, I certainly will."

He lowered his head to kiss her. When he surfaced, they were both breathing hard and knew it would be a while yet before they got out of bed. He gave the clock another glance. "Around nine," he murmured, "remind me to make a couple of phone calls. I need to cancel the kidnapping plans."

She laughed, and kept laughing until his strong thrust into her body changed the laughter into a soft cry of pleasure, as he turned that relentless focus to the task of bringing them both to the intense ecstasy they found only with each other. She had been so afraid of that part of him, but now she knew it was what made him a man she could depend on for the rest of her life. As she clung to his shoulders, a dim echo of thought floated through her brain: "God bless overloads!"

LINDA HOWARD

Writing a bio has to rank right up at the top of anyone's list of most boring activities. My past and present life was and is so centerline normal that it's hard to come up with any interesting stuff, though as someone once pointed out, what we consider normal in our family would make most people think they've stumbled into a combination of the Addams Family and the A-Team.

Here's the regular stuff: I'm the second-eldest of six children. My parents were very balanced about it, producing two girls, then two boys, then twins of one each. Both identical and fraternal twins run in the family, which causes a certain amount of anxiety whenever there's a pregnancy, until technology can assure the frantic mom-to-be that yes, indeedy, there's only one in there.

I attended a small rural school, then a small community college. I'm a college dropout and have no desire to drop back in. My education is an ongoing process, but it's self-directed. I read heavily, on almost any subject, from astronomy to zoology. Cooking and housekeeping are two things I do *not* study.

After leaving college, I worked for a trucking company for seventeen years. I began writing when I was nine, and despite what I did for a living, I always thought of myself as a writer. I did one short story when I was nine, then leaped immediately into book length. Since there were no other writers around, there was no one to tell me how hard that was, so I happily wrote and wrote, not knowing that it was supposed to be difficult. When I decided to learn how to cross-stitch, I typically jumped in at the deep end. Did I pick a flower as my first project? A sampler? Of course not. Oblivious to the obvious, as usual, I simply chose the pattern I liked, which was 2 × 3 *feet* and contained 55,000 stitches. I didn't realize that wasn't the normal route to learning cross-stitch until I took it in to be framed and the craft lady was agog. Anyway, I've been writing professionally since 1980 and full-time since 1986. I've never wanted to do or be anything else, and it certainly set me free to study all of my other interests.

I've lived in northeast Alabama all of my life, amid mountains and lakes and rivers. Maybe it's the Cherokee in me, but the sight of a misty mountain doesn't bring to mind the freshness of it all, but how incredibly ancient it is, how it has endured hundreds of thousands of years before the existence of humankind. Growing up in a rural environment was great. We always had chickens and dogs and cats, and for a few years we raised our own bacon. Though seldom seen, there were also bears, wolves and mountain lions, as well as deer and wild turkeys. We had a pet rooster that thought it was a dog, which taught us the meaning of the term "birdbrain." Our menagerie also included turtles and terrapins, and a scorpion named Eric the Red. Frankly, reptiles and scorpions have limited repertoires.

Southern summers are childhood magic, long and hot and slow. Hmmm. Guess it's pretty good for adults, too. And since it is the South, there are, of course, a multitude of cousins in the near vicinity. I don't know why the parents didn't do whatever they could to keep the different sets of cousins apart; each group was volatile enough on its own, but put us together and things reached critical mass.

It must be genetic, but we were always interested in fire and explosives. Some kids play with matches; we made Molotov cocktails. Some kids catch fireflies in jars; we blew them up. The jars, not the fireflies. I guess it isn't your normal childhood occupation, but I can't remember when I *didn't* know how to make a Molotov cocktail. We used soft-drink bottles. Somehow, long before any of us studied chemistry, we knew what common household items could be mixed together to make a very satisfactory explosion. We destroyed countless bottles, jars and tin cans. We set off explosions in the big drainage pipes that run under driveways; we used smaller hollow pipes to make crude bazookas, aiming projectiles (rocks, sticks, whatever was handy) at selected targets. We would painstakingly dissect packs of firecrackers in order to collect enough gunpowder to give us the desired power. What I *can't* remember is any of the parents being particularly concerned by or interested in the muffled booms. Like I said, a combination of the Addams Family and the A-Team.

One summer we were visiting cousins and our attention was attracted by a big, hollow tree in their front yard. There was, of course, the usual supply of firecrackers, cherry bombs and M-80s. Life as we knew it wasn't possible without gunpowder. I don't remember if we were going to use the hollow in the tree as a holder for a rocket launcher, or if we were trying to blow up the tree itself. Minor detail. At any rate, there was a huge, satisfying BOOOM that rattled windows, though the tree remained upright and whole. We went happily in search of our next target, but after a few minutes noticed the smoke drifting from the top of the tree. This forty-foot tree was on fire. Inside. And it stood right next to the house.

Self-sufficient little devils that we were, we handled things ourselves. A ladder, a water hose, and it was taken care of, though the smoke did get a bit thick. Our uncle came outside and stared at the smoldering tree as we industriously sprayed it with water.

"What are y'all doing?" he asked, a bit irritably. Looking back, I can see why.

It seemed pretty obvious. "We're putting out the tree."

"Just how did it catch on fire?"

One of our cousins looked up at the blue, cloudless summer sky, then back to his father. "Lightning," he said.

Ah, summer.

Linda Howard

HOT COPY

Carole Buck

Chapter One

July 21, 1993
6:39 a.m.

Christine Marie Kavanaugh—the distaff half of the top-rated news anchor team in one of the largest local television markets in the southeastern United States—had always been a bridesmaid, never a bride.

Until now.

She couldn't help wondering why she hadn't had the good sense to leave well enough alone. She and Mitch Nelson, the man she was about to wed, had something special. It was something that had survived sixteen years' worth of stress and strain, mistakes and misunderstandings.

Was it *really* necessary for them to trade "I do's"? she asked herself. Getting married was bound to change their relationship. What guarantee did either of them have that the change would be for the better?

I love you, Mitch, Christy thought. But I don't know if I can—

"Darling, you look adorable!" someone behind her suddenly cooed.

Christy knew sarcasm when she heard it. Stung, she whirled around. Or, rather, she *tried* to whirl around. The elaborate, white lace gown she was wearing—a gown she couldn't recall picking out, purchasing or putting on—didn't lend itself to sudden movement. The huge hoop skirt of the dress seemed to have created some sort of suction effect, making it virtually impossible for her to shift position.

Muttering several of the words the Federal Communications Commission had declared were not fit for public airwaves, Christy twisted her body and yanked at the bottom half of the Scarlett O'Hara-style garment with both hands. After a few moments, the reinforced hem of the hoop skirt abruptly parted company from the floor.

Christy staggered a step or two, but managed to retain her balance. Then, teetering on a pair of heels that were at least two inches higher than anything she'd ever worn before, she turned and confronted the source of the pseudocompliment about her appearance.

The woman standing before her was serene. And stunning. And stylish. She seemed to be everything Christy—who was sweating profusely beneath her frilly bodice and feeling faintly nauseated—wasn't.

Including tall. Somehow, that was the worst of all. The woman, whoever she was, was at least five foot ten to Christy's barely five-four.

Christy cocked her chin and prayed she didn't topple off her stiltlike shoes. "Do I know you?" she challenged, using the inquisitorial tone she'd developed during a stint as an investigative reporter.

Unfortunately, the woman seemed more amused than intimidated. She smiled. "I'm Amanda. Mitch's ex-wife."

The fact that Mitch had been married before came as no surprise to Christy. She was aware that the man she'd finally agreed to wed had an ex-wife lurking in his background. It was something she'd accepted—and tried to ignore.

"Exactly what are you doing here...Amanda?" Christy wasn't about to address the other woman as "Mrs. Nelson." That title—for better or worse, for richer or poorer, et cetera and so forth—was going to belong to her in just a short while. She didn't intend to share it or the man who would be bestowing it upon her with anyone!

"I'm your matron of honor."

Christy nearly choked.

"It was Mitch's idea," Amanda added in a cordial coup de grace.

"Ninety seconds," an authoritative male voice declared. "Everybody settle down."

Christy went rigid. The voice belonged to Wayne Jackson. He was the floor director for the WEZE-TV newscasts she'd been co-anchoring, Monday through Friday at 6:00 and 11:00 p.m., since April. But what in heaven's name—?

She glanced around, focusing on her surroundings for the first time. Her stomach knotted. The setting for her impending nuptials was WEZE's main broadcast studio! And if that wasn't bad enough, the place was crawling with her newsroom colleagues!

But how could that possibly be? She and Mitch had agreed that they'd have an ultraquiet wedding—a bare bones, civil ceremony in a judge's office. They'd also agreed that no one from the station would be told anything about their marriage until after it and the honeymoon had taken place.

Obviously, something had gone wrong. Very wrong.

"So, babe," another distressingly familiar male voice said. "Are you all set?"

It can't be, Christy told herself desperately. Pivoting on wobbly heels, she turned toward the source of the question. It *can't* be!

But it was.

The man who'd addressed her was her co-anchor, Brent Harper. As much as she disliked him personally, Christy was willing to concede that Brent had what it took to be extremely successful at his job. His primary assets: golden hair, a silver tongue and an iron butt. In other words, he looked great, sounded better and had unlimited stamina when came to sitting down in front of a camera.

"What are you doing here?" Christy croaked. Brent was togged out in his favorite tax-deductible tuxedo. That did not bode well for the situation at hand. He was also sporting pancake makeup, bronzing powder and a teeny tiny touch of eyeliner. That boded even worse.

"I'm giving you away."

"You're *what?*"

"One minute," Wayne Jackson called.

"I'm giving you away," Brent repeated. His gaze strayed toward Amanda Nelson. He preened and turned his head, displaying his profile. It was a characteristic ploy. Brent considered himself God's gift to women and he made an effort to bestow himself on as many of them as possible. Since her arrival at WEZE, Christy had discovered that there were quite a few seemingly intelligent females who did not object to being the recipients of his sexual largess.

"Was this—" she swallowed hard "—Mitch's idea?"

"Of course not. It's in my new contract."

"But I thought you were still negotiating!"

"My agent settled the deal this morning." Brent flashed a set of the finest capped teeth money could buy. "If my co-anchor—that's you—marries my news director—that's Mitch—I have a contractual right to be in the wedding party."

Christy considered this outrageous assertion for several seconds, then said the only thing that seemed to make any sense.

Her co-anchor's eyes widened. "What do you mean 'no'?"

"I mean no, Brent. I do not, repeat, not want *you* giving me away."

"Thirty seconds, people."

"It's a little late for that, don't you think?" Brent huffed. "Whom *do* you want?"

"Nobody!"

"Oh, great. And next you'll be telling me you've decided you don't want to get married!"

"Fifteen seconds to broadcast."

"Well, maybe I *don't* want to—" Christy broke off abruptly, appalled by what she'd been on the verge of admitting. A split second later, she registered the implications of the countdown Wayne Jackson had been calling out. "Fifteen seconds to *what* broadcast?" she demanded.

"What broadcast do you think?" Brent snapped. "Jeez, Christy. Haven't you been listening to the promos? WEZE's preempting network programming to go live with your wedding."

Suddenly, Christy couldn't breathe. The bodice of her gown tightened around her chest like an iron corset. A white lace veil settled over her face, clouding her vision. She gasped. Filmy fabric filled her mouth.

"Ten seconds."

Panicking, Christy struggled to bat the veil away. Mitch, she thought. She needed Mitch.

"Christy?"

It was Mitch's voice. Cool. Competent. Compelling. When everyone else around him was losing his head, Mitchell Thomas Nelson inevitably kept his. That was one of the first things she'd learned about him.

"Five seconds."

"Sweetheart?" There was a *click*. The sound of a light being switched on. "What's the matter?"

Oh, God. She could hear Mitch, but she couldn't see him! She could feel his presence, but she couldn't find him!

"Four seconds."

"No," Christy protested, fighting against the suffocating veil. Someone—was it Brent?—caught her hands. Somehow, she managed to yank free.

"Three seconds."

"Christy, come on." It was Mitch again.

"No." She shook her head wildly. She wasn't sure what she was saying no to. She only knew she felt impelled to say it. "No."

"Two seconds."

Fingers gripped her upper arms. "Christy! Wake up!"

Christy opened her eyes. *"No!"* she cried out, surging to a sitting position. Her heart was hammering. She was trembling violently.

A pair of strong male arms encircled her. Embraced her. Gathered her shaking body close against a warm, well-muscled chest.

"Easy," Christy heard Mitch say. His voice—so fiercely commanding only an instant before—was soft and soothing. "It's all right, Christy."

She felt the tender stroke of his hands against her back and the teasing stir of his breath against her hair as he repeated the reassuring words over and over. She inhaled deeply, savoring the familiar, faintly musky scent of her lover's skin, then exhaled on a sigh.

"Easy," he murmured. "Easy. I've got you."

The aftereffects of her nightmare—for that's all it had been, just a stupid nightmare—gradually receded. The tremors running through Christy's body stilled. Her pulse slowed to something approaching its normal rhythm.

It's all right, she told herself. You're in your bed. In your apartment. And you're with Mitch. Everything's all right.

"Okay?" Mitch eventually asked, brushing his lips against her temple.

"Okay," Christy affirmed. After a second or two, she shifted away from the man she had pledged to marry before the day was out. The temptation to do the opposite—to snuggle intimately against him—was very strong. But with her recovery had come a sense of embarrassment. She'd obviously been tossing, turning and talking in her sleep. She wondered uneasily what she'd said and how Mitch had interpreted it.

There was only one way to find out. Gathering her nerve, Christy lifted her head and gazed up into the hazel eyes of the man who'd played a crucial role in some of the best—and a few of the worst—moments in her life.

Although he had the vitality of a man half his age, Mitch looked every day of his forty years. While his dark brown hair was as thick as it had ever been, it was liberally threaded with silver. There were fine lines radiating out from the corners of his eyes. Much deeper grooves bracketed his mouth.

Mitch wasn't classically handsome by any stretch of the imagination. He'd once jokingly described himself as having a great face for radio. There was a certain validity to this self-deprecating assessment. His angularly irregular features—the strongly sculpted jaw, the hawkish nose, the crook-cornered lips—were not particularly telegenic. However, they did add up to an emphatically masculine whole.

"I don't know what Mitch Nelson has," Christy had once overheard one of WEZE's production secretaries say to another, "but whatever it is, it makes all the other guys around this place seem like wimps."

"Christy?"

She moistened her lips. "I'm sorry, Mitch."

"For what? Having a nightmare?"

"Well..."

"It must have been a doozy."

The remark sounded wryly rhetorical. But Christy knew there was an implied inquiry embedded in the observation.

"Brent Harper was in it," she said after a few moments.

Mitch cocked a brow. "What was he trying to do?"

Christy hesitated, then opted for the truth. Part of it, at least. "Give me away."

"Huh?"

"He was at our wedding. He said he had a contractual right to give me away."

Mitch studied her for several seconds. Then, suddenly, he chuckled. "A contractual right?" he repeated. "No wonder you kept saying 'no.'"

Christy managed a small laugh. "Did I?"

"Yeah." Another deep-from-the-chest chuckle, punctuated by a lopsided grin. "I was afraid you were saying it to me."

This remark cut dangerously close to the bone. Christy reacted without thinking. "No!"

The smile disappeared. The chuckling stopped. Mitch seemed genuinely taken aback by her vehemence. "No?"

"I didn't," Christy tried to explain. "I mean, I wouldn't." Lord. She was babbling like a guilt-ridden idiot! "That is, I wasn't."

"You weren't what, Christy?"

She gestured. "Saying no to you, Mitch. In...in the nightmare."

There was a silence at this point. Christy never knew precisely how long it lasted. She sufficed to say it was long enough for her to become acutely aware of the fact that both she and Mitch were naked.

Not that she hadn't been conscious of their mutual state of undress prior to this silence. She had eyes. She could see. She could see plenty. She could also remember the feel of her body pressing against Mitch's when he'd held her, heart-to-heart, after she'd woken up from her nightmare.

Still. The awareness that blossomed during the silence was unsettling. It was also very arousing.

"What about in real life?" Mitch finally asked. It was evident that she wasn't the only one who'd been affected by the last few moments. There was a hint of huskiness in his voice. His gaze strayed downward from her face for an instant, then returned to focus on her mouth. The green flecks in his changeable eyes glinted like shards of emeralds.

Christy swallowed, feeling the tips of her breasts tighten. There was an odd, expectant fluttering in the pit of her stomach. "Real—" she swallowed a second time "—life?"

"Uh-huh." He brought his hands up to cup her shoulders. His fingers were faintly callused. His palms were warm. "Are you going to be saying no to me a lot in real life?"

It was impossible for Christy to be touched by Mitch without wanting to touch him in return. She lifted her hands, pressing them against his hair-roughened chest. "That depends," she responded, stroking upward.

"On what?"

Christy closed her eyes as Mitch began to caress her breasts. He brushed the pads of his thumbs across her nipples, triggering an explosion of pleasure deep within her. The breath she hadn't even realized she'd been holding escaped her lungs in a rush. She opened her eyes.

"What does it depend on, Christy?" Mitch prompted. A flush of excitement rode high on his sharply hewn cheeks.

"On...mmm...circumstances." Like most of the women she knew, Christy was plagued by insecurities about the size and shape of her body. These insecurities evaporated when she was alone with Mitch. He made her feel as though she were the most exquisitely made female in the world.

"What about *these* circumstances?" The movement of his long, lean fingers became more explicitly erotic.

Christy dipped her head and pressed a kiss against Mitch's throat. She felt the jump of his pulse against her lips. She licked his skin, savoring its resilient texture and faintly salty taste. "What about them?"

"Are these the kind of circumstances that would make you say no to me?"

Considering that Mitch began maneuvering her from a sitting position to a supine one even as he asked this question, it was obvious what he assumed her answer was going to be. Given the shameless way she cooperated with his handling, Christy was prepared to admit that his assumption was justified.

"No," she replied huskily.

"Which means?"

Christy locked her arms around Mitch's neck. She wove her fingers through his thick, dark hair and pulled his face down toward hers. "Exactly what you think it means."

He showed his teeth in a very male smile. "Good."

And then he kissed her. Hotly. Hungrily. She kissed him back the same way. He nipped at her lower lip. She responded in kind.

The kiss went on and on. Their breaths blended. Their tongues mated in a bone-liquifying evocation of the joining still to come.

There was nowhere the man who'd been Christy's first lover hadn't touched her in the past. There was nowhere he didn't touch her now. Somehow, the sensations he evoked seemed more intense than ever before. She went from willing to wanton in a matter of moments.

Mitch sought and found the most sensitive part of her feminine core. Christy cried out, arching against his palm. Her fingers flexed in a response she couldn't have controlled if she'd tried. Her nails bit into the tautly muscled flesh of his broad shoulders.

"Yes," she gasped on a shuddery breath.

"*Yes,*" he echoed hoarsely several seconds later when he entered her with one smooth, powerful stroke. Christy lifted her hips, sheathing him inside her as deeply as she could. Mitch gave a guttural groan then claimed her lips once again.

There was no hesitation. No holding back. They moved together as one. Pleasuring. Possessing. The give-and-take was searingly sweet.

Then, without warning, Mitch stopped.

Christy whimpered his name. She was close. So close. Fulfillment beckoned with a white-hot promise. But she couldn't reach it alone!

"I just... thought... of something, sweetheart."

"You can *think* at a time like this?" Her voice shredded halfway through the question. Fevered and frustrated, she attempted to shift her position. Mitch held her fast.

The rigidity of his sweat-sheened body and the raggedness of his breathing made it clear how much his stillness was costing him. The force of his will was a palpable thing.

"Isn't it supposed to be...bad luck...for the groom to see the bride before the ceremony?" he questioned.

Christy blinked several times, trying to make sense of this inquiry. Bad luck? she asked herself. How could the groom seeing the—

Oh. Yes. Yes, of course!

"It's only b-bad luck if the bride's wearing her wedding g-gown," she said unsteadily. She thought fleetingly of the hoop-skirted horror she'd had on in her nightmare and shuddered. "But since I'm not wearing—oh...ohhhh." Her shudder gave way to the first glorious spasm of release as Mitch stopped restraining himself and began to move inside her once again. "Oh...*yes!*"

Christine Marie Kavanaugh never managed to finish her explanation.

It didn't really matter. The man she was supposed to marry had obviously understood the point she'd intended to make.

Chapter Two

Mitchell Thomas Nelson had first proposed to Christine Marie Kavanaugh in New York City on May 30, 1978. They'd been lovers for nine months. He'd been twenty-five. She'd recently graduated from college and had been about to celebrate her twenty-first birthday. She'd also been on the verge of leaving him—and the Big Apple—for a reporting job.

In all honesty, matrimony hadn't been on his agenda at that point in his life. He'd been stunned when the words *marry me* had come tumbling out of his mouth. He knew Christy had been stunned, too. He'd seen the astonishment on her face.

And after the astonishment he'd seen anger, as well as several other emotions he hadn't been able to interpret until much later. His impulsive proposal had been adamantly rejected. The quarrel that had erupted out of the rejection had been bad. The parting that had followed, even worse.

He'd proposed to her again on July 9, 1993—roughly three months after she'd joined the WEZE news team and precisely twenty-eight days after they'd resumed the physical relationship they'd broken off the night she'd refused his first offer of marriage.

"But...what's wrong with what we have now?" Christy had asked when he'd finished the speech he'd been rehearsing in his head for more than a week. Her normally mellifluous voice had been tight. There'd been something close to panic in her long-lashed, dark brown eyes.

"It's not enough, Christy," he'd told her. "I thought it would be. But it's not. I love you. I love you and I want you to be my wife."

"I love you, too, Mitch," she'd responded. "But—"

Clamping down on a flash of temper at the caveat, he'd silenced her with a quick, claiming kiss. "You don't have to answer right away," he'd murmured against her lips. "Just think about it."

She had.

Mitch had made his proposal on Friday night. Christy hadn't given him her response until the following Sunday afternoon. There'd been moments during the interim day-and-a-half when he'd come very close to exploding with frustration. Only the memory of past mistakes had enabled him to keep his emotions in check.

Finally...

"All right," she'd said to him in the languid aftermath of lovemaking.

The answer had come out of nowhere. His first thought had been that Christy was offering an assessment of the ecstasy they'd just shared. But...all right? Just *all right?* Such a description had struck him as understatement bordering on insult.

He'd levered himself up on one elbow and studied Christy. Her cheeks had been flushed, her short brown hair tousled and her coral pink lips faintly swollen. She'd been deliciously disheveled—a provocative contrast to the impeccably groomed image she presented in her professional life.

"All right, what?" he'd asked after a few moments, savoring his private view of a very public woman.

"All right, let's get married."

His breath had jammed somewhere between his lungs and his lips. "Christy," he'd eventually managed to get out. "Are you... are you *sure?*"

She'd laughed shakily. "It's what you want, isn't it?"

"Yes," he'd instantly affirmed. "God, yes. I want it more than anything. But you have to want it, too."

She'd reached up and stroked her fingers lightly against his face. He'd felt the feathery caress clear down to the soles of his feet. His body had begun to harden, his blood had started to hum. "What I want is you," she'd told him. "I want you very much, Mitch."

"Enough to marry me?"

"Yes."

The world had seemed to tilt. He'd struggled to keep his bearings. His heart's desire had been within his grasp and yet...

"When?" he'd demanded.

He'd braced himself for hesitation—for a lot of hemming and hawing about arrangements. But Christy hadn't batted an eyelash.

"What do you think about Wednesday, July twenty-first?" she'd asked steadily. "We're both scheduled to be on vacation that week. I know you've got a broadcasters' convention to go to, but it'll be over on the twentieth. We can have a quiet wedding on the twenty-first, then go away together for a few days."

"How...quiet...a wedding?"

"You. Me. A judge. Two witnesses." Her tone had been crisp and unequivocal. "No mess. No white lace fuss. No flung rice."

"No family?" He hadn't been sure why he'd asked this. His parents were dead and he was an only child. As for her relatives, well, given what he knew, he would have been amazed if Christy had wanted to invite them.

"No."

"No friends?"

"No."

"No colleagues from work?"

"Definitely not."

"We *are* going to tell people afterward, though."

"Tell people?" She'd seemed puzzled by the inquiry.

He'd nodded. "I've gone along with your wanting to keep our involvement a secret because I know the kind of gossip there'd be if people at the station found out we were having an affair. But our getting married is something else. If you're hoping to hide—"

"Oh, no," she'd interrupted, a hint of throatiness entering her voice. "Never. If I marry you—"

"When," he'd corrected fiercely. "*When* you marry me." He'd bent his head and kissed her. The taste of her mouth—and of the sense of triumph he'd been experiencing—had been very, very sweet. "As for what I think about having Wednesday, July 21st for a wedding date—" He'd kissed her again. Deeper. More demandingly. "—sweetheart, it can't come soon enough."

July 21, 1993
5:16 p.m.

"This waiting is driving me nuts!" Christy exclaimed, tossing down her purse and springing up from the seat she'd taken barely thirty seconds before. She began pacing around the office of the Right Honorable Judge Josiah Patterson Burnside.

Mitch remained seated on the leather couch his wife-to-be had just deserted. He checked the clock that was hanging on the wall behind the judge's desk. "We've been here less than fifteen minutes," he pointed out.

"Well, it seems longer," came the irritable reply. "Much longer."

Mitch watched silently as Christy roamed restlessly around the office. Despite her agitation, her movements were graceful. The elegantly simple cream dress she was wearing flattered her slender shape. It subtly hinted at, rather than blatantly hugged, her fluently feminine curves.

"How late do you suppose Judge Burnside is going to be?" she eventually asked, glancing in his direction.

"Your guess is as good as mine," Mitch replied, smothering his own impatience.

"What if we miss our flight?"

"It doesn't leave until eight o'clock, sweetheart."

Christy fluffed at her light brown hair and made an inarticulate sound of frustration. "I just want to get this thing over with!"

Mitch knew there'd been a time when he would have taken umbrage at her use of the phrase "this thing" to describe their impending wedding. Fortunately, that time had passed. He understood—far better now than he had fifteen years ago—why Christy was so terribly wary of marriage.

The woman he loved was the product of a psychological war zone. A variety of pressures, including the insidious ones labeled "maintaining appearances" and "staying together for the sake of the children," had kept her wealthy, socialite parents locked in a poisonous relationship for twenty years. They'd finally separated the week Christy, the oldest of their three daughters, had turned eighteen.

"The news that my mother and father were filing for divorce was the best birthday present I ever got," she'd once confessed to him. The expression in her eyes had been bleak to the point of bitterness.

He'd had to wait a long time for Christy to open up about her parents' marriage. Yet even after she had, it had been difficult for him to imagine the environment in which she'd been raised. His own parents had shared eighteen years of love and laughter before they'd been killed by a drunken driver. The memory of the joy they'd had together had sustained him through his grief at their untimely deaths.

Christy had moved to stand in front of one of the office's two windows. She was toying with its venetian blinds. Her body language—the rigid spine, the stubbornly squared shoulders—spoke of great stress. So did the trembling of her fingers.

Mitch got up from the couch. He crossed the room in a half dozen long strides, his footsteps muffled by the office's wall-to-wall carpeting.

Christy started slightly when he slid his arms around her waist. While she didn't resist when he drew her back against him, she didn't exactly relax into his embrace, either.

The crown of her head just reached Mitch's chin. He brushed his lips against her hair, savoring its silken texture. Christy's bridal coiffure—an artless arrangement of feathery curls—was infinitely more touchable than the heavily sprayed "hair helmet" required by her anchoring chores.

"I know you're nervous," he murmured. The spicy-sweet scent of her perfume teased his nostrils. He felt a stir of response in his groin. "I am, too."

She made a sound that was somewhere between a choke and a chuckle. "How can you be nervous? You've done this before."

The reference to his first marriage caught Mitch completely off guard. "I—uh—"

Christy turned in the circle of his arms and looked up at him. "What was Amanda like? Was she beautiful?"

Mitch didn't know what to say. Or maybe he did, but didn't know how to say it. To put it bluntly, his ex-wife had been like Christy in a lot of ways. Both of them had brown hair, brown eyes and flawless, faintly tawny complexions. Both of them had even, finely drawn features. Both of them had flashing smiles that revealed flirtatious sets of dimples.

But Christy had a special spark—a unique complexity of spirit—that Amanda had never possessed. This missing spark had been one of many reasons he'd been willing to agree to the divorce she'd demanded barely two years after they'd traded "I do's." One of the others had been his recognition that whatever her deficiencies, Amanda deserved better than a husband who put her a distant third to his work and the memory of another woman.

"Mitch?" Christy prompted.

"Amanda was . . . is . . . attractive."

"Tall?"

"Uh—no. About your height."

An odd expression flickered across Christy's face. "Really?"

Mitch frowned, trying to figure out what had prompted this uncharacteristic curiosity about his ex-wife. While he'd always been prepared to talk about Amanda, Christy had never pressed the subject before. His basic reaction to this apparent lack of interest had been relief. He was acutely aware that the story of his marriage was not likely to bolster Christy's shaky opinions about the institution.

"Where did you get the idea Amanda was tall?" he asked.

A tiny shrug. Another odd expression. "Just an impression."

She was hiding something. He could feel it. Unbidden, his mind jumped back to the nightmare she'd had that morning. She'd been hiding something about that, too. "Christy—"

At that moment, the office's overhead lights went out. It happened suddenly. There was no warning flicker. They just shut off, as though someone had thrown a switch. The muted hum of the air-conditioning system fell silent in the same abrupt fashion.

Mitch glanced at the clock on the wall. Its hands were frozen at twenty-three minutes past five.

5:45 p.m.

"I have a bad feeling about this."

Mitch knew precisely what Christy meant. He, too, had a bad feeling. But he wasn't going to admit to it. He wasn't going to admit it because he had an even *worse* feeling about what might happen if he did.

"You heard what Judge Burnside's secretary said when she came in here a few minutes ago," he responded, loosening his tie with a quick tug of his fingers. The temperature in the office seemed to have risen four or five degrees since the air-conditioning had gone off. Hardly surprising, given the sizzling summer weather outside. "There's a lot of construction going on in this area. Somebody probably made a mistake and cut through a cable."

"Maybe, but I don't think so."

"It happens all the time. Then again, there could be a system overload. This heat wave we're having has pushed power companies to the limit."

Christy remained silent for several seconds. Mitch watched her eyes stray toward Judge Burnside's desk. He knew exactly what was drawing her attention. It was a telephone.

Christy looked back at him. "We really should call the station."

He shook his head, willing himself not to glance toward the judge's desk. "We're on vacation."

"I know that, but—"

"We're here to get married, remember?"

"Of course, I remember. But—"

"Look," he cut in sharply. Christy's use of the word *but* bothered him. It bothered him a lot. "It's a quarter to six. Fifteen minutes 'til air time. We both know that the last thing the newsroom needs right now is one of us phoning in to check out some minor power failure."

"What if it *isn't* minor? What if—what if power's out all over the city? Don't you think Dave and Gus would appreciate a call?"

The "Dave" in question was David Bauman, producer of WEZE's award-winning 6:00 and 11:00 p.m.

newscasts. The "Gus" was Augustus Mulroney, the station's assignment editor.

"If power's out all over the city," Mitch said flatly, "Dave and Gus aren't going to have time to appreciate *anything*."

Christy acknowledged his point with a grimace, but didn't abandon her argument. "Even so—"

Goaded by an emotion he couldn't—or wouldn't—put a name to, Mitch interrupted her. "Okay. Supposing we *did* call the station. And supposing somebody told us the whole city's blacked out. What would you want to do, Christy?" He searched her face for a moment or two. Something knotted deep inside him. "Would you want to forget the wedding and—"

"Forget...the weddin'?" a sonorous, very Southern sounding male voice queried from the doorway of the office.

Mitch turned. So did Christy. "Judge Burnside!" they exclaimed.

"In the flesh," the judge affirmed, mopping his brow with a large white linen handkerchief.

"Are you all right, Your Honor?" Christy questioned.

"Fine. Fine. Just a bit...winded...after bein' required to climb five flights of stairs." The judge dragged the handkerchief across his forehead again. "Oh. It's not just the city...that's blacked out. It's practically the whole southeastern United States!"

"*What?*" The question came from both of them, simultaneously.

"One of the bailiffs downstairs...had a radio. There's...all kinds...all kinds of confusion. Electricity's off everyplace. Heard something about sunspots. Some kind of...solar stormin'."

Mitch glanced at Christy. He knew they were thinking the same thing.

A multistate power failure affecting millions of people.

It was one *hell* of a story.

He shifted his gaze to the telephone on the desk, mentally reviewing WEZE's resources. "Judge Burnside," he said, "would you mind if I used—"

Beep. Beep. Beep.

It took Mitch a split second to recognize the annoying, high-pitched sound for what it was and to realize that it was emanating from his left pants pocket. By that time, the damage had been done.

"You brought your beeper to our wedding?" Christy gasped, her dark eyes flashing a volatile mix of accusation and indignation.

"Christy, please—" Mitch fumbled in his pocket.

"You stood there trying to make me feel guilty about wanting to call the station and all the time—*all the time!*—you had your *beeper* with you?"

"A mistake," he protested, still trying to shut off the beeper. He couldn't find the Off button.

"Oh, I'll say it was a mistake!" Christy pivoted away from him.

Mitch finally succeeded in silencing the insistent *beep-beep-beep* of his electronic pager. Reaching out, he caught his infuriated fiancée by the arm and forced her to turn back to face him. She tried to jerk free. He wouldn't let go. He had the feeling that if he did, he might very well lose her forever.

An excuse, he thought suddenly. She's just looking for an excuse to call this wedding off.

"For God's sake!" he exclaimed. "I didn't mean to bring the damned beeper with me. I don't even remember sticking it in my pocket!"

"Do you really expect me to believe that?" she shot back, still struggling to break loose from his grasp. "Of all the—"

It was at this point that *Christy's* beeper went off.

Chapter Three

"Honestly, Mitch. I didn't know I had it with me."

"I believe you, Christy."

"I mean, I have absolutely no idea why I put my beeper in my purse."

"Let's just forget it, okay?"

Christy sighed heavily and wished she could do just that. She glanced downward, focusing on the fingers of her left hand. The *ringless* fingers of her left hand. A peculiar pang of emotion lanced through her.

It's not my fault we didn't get married, she reminded herself. Mitch was the one who suggested postponing the wedding, not me.

Sighing a second time, Christy lifted her gaze and surveyed the tangle of traffic she and Mitch had been trapped in for nearly twenty-five minutes. The city's version of evening rush hour was bad enough under the best of circumstances. But with every single traffic light out and scores of desperate-to-be-home commuters jamming the streets...

The driver of the car behind theirs began honking his horn. Christy glanced left. Mitch was staring straight ahead. His hands—ringless like hers—held the steering wheel in a white-knuckled grip.

"I'm sorry about what happened back in Judge Burnside's office," she said softly.

He kept his eyes on the road. "Are you?"

She blinked, taken aback by the challenging tone of this response.

"Of course I am," she asserted after a second or two.

"Fine" came the terse reply. "Apology accepted."

"But—"

"Why don't you take another shot at calling the station?"

Christy hesitated briefly, then decided that this was neither the time nor place for them to hash out what had happened in Judge Burnside's office. They'd have plenty of opportunity to do that later.

Leaning forward, she picked up Mitch's car phone. She punched in a string of numbers, then put the receiver to her ear. She heard nothing but a faint crackle of static. Disconnecting, she repeated the process. Again, she heard nothing but static. She got the same results on the third try.

"Still no luck," she finally reported, returning the receiver to its cradle. She eyed the rectangular opening in the dashboard where there should have been a radio. Unfortunately, Mitch's was in the shop for repairs.

"Dammit," she heard him mutter. "I wish I knew what was happening."

Christy tried to think of something soothing to say. She failed miserably. Instead, she kept recalling what Mitch had related to her about the phone conversation he'd had with Gus Mulroney right before they'd made their exit—unwed—from Judge Burnside's office.

"What's this about people being stuck in an elevator?" she'd asked anxiously as she and Mitch had trekked down the fire stairs of the municipal building in which the judge's office was located. Although she'd only heard Mitch's side of the exchange with WEZE's assignment editor, it had been more than enough to alarm her.

"Gus says two cars are stopped between the newsroom floor and the broadcast studio," he'd answered.

"Is anybody hurt?"

"I don't think so."

That, at least, had been something to be grateful for. "Do you know who—?"

"There are seven guys in one car. Four techs, including the TelePrompTer operator, plus Rick Bennett from Special Assignment, and Jack and Pete from Sports. Brent and Linda are in the other one."

It had taken Christy a moment to grasp the professional implications of the last sentence. The "Linda" Mitch had mentioned was Linda Shawcross, the cohost of WEZE's noontime talk show. She was also Christy's vacation fill-in. And if both she and Brent Harper were—

"My God!" she'd exclaimed. "Who's anchoring the six o'clock newscast?" She'd taken it as an article of faith that—power failure or no—WEZE would be on the air with a six o'clock newscast.

A fractional pause. Then, succinctly, "Wally."

"Wally . . . the *weatherman?*"

"It was either him or Delia."

Christy had grimaced. Delia Reynolds was the newest member of the WEZE on-air staff. She was also the girlfriend of the station's owner. A blond and buxom ex-beauty queen, Delia had a certain talent for turning out fluffy little features about adorable little animals and cute little kids. But when it came to coping with breaking news . . .

"That was my reaction, too," Mitch had concurred dryly.

They'd reached the lobby level of the municipal building at that point and gone outside. The early evening air had been hot and heavy and humid. Within seconds, Christy had felt herself start to perspire. Mitch had taken off the suit jacket he was wearing and slung it over his arm.

"It could've been worse," he'd commented as they'd headed toward the lot where he'd parked his car.

"Worse than a choice between Wally and Delia?"

"No. Worse than nine people trapped in two elevators. According to Gus, the building's third car just reached the twenty-fourth floor when the power went out. Luckily, somebody managed to pry the doors open."

"Were there passengers?"

"Dave Bauman. The new robo-cam operator, Scott. Your favorite floor director, Wayne Jackson and SueBee Hawkins."

The last name had caused Christy to check herself in midstride. "SueBee Hawkins?" she'd repeated incredulously. "I thought she was finally going on maternity leave this week."

"She did. But the substitute makeup artist was hospitalized last night. SueBee apparently agreed to come back and fill in for a few days."

"For heaven's sake, Mitch! She's due at the end of this—"

The blare of a car horn jerked Christy back into the present. She turned toward Mitch. Every element of his expression—from the sharp V of his drawn-together brows to the quilting of the small muscles along the side of his angular jaw—communicated frustration. And there was something more. Something darker. More... disturbing.

"Why don't I try calling the station again?" she offered.

He slanted her a look she wasn't certain how to interpret. It was very similar to the look he'd given her when she'd seconded his suggestion that they postpone their wedding.

"Good idea," he said after a moment.

She leaned forward and picked up the mobile phone. "At least Gus knows we're on our way to the station."

Mitch sounded his car horn. "Too bad only God knows when—or if—we'll get there."

7:17 p.m.

"Mr. Nelson! Miz Kavanaugh!" The exclamation came from the retired police officer who guarded the lobby of the glass-and-metal high rise that housed the business offices and studios of WEZE-TV. "What're y'all doin' here?"

"Going to work, Joe," Mitch answered. "There's a big story to cover."

"Can you fill me in on what's goin' on?"

Mitch nodded at the radio he'd spotted sitting on the guard's desk. "You probably know more than we do if you've been listening to that."

The grizzled old guard looked disappointed. "I been tryin' to tune in some news ever since the lights went off, but it's been real hard pickin' anythin' up. I *did* hear that it's not just us that got hit with this blackout, though. Six, seven, maybe eight states are dark. There was some scientific expert on claimin' it's all because of sunspots." A skeptical snort. "Sounds kind of fishy to me. Anyway, the mayor's declared we're havin' some kind of emergency." A second snort, this one scornful. "Like we need some overpaid politician to tell us that. The governor's gettin' in on the declaration act, too. Probably have the President doin' the same thing before too long."

"What's the situation in the building?" Christy asked.

Joe scratched his forehead. "Everybody's out 'cept you news folks. Elevators are at a dead stop. Whole bunch of people got trapped—"

"Yes, we know about that. Are they all right?"

"Last I heard. I keep tryin' to call 911. To get some help rescuin' 'em, you know? But the number's always busy. As for the rest, well, the air-conditionin's completely off. Place's goin' to be like an oven in another few hours. But at least it won't be totally dark. We got lights operatin' on batteries here and there."

"Is WEZE's emergency power still on?" Mitch questioned. One of the few pieces of good news he'd gotten from Gus Mulroney was that the station's diesel-fueled backup generators had kicked in as they were supposed to.

"I guess. I haven't checked it personal. I mean, a man of my age? Tryin' to climb up to the top of this place?"

Mitch glanced at Christy. It was obvious from her expression that the guard's words had registered with her in the same way they'd registered with him.

WEZE's newsroom was on the eighteenth floor. Its studios and most of its production facilities were six floors above that.

Twenty-four floors.

Two flights per floor.

Twelve, maybe fifteen, steps per flight.

Ouch!

"I forgot about the stairs," he admitted, forking his right hand back through his hair.

"Me, too." Christy plucked at the front of her cream-colored dress. Mitch could see that the gently draped bodice was damp with perspiration. "Still. Better stairs than a subway tunnel like last time."

"Last time?" Joe echoed. "You two been through somethin' like this before?"

"The New York City blackout of 1977," Mitch said, not wanting to elaborate. His mood at the moment was anything but nostalgic.

"You were in a *subway* tunnel?"

"Mitch and I happened to be sitting next to each other in a train that got caught between stations when the power failed," Christy explained. "I grabbed his hand. I was still holding on to it five hours later when a team of transit workers finally showed up to evacuate us."

7:24 p.m.

Midway between the seventh and eighth floors, the anger that had been building inside Mitch coalesced and achieved critical emotional mass.

She said she loved him, but...

She said she was willing to marry him, but...

She was always setting limits, making excuses, imposing conditions. She was always holding something back!

Outside of bed, the only time Christine Marie Kavanaugh had ever turned to him without reservation had been in the darkness of a stalled New York City subway car on the night of July 13, 1977. She'd taken his hand—the hand of a stranger!—and she'd *clung* to it.

Mitch's mind suddenly replayed the hypothesis he'd thrown at Christy in Judge Burnside's office.

"Supposing we did call the station," he'd challenged. *"And supposing somebody told us the whole city's blacked out. What would you want to do Christy? Would you want to forget the wedding and—"*

"Well, I guess I didn't need to complete the question to get your answer," he said.

Christy, who'd reached the eighth-floor landing a few steps ahead of him, paused and turned around. "What?"

Mitch stopped where he was and looked up at her. "Back in Judge Burnside's office, I started to ask you what you'd want to do if we called the station and found out the whole city was blacked out. The first option—which I never got to finish—was to forget the wedding and go to work."

The stairwell they were in was equipped with the battery-powered lights Joe, the guard, had mentioned. Although the illumination from these lights was weak, it was sufficient enough to reveal an abrupt loss of color in Christy's face.

"The wedding's not forgotten," she disputed. "It's just postponed."

"Until when?"

"Until, until, I don't know exactly." Christy gazed down at him for the space of several heartbeats then said pointedly, "*You're* the one who suggested we wait, Mitch."

He advanced to the landing. "An idea you were more than happy to endorse."

"Well, what did you want me to do? Demand that Judge Burnside marry us right then and there?"

The truth clouted him like a two-by-four. Yes, he realized. Yes, dammit! That's *exactly* what he'd wanted her to do. He'd wanted her to make an unequivocal commitment to him—no ifs, ands or buts.

He recalled his assessment of Christy's reaction to the discovery that he'd accidentally—and it had been accidentally!—brought his beeper to Judge Burnside's office.

An excuse, he'd thought. *She's just looking for an excuse to call the wedding off.*

Christy's lips parted on a rushing exhalation of breath. Her dark eyes widened. It was obvious that she'd sensed the flavor of his thoughts.

"When you suggested—" she broke off, shaking her head as though rejecting the possibility she'd been about to raise. Mitch stayed silent. Finally, she resumed speaking. "Was that . . . was that some kind of *test?*"

The accusation in her voice flicked him on the raw. "If it was," he snapped, "you failed." Brushing by her, he continued up the stairs.

"That's not fair!" Christy called after him.

It wasn't and, deep down, he knew it. But fairness wasn't the point anymore. He kept climbing, increasing his pace a bit. After a moment, he heard Christy's footsteps behind him. The sound of shoe heels hitting cement echoed eerily through the stairwell.

She caught up with him on the twelfth-floor landing. They were both huffing and puffing by that time. Christy's previous pallor had given way to a flush of color that had as much to do with anger as exertion.

"It's not . . . my fault, Mitch."

"What . . . isn't your fault?"

"That we didn't . . . get married. I was ready—"

"Oh, yes." He sucked in a deep breath. "So ready, you jumped at the first little excuse to put the ceremony off."

She glared at him, her breasts heaving. "I wouldn't call what may be the worst blackout in U.S. history a 'little excuse'!"

"Oh, of course not," he fired back. A phrase from their mutual past popped into his mind. "*You'd* call it a major journalistic opportunity!"

She flinched. It was obvious she recognized the words as her own. "Well, what if I would?" she returned, her voice rising. "Are you going to pretend you don't think this is important? I mean, did I or did I not hear you tell Joe we were here because there's a big story to cover?"

"That's not the same thing."

"Of course it is!"

He gestured dismissively. "Have it your way. You always do."

"And what's *that* supposed to mean?"

"Figure it out for yourself!" He started climbing once again. His chest was tight. His temples were throbbing. He could feel sweat trickling down his back and chest. He yanked open a few shirt buttons.

"Mitch!"

He kept going. And he would have kept going straight to the top if a stitch in his left side hadn't forced him to stop on the twenty-first floor landing. The sudden stab of pain nearly had him doubled over. He leaned forward, trying not to think about the series on stress and heart attacks WEZE's medical reporter had done several months before.

"Mi...itch?" It was Christy. She was gasping for air.

He jerked upright when he felt her touch him. "I'm...fine!"

She reached out to touch him again but something in his expression must have warned her against it. She lowered her arm. "No—" she struggled to fill her lungs "—you're not."

"Yes." He edged back, gritting his teeth. "I...am." He stared at her, his thoughts as disjointed as his breathing was disordered. "Why are you so damned sure our getting married would be...a mistake?" he asked rawly.

For a moment, she seemed too stunned to speak. Then, falteringly, "I n-never—"

"Don't deny it." Mitch inhaled and squeezed his arm tightly against his side. The stitch seemed to be easing. His mind veered off on a dangerous tangent. "Not all marriages...are like your parents'."

"I know th-that," Christy responded shakily. "Some marriages...are like my sisters'. They've already had five between them." She paused, her chin going up a notch. "And some...and *some* marriages are like yours! It lasted—what, Mitch? Two years?"

Mitch was beyond censoring himself. "I only married Amanda because she reminded me of you! Dammit, Christy. I love you!"

"And I love you!" She threw the words at him like rocks. "But that doesn't mean—"

Mitch suddenly understood the meaning of the phrase "seeing red." He caught Christy by the arms. "You can't stop saying it, can you?" he demanded.

"Wh-what?"

"*But.*" He spat the syllable out. "It's always there. Your little escape clause. You love me...*but*. You'll marry me...*but*."

"Bu—" She stopped herself a split second too late.

Mitch cursed. He tightened his grip for an instant, then opened his hands. Christy staggered back a step. "Forget it," he said. "Just forget it. Forget us and forget the wedding. Forget all of it!"

There was a disastrous silence.

Dear God, Mitch thought, appalled. *What have I done?*

There was no need for him to search for the answer to this question. All he had to do was to look at the expression on Christy's face.

"Fine," she said after a moment, her voice as brittle and colorless as a piece of plate glass. "If that's what you want." Then she turned away from him and began walking up the stairs again.

"Christy!"

She didn't stop.

He didn't blame her.

Mitch's recollection of what happened during the next few minutes was never clear. Had someone told him he'd finished the climb to the twenty-fourth floor on his hands and knees, he probably would have believed it.

He caught up with Christy at the top of the stairs. They struggled briefly—breathlessly—over which one of them would open the door, then they staggered out into the hallway that led to the WEZE news studios.

"Mitch! Christy! I didn't know you were together!"

The source of this salutation was an eager-beaver production assistant nicknamed "Eye Chart." The moniker was the product of jokes about his surname, which was an unwieldy combination of consonants and vowels: "the fourth line of an eye chart," according to one of the station's resident wags.

Mitch saw Christy nail the unfortunate young man with a single look.

"We . . . *were* together," she panted. "We're not . . . anymore!"

And with that, she went stumbling down the hall.

"Jeez!" Eye Chart gasped. "What'd I say?"

"The wrong...thing," Mitch answered, leaning against the wall. He felt sick.

"But—"

"Don't, Eye Chart. That's the...wrong thing...to say, too." Mitch lifted his left arm and stared blearily at his wristwatch. It took him a moment to make sense of the digital readout.

8:06.

Mitch frowned. There was something about the time...

Then he realized. The flight he and Christy had booked for their honeymoon getaway had been scheduled to leave six minutes ago.

Chapter Four

Christy sought refuge in WEZE's greenroom—the space where the station's on-air guests waited prior to making their appearances. She understood she didn't have much time. There was a job to be done. A big story to be covered. Still, if she could just have a few minutes alone...

The greenroom was dark once she closed the door. Christy felt her way to a chair and collapsed into it. Hugging herself, she hunched forward.

"Forget it," Mitch had said. *"Just forget it. Forget us and forget the wedding. Forget all of it!"*

"F-forget it," Christy repeated unsteadily. The bridge of her nose ached with the pressure of unshed tears. "Forget...all...of it."

Even if she'd wanted to, there was no way—

Mitch had asked for her telephone number once they'd been evacuated from the subway tunnel. As she'd scribbled it on a scrap of paper she'd found in her purse, she'd succumbed to an uncharacteristic urge to flirt, and teased him about having waited to make his request until after he'd had a chance to see what she looked like.

"I knew what you looked like hours ago, Christy. I spotted you the second I stepped on the subway," he'd responded, his voice soft, his gaze steady. "And I elbowed two guys out of the way to make sure I ended up in the seat next to yours. I was trying to think of something to say to you when the lights went out."

This comment—and the memory of the almost electric sense of connection she'd felt when she'd first grabbed Mitch's hand—had given her plenty to think about during the long trek from the subway station to the East Side apartment she shared with two other girls. Mitch had insisted on escorting her to her front door, but refused her invitation to come inside. She hadn't taken the refusal personally. One of the many things she'd learned about him during their hours in the darkness was that he was employed as an associate producer at a local television station. As an aspiring broadcast journalist herself, she'd empathized with his hunger to get involved in covering what was bound to be one of the biggest stories of the year.

A week had passed before she'd heard from Mitch again. By the time he'd finally called, she'd given up hope that he'd ever make use of the telephone number she'd so willingly provided. She'd told herself she'd been foolish to mistake the kindness of an attractive stranger for personal interest.

"Hello?" she'd said flatly when she'd answered the phone.

"Christy?"

She'd recognized his resonant voice instantly. "Mitch?"

"Yeah. That's right." He'd sounded both surprised and pleased that she'd identified him on the strength of two syllables. "How are you?"

"Fine."

"Any aftereffects from being stuck in the subway?"

She'd decided not to mention the erotic dreams that had invaded her slumbers for several nights running. "None so far. How have you been?"

"Okay. Busy as hell, though."

There'd been an uncomfortable pause. Recalling how easily she and the man on the other end of the line had talked with each other the night of the blackout, she'd wondered at the awkwardness.

Finally, Mitch had cleared his throat and said, "You've, ah, probably wondered why I haven't gotten in touch before this."

"A little," she'd conceded, not wanting him to think she'd been lingering by the phone, longing for his call. "I mean, after what happened . . ."

"Yeah, well, that's why I held off."

"I don't understand."

"What went on between us was pretty intense, Christy." The sudden huskiness of his voice had sent a quiver running through her. "I thought it might be a good idea if we each had a little time to step back."

"I . . . see."

There'd been another pause.

"Christy?"

Her heart had been beating very rapidly. "Still here."

"Look, if you're not doing anything Saturday night, would you like to spend a few hours holding hands in the dark?"

She'd been surprised into laughter. "Haven't we already done that?"

"That was in a subway. This would be at the movies. Your all-time favorite, *Citizen Kane,* is playing in the Village."

"How did you know—?"

"You mentioned it the other night."

"Oh." It had been her turn to be both surprised and pleased.

"So, what do you say?"

What she'd said had been, "Yes."

They'd become lovers roughly six weeks later. They'd had more than a dozen dates by then. She'd finished the summer job she'd had in one of the network news departments and begun her final year at Barnard College.

Their "dates" had not been particularly romantic. Indeed, they'd spent much more of their time together debating political issues and discussing their professional ambitions than flirting. Still, not all the sparks they'd struck off each other had been intellectual ones.

Her awareness of how carefully Mitch had been controlling himself when they were together had dawned rather late. While not ignorant about the facts

of life, she'd had very little real-life experience with the
opposite sex. She'd been an overweight wallflower
during her adolescence. Although she'd dropped the
excess poundage when she'd gotten to college, she
hadn't been able to overcome her sense of social in-
adequacy. Not that she'd made much of an effort to.
She'd preferred to remain aloof—apart—and devote
herself to achieving her career goals.

Given this, she'd been grateful that Mitch hadn't
tried to push the pace of their relationship—that he'd
left the crucial questions of how far, how fast, up to
her. Yet, at the same time, there'd been a part of her
that had resented his self-discipline. Deep down, she'd
wanted to be overwhelmed. To be relieved of the responsibility and risk that went with saying yes to intimacy.

Ultimately, she'd discovered that there was a way to
strike a balance between her seemingly contradictory
emotions.

It had been a Saturday night. She and Mitch had
been strolling around Greenwich Village after a delicious meal at a little Italian restaurant they'd discovered.

"So, Christy," he'd said, draping a companionable
arm around her shoulders. His touch had triggered a
familiar tremor of response in her. "Your place or
mine?"

The clichéd line had become a running joke with
them. Mitch had used it the first time one of their
kisses had caught fire and threatened to burn out of
control. By making it clear that he didn't expect the

inquiry to be taken seriously, he'd managed to cool things off. At the same time, he'd obliquely acknowledged the incendiary implications of their sexual chemistry.

In the past, Christy had always responded to the query with a quip. Not this night. She'd stopped walking. Mitch had stopped walking, too. He'd been smiling. Their eyes had met and his smile had faded. In that moment, she'd made her decision.

"Christy?" he'd asked.

She'd lifted her right hand and laid it against Mitch's chest. She'd been conscious of a sense of possessiveness she'd never previously known.

"Since I have two roommates and you live alone," she'd answered, "I think it should be yours."

Mitch's left hand had come up to cover her right one. She'd moistened her lips and seen his eyes spark with dangerous green fire.

"Are you sure?" he'd asked, his voice deeper and darker than it had been a few seconds before.

"Yes," she'd said. "Oh, yes."

Mitch had asked her the same question—a bit more insistently—some time after their arrival at his small, spartanly furnished apartment. She'd given him the same answer. Because she *had* been sure.

Yet as certain as she'd been about the rightness of what she'd intended to do, there'd come an instant when an instinctive feminine fear had welled up inside her. Mitch had sensed her change of mood instantly. "Christy?" he'd questioned, easing back from a long, lingering kiss. "What is it?"

Somehow, his obvious attunement to her had served to increase her uneasiness rather than ameliorate it. Her impulse had been to look away. She'd started to avert her head but his fingers had caged her face with tender implacability, preventing her from evading his gaze or the issue.

"Christy?" he'd repeated. "What's wrong?"

"I—I've never done this before, Mitch."

She'd expected him to be surprised by—perhaps even a little ambivalent about—this admission. But he hadn't been. In fact, the expression she'd glimpsed in his eyes had told her that the possibility she was a virgin had already occurred to him.

A new fear had comingled the first. Her cheeks had gone hot with an unfamiliar kind of mortification. "Is it that obvious?" she'd asked.

Mitch had dipped his head and licked her lower lip, then stroked the moisture he'd left with the ball of his thumb. "Not the way you mean."

"But—"

"Shh." His breath had misted her lips. "You were made for this, sweetheart. We both were."

He'd claimed her mouth then, more deeply than before. She'd parted her lips. A moment later, she'd felt the rough-velvet insinuation of his tongue. Every vein in her body had seemed to expand, releasing wave upon wave of warmth. It had prickled along her skin, puckered the nipples of her breasts, and pooled between her quivering thighs like molten honey.

He'd kissed his way down her throat. She'd tilted her head back with a long, drawn-out sigh and closed her eyes.

Mitch had dealt adeptly with the buttons of her blouse, the zipper of her skirt, the tiny clasp at the front of her bra. Before she'd fully realized what was happening, she'd been reduced to wearing nothing but a pair of lace-trimmed panties and a scattering of goosebumps.

She'd opened her eyes, shivering as awareness of her near nudity had swept through her. A sense of insecurity had seized her. She'd started to lift her arms up to shield her body.

"No," Mitch had said, forestalling her effort by capturing her wrists. His gray-green eyes had moved over her. "Don't. You're so . . . sweet heaven, Christy, do you have any idea how beautiful you are?"

"Beautiful" had never been a word Christine Marie Kavanaugh had associated with herself. But in that instant, she'd been utterly persuaded she was.

She'd lowered her arms. Mitch had stroked his hands up. Her knees had nearly given way when he'd taken full-palmed possession of her breasts.

Kisses. Slow and searing.

Caresses. Ardent and arousing.

His clothing had become a source of frustration to both of them. She'd tried to rectify the situation. The shakiness of her fingers had undercut her eager efforts to help him undress.

"Oh, G-God—" Mitch had groaned as she'd fumbled at the front of his jeans. "Please. *Sweetheart*. Let me do it."

She had. Seconds later, he'd been naked. He'd opened his arms. She'd gone to him.

After an unknowable number of minutes, Mitch had swept her up and carried her to the alcove that held his bed. He'd laid her down like some priceless treasure, then stroked her from throat to breast, from breast to hip. She'd reached up, wanting to draw him down beside her. Evading her hands, he'd straightened and stepped back.

"Wait," he'd said.

She'd spoken his name in protest, struggling to lever herself into a sitting position. She'd watched, befuddled by sensation, as he'd crossed to a small bureau, opened its top drawer and taken something out. After a few moments, he'd turned back to face her. He'd been wearing a condom.

She'd flushed, embarrassed by the sudden realization that she'd given no thought to birth control. "I didn't—"

"It's all right," Mitch had interrupted, moving back toward the bed with lithe, athletic strides. He'd gazed down at her for a moment. "I did."

The mattress had sagged a little under his weight when he'd stretched out beside her. She'd shivered with anticipation as he'd taken her into his arms once again. He'd begun to explore her with his hands and mouth, worshipful and wanton at the same time.

"Touch me," Mitch had urged. "Please, Christy. Touch me."

She had. Emboldened, she'd touched him everywhere. Instinct had guided her most of the way. Mitch's responses—the sudden groan, the shattered breath—had taken her the rest of the way.

She'd cried out as he'd feathered his fingers against the aching apex of her body. Something within her had clenched like a fist, then released into a melting spill of pleasure.

"Mitch," she'd pleaded.

"Soon," he'd promised.

She'd felt him shift his weight. His hands had slid around to her back then moved down to cup her buttocks. He'd lifted her. She'd opened to him without hesitation.

Nothing had prepared her for the swift, sure thrust that Mitch had used to bring them together. There'd been an instant of discomfort followed by an indescribable sense of fullness. And beyond that sense of fullness there'd been something more. It had summoned her with a pulsating radiance.

"Oh..." she'd gasped, straining upward. "Oh..."

"Easy, Christy," her lover had whispered. "Just let it happen."

"I...can't..."

"Yes, you can."

He'd moved then, and she'd moved with him. Meeting. Matching. Mating. Merging. The earth had moved, as well, or so it had seemed.

"Mitch!" she'd cried out, clutching at the man who was the center of a wildly spinning universe.

"I'm here, sweetheart. I'm—"

July 21, 1993
8:14 p.m.

"—here, Christy?"

Christy started violently, her body throbbing with echoes of remembered ecstasy. "W-what?" she stammered, blinking as the beam from a flashlight hit her squarely in the eyes.

"Don't worry," a familiar feminine voice drawled. "It's only me."

The flashlight beam shifted. Christy squinted toward the doorway of the greenroom. The short, bulging-belly figure she saw standing there was as recognizable as the voice. "SueBee?"

"That's right. Mitch asked me to find you."

Christy swallowed. "Did he?"

"Uh-huh. I'm s'posed to make you up for the next cut-in. Then I've got to practice using the Tele-PrompTer machine. I don't know if you've heard, but the regular prompter operator's stuck in an elevator with a half dozen other people, so I'm fillin' in for him. I've got my makeup set up in the main studio. 'Course, with no air-conditionin', the foundation's goin' to melt right off you. I tried sprayin' Wally's bald spot with deodorant earlier, but it didn't do any good. I swear, that man's forehead looked like a baked ham on air. Oh, before I forget—I had somebody go down to the eighteenth floor to get that navy blazer you keep in your office. I figured you might need somethin' fresh to wear."

"Thank you." Christy got to her feet. She felt weak.

"You all right?" SueBee inquired solicitously.

"I'm fine," Christy answered, steadying herself by sheer force of will. She walked to the door with slow, careful steps.

They began making their way down the hall. The only sources of illumination were SueBee's flashlight and the flickering glow emanating from the TV monitors in the edit bays that lined the long corridor.

"Eye Chart said you and Mitch came in together," the makeup artist commented after a few moments. "Must have been somethin'—havin' to climb up twenty-four floors."

"Oh, yes," Christy agreed tightly. "It was something."

"You can't stop saying it, can you?" Mitch had demanded, his voice harsh, the grip he'd had on her arms almost hurtful.

"Wh-what?" she'd asked, not understanding.

"But," he'd responded. *"It's always there. Your little escape clause. You love me . . . but. You'll marry me . . . but."*

He'd been so angry, she thought, clenching her hands. Her nails bit into the flesh of her palms. She'd never seen him so angry! Not even fifteen years ago when—

A grunt of distress penetrated Christy's turbulent recollections. She checked her stride, suddenly realizing that SueBee had come to a halt in the middle of the hall. The blond-haired makeup artist was pressing one hand against her rounded belly.

"What's wrong?" Christy questioned, genuinely alarmed.

SueBee took her hand away from her belly. "It's just a contraction."

"A...contraction?"

"It's nothin' to worry about. I've only had a couple."

"SueBee!"

"I'm not goin' to have my baby tonight, Christy," the makeup artist declared, resuming her waddling progress down the corridor. "Now, let's go get you ready to do TV."

Chapter Five

Mitch scanned the five people who were gathered at the conference table with him.

Seated to his left: producer Dave Bauman, a lean, coiled spring of a man who occasionally vented his professional frustrations by throwing telephones but never raised his voice. Next to him, assignment editor Gus Mulroney. Short, squat and sarcastic, Gus had long ago mastered the art of screaming while chain-smoking cigarettes and swilling black coffee.

Seated on the other side of the table, to Mitch's right: WEZE's balding butterball of a weatherman, Wally Parker. Next to him, chief engineer Andy Castle, a handsome black man who'd learned electronics in the army.

Seated at the far end of the table, directly opposite Mitch: anchor Christine Kavanaugh, the woman who was supposed to have become his wife more than four hours ago. She was the only one in the room who wasn't looking at him. Her eyes were fixed on the spiral-bound notebook in front of her.

Mitch bit back the urge to ask Christy what she found so fascinating about the page she kept staring at. As far as he could see, the damned thing was blank.

"Okay," he said, running a hand back through his hair. He felt a trickle of sweat course down the line of his spine. "The last cut-in was good. And just in case you're wondering—yes, we do have an audience. We've been getting calls from people who're watching us on battery-powered TVs."

"Any Nielsen families?" Dave Bauman queried wryly, referring to the all-important television ratings system.

Mitch smiled briefly. "Let's hope so. In any case, I've made a decision about the next couple of cut-ins. I want to do them with Christy voicing from the announcer's booth. We can switch in any live shots we've got from the field. We're using too much juice and generating too much heat when we light up the studio. Some of the equipment's starting to act up. I don't want to jeopardize the eleven o'clock newscast."

There were concurring comments from Gus, Dave, Andy and Wally.

"Christy?" Mitch questioned, working to keep his voice neutral.

She lifted her gaze. "If you want me in the announcer's booth, you've got me in the announcer's booth."

Mitch's body tightened. *If* he wanted her...

"Fine," he said tersely, breaking eye contact. He looked at WEZE's chief engineer, forcing himself to focus on professional matters. "What's the situation with our folks in the elevators?"

"Pretty good, all things considered," Andy Castle replied in his deep bass voice. "Like I told you when you got here, the hatches on the tops of both cars are open and so are the shaft doors on this floor. They're blocked off, but we've fixed up a pulley system so we can lower stuff down. All the comforts of home—assuming home happens to be a cave somewhere along the equator."

"What about the audio link?"

"There's some interference, but it's basically okay. The biggest problem is that Brent doesn't know the difference between *send* and *receive*. He's also ticked off you won't let him do live reports on the trauma of being trapped in an elevator."

"Does he sound traumatized?" Mitch inquired dryly.

"Nah. Just his normal unpleasant self."

"So you don't think he's likely to emerge from this ordeal a better person?" Gus Mulroney was the source of this sardonic query.

"No way." Andy chuckled, then looked at Mitch once again. "The bottom line is, everyone in the elevators seems to be all right. We've got the sound from both cars routed through the control room."

Mitch nodded his approval. "Gus, what's the latest from the field?"

The assignment editor rattled off the requested information with machine-gun rapidity.

"Okay." Mitch glanced at Dave Bauman. "Have we got a definite time on the power company news conference?"

"They're still saying around eleven," the producer answered. "It's going to be a mob scene."

The word *mob* triggered a thought. Mitch looked at Gus Mulroney again. "What's happening with those disturbances on the South Side?"

The assignment editor fanned his ruddy face with one hand. "The latest we've picked up on the police scanner sounds like pretty minor stuff. Some looting. Some vandalism. I've got a crew on the way. No reporter."

Mitch proceeded to the next item on his agenda. "Wally, how's the report on the cause of the blackout coming?"

The rotund weatherman straightened in his chair and stroked a hand across his receding hairline. He then launched into a complicated recitation larded with terms like "atomic nuclei and electrons," "solar cosmic rays," "step-up transformers," "subtransmission substations" and "load dispatchers."

"Are you going to be able to boil this down to a couple of minutes?" Mitch questioned when Wally paused to breathe.

"More to the point," Gus Mulroney inserted, "is anybody going to be able to understand it once you do?"

The weatherman looked abashed. "It'll be better with pictures," he promised. "We've got some great file tape of solar flares."

"Okay, Wally," Mitch said. "Just keep it simple."

There were a couple more minutes of discussion. Except for an expression of concern about the very pregnant SueBee Hawkins, Christy contributed nothing to the conversation.

Andy, Dave and Wally left the room as soon as the meeting ended. Gus stayed put at the table. Mitch remained seated, as well, watching Christy gather her things and get up from her chair.

She had to pass within touching distance to reach the door. Unable to stop himself, Mitch caught her by the hand. He said her name.

She froze in her tracks, but didn't attempt to pull free of his grasp. She just turned her head slightly and looked at him. Beneath the tan-toned pancake and powder she was wearing, she was very pale.

Mitch tightened his hold for an instant, then let go. An expression he cou'dn't interpret flickered across Christy's face. He saw her swallow.

"What?" she asked after a second or two.

Words clogged his throat and clotted on the tip of his tongue. Apologetic words. Angry words. Words of accusation and explanation.

"Was that . . . was that some kind of test?" she'd asked him.

"If it was," he'd returned, *"you failed."*

And she had, in a sense. But he'd failed, too, hadn't he? He'd been so certain what he wanted for them was right that he'd pushed and pushed—

"I meant what I said before," he abruptly declared. "About the last cut-in. It was good. And you were great."

Her chin went up. Something deep inside him ached at the familiarity of the movement. "Thank you," she replied. "But you know me, Mitch. If I see a major journalistic opportunity, I take it."

And with that, she left the room.

"Trouble in paradise?" Gus inquired after a few moments.

Mitch's first impulse was to deny everything. Then he took a look at his colleague's ruddy face and understood denial wasn't going to do any good.

"What do you think you know, Gus?" he asked carefully.

"Same thing that everybody else around the station thinks they know. Except for Eye Chart, of course. Don't get me wrong. I like the kid. He's a hard worker. But he can be dumber than a box of rocks about human nature."

"I see." Mitch shifted, trying to adjust to the idea that the affair he and Christy had believed they'd kept under wraps apparently was common knowledge. How had they revealed themselves? he wondered.

"Don't waste time trying to figure out how people figured out, Mitch," Gus counseled. "It wasn't anything either one of you said or did. It's just that there's been this—this *buzz* between you and Christy ever since she joined the station."

"Look, there was nothing going on between Christy and me when I hired her," Mitch snapped. "We were friends, yes. But if anybody's suggesting—"

The assignment editor held up a hand. "Nobody's suggesting anything, Mitch. Least of all that Christine Kavanaugh got her anchoring job at WEZE by sleeping with the news director." He cocked his head, considering. "I'd say that little development broke about...mmm...maybe five weeks ago."

The guess was unnervingly close to the mark. "God, Gus," Mitch said, with a ragged laugh. "Have you been spying on us?"

"I've got an instinct for certain things," Gus replied, shrugging. "Even so, I wasn't absolutely sure about the two of you until a couple of minutes ago. I mean, it's not like you and Christy got caught playing Make Friends with Mr. Salami on company time."

Mitch understood the reference. One of the first bits of WEZE gossip he'd picked up had been Brent Harper's nickname for a certain part of his anatomy. "Has our ace anchorman been up to something at the station?"

"Yeah. You might say that. On Monday—when you were out of town—Eye Chart neglected to knock before he opened the door to the anchor office. He, ah, tripped over Brent and Linda."

Mitch got the picture. Vividly. "Oh, man."

Gus shook his head disgustedly. "'Mr Salami,' my ass. Talk about having delusions of grandeur. Brent's barely a cocktail frank!"

Mitch had to laugh. For a moment, the weight he was carrying seemed to lift. Then he stopped laughing and the weight pressed down once again.

Christy, he thought. Oh, Christy...

"You want to talk about it?"

Mitch sighed and rubbed the back of his neck. After a few seconds, he looked at the assignment editor. Beneath his prickly exterior, Gus Mulroney was a very perceptive person. He was also a good friend. "Do you know Judge Burnside?"

A nod.

"Christy and I were in his office when you beeped us. We were . . . supposed to be getting married."

Gus didn't even blink. "You were supposed to, but you didn't?"

"No." Mitch shook his head, the taste of the single syllable he'd just uttered bitter on his tongue. "We didn't."

"Because I beeped you?"

"Because after I talked to you, I suggested to Christy that we postpone the wedding and go to work."

"Why the hell did you do a stupid thing like that?" Gus demanded. Then he frowned, his eyes narrowing. "Unless you didn't really want—"

"I've wanted to marry Christy for fifteen years," Mitch cut in. He gestured. "I *still* want to marry her."

"But?"

Mitch winced. Lord, if he ever heard that word again—

"*But?*" Gus prodded.

Mitch debated with himself. Then, briefly and bluntly, he related what had happened during the climb up to the twenty-fourth floor.

Gus let several seconds tick away. "Well," he finally said, his tone reflective, "I guess you can't keep fifteen years' worth of frustration bottled up forever."

"And what's *that* supposed to mean?"

"It means that in the four years you've been at WEZE, I've seen you lose your temper three, maybe four, times. It takes a lot to get you to the boiling point, Mitch. Even more to get you to blow off steam. But when you do. . ."

"You don't know what you're talking about, Gus."

"Did you propose to Christy fifteen years ago?"

Mitch hesitated, then told the truth.

"And?" Gus prompted.

"And, what do you think? She turned me down."

"So?"

"So nothing!"

"You haven't been carrying around some sort of grudge?"

"No!" Mitch closed his eyes, struggling against a sudden onslaught of memories. "At least, not anymore. . . ."

He and Christy had made a date to meet for dinner at their favorite Italian restaurant in the Village. She'd breezed in more than a half hour late. She'd been incandescent with excitement. There hadn't been a man in the place who hadn't stared at her, including him.

She'd reached the corner table where he'd been sitting, stewing, for thirty minutes and kissed him on the mouth. His response to this unusually public display of affection had been equal parts of arousal and anxiety.

"I'm sorry I'm late," she'd said, sitting down opposite him.

"No problem," he'd answered. "You look... happy."

He'd been conscious of an odd sense of resentment as he'd spoken the adjective. Christy had been *glowing*. Yet as far as he'd been able to tell, it had had nothing—not a damned thing!—to do with him.

"I am happy." She'd leaned forward. "I've got a job, Mitch."

"A job?" It had been his understanding that Christy intended to return to the researcher's slot she'd had the previous summer. He'd known she wasn't entirely happy with the situation because of the role her father had played in securing the position for her. Still, he'd thought she'd vowed to prove to her colleagues that while she might have gotten the job through family connections, she was more than capable of succeeding at it on her own.

She'd nodded, her toffee-colored hair rippling over her shoulders. "At the public broadcasting station in Boston."

"I didn't realize—"

"I know." Christy had reached across the table and touched his hand. "I was going to tell you, but I was afraid of jinxing my chances. I'm still having trouble believing the station actually picked me. I mean, well, *you* know the kind of work they do there. And I landed this all by myself. It's not like the slot at the network, with my father pulling strings. This is more than just a job, Mitch. This is a...a major journalistic opportunity!"

She'd smiled at him then, the sweet curve of her lips seeming to mock the pomposity of her final words. But the determined sparkle in her eyes and the confident uplift of her chin had sent another message.

He'd experienced a rush of pride followed by a sudden constriction in his chest. I'm going to lose her, he'd thought. I'm going to lose her to a job in Boston.

"What about us?" he'd asked, pulling his hand out from under hers.

Her smile had vanished. "Us?"

"Yeah. You and me. The past ten months. Us."

"But this won't—Mitch! It's only *Boston*. We can still see each other on weekends. Given the schedule you've been working, weekends are about the only time we've had together anyway."

"Are you complaining?"

"No. Of course not. I know how important your career is to you." Christy had paused, her gaze very steady. Then she'd added, "It's as important to you as mine is to me."

He'd found himself squirming and he'd blamed her.

"Look, I realize it's going to be complicated—living in two different cities," she'd gone on. "But it's not as though I'm talking about moving to, to, oh, I don't know! To Seattle or someplace like that."

Her choice of cities had been unfortunate. Because he, too, had been under consideration for a "major journalistic opportunity." And he, too, had been keeping superstitiously silent about it.

Christy had gone still. Her eyes had flicked back and forth, reading his face like a printed page. "What?" she'd asked.

There'd been no point in evasion.

"There's a producer's slot opening up on the late news at the number two station in Spokane," he'd answered flatly. "They like my resume tape. They want to fly me out for an interview next week."

"I see." She'd arched her brows. "Congratulations."

"I was going to tell you."

"Oh, really? When?" Her tone had been as sweet and as sharp as a sugar-coated razor. "At the airport?"

"No! For God's sake, Christy. I'd want you to come with me."

"To Spokane, you mean."

He'd felt like a driver who'd suddenly discovered he had no brakes. All he'd been able to do was to steer as best he could for as long as he could and to pray that the inevitable crash wouldn't be fatal.

"Yeah," he'd said, nodding. "If I get the job."

"Oh, you'll get it. But what about *my* job, Mitch?"

"Look, I didn't know about 'your job' until five minutes ago."

"You expect me to give it up, don't you?"

"I want us to be together!"

"What about what *I* want?"

"Dammit, Christy, I love you! I—" He'd reached across the table and caught one of her hands. And then he'd said it. "Marry me."

"W-what?" she'd stammered after a stunned silence.

He'd said it again.

"Are you out of your mind?"

Maybe he had been....

July 21, 1993
9:43 p.m.

... and maybe he still was.

Mitch opened his eyes. He looked at Gus Mulroney, uncertain how long he'd been tangled in the web of memory.

The assignment editor didn't say anything. He just sat there.

"I proposed to Christy in New York," Mitch finally told him. "We'd known each other about ten months." His mouth twisted. "We'd met during the '77 blackout."

That made Gus sit up a little straighter. "No kidding?"

"No kidding. It just ... happened."

"The blackout or the meeting?"

"The proposal."

"Are you saying you didn't mean it?"

"Oh, I meant it. Once it came out and I realized what I'd said, I meant it." Mitch gestured. "Christy had this job offer in Boston. I was close to getting one in Spokane. She, well, she ended up thinking I wanted her to put her career second to mine."

"Did you?"

The admission didn't come easily. "Yeah. Deep down, I did. But that wasn't why I asked her to marry me. The proposal wasn't supposed to be some kind of consolation prize for her giving up a great job. It was for me, Gus. The proposal was for me."

"Huh?"

Mitch inhaled sharply through his nostrils. "My parents died when I was seventeen. I was pretty much on my own after that. I worked my way through college in three years, then busted my tail to land a decent job. I didn't have the time—or the inclination—to get involved with anybody."

"Until Christy."

"Until Christy." Mitch averted his gaze. "I knew what that job in Boston meant to her. But it didn't matter to me. I was so damned scared of losing her. Of losing somebody else I loved...." He looked back at Gus. "Marriage was the only way I could think of to hold on to her. But instead of keeping her close, I ended up driving her—"

Mitch broke off as he caught the sound of someone pounding down the hallway that led to the room where they were sitting. A second later, Eye Chart skidded through the doorway.

"Mayor's...news conference," he panted. "Five minutes."

Chapter Six

10:45 p.m.

Mitch checked his wristwatch as he moved swiftly down the hallway that led to WEZE's main control room and broadcast studio.

Fifteen minutes to air.

He knew that to most people this probably seemed like a very modest chunk of time. But to him, a veteran of an industry where every single second was squeezed to the limit, it was an eternity.

He inhaled sharply. If he could get fifteen minutes alone with Christy, maybe he could begin to—

"WEZE's eye-in-the-sky camera was over the city when the power—"

"Dammit!"

The first voice, poised and pleasant, was Christy's. The sound of it had a profoundly disruptive effect on Mitch's pulse. The second, fierce and frustrated, belonged to Dean Yaeger, one of the station's best tape editors. The sound of it made Mitch's nerves tighten.

Both voices had issued from the edit bay he'd just passed. Mitch pivoted, backtracked, then stepped into the small workspace.

"What?" he demanded of the T-shirted man who was hunched in front of a pair of editing machines.

The air was redolent of stale cigarette smoke and deadline-induced sweat. There was a can of grape soda perched atop one of the room's two TV monitors, a blatant violation of the station's prohibition against food or drink in the production area.

"A few more hours without air-conditioning and every piece of equipment in this place is going to go down," the frizzy-haired editor grumbled. "The damned edit points keep slipping."

Mitch grimaced. The report Dean was working on was a blackout overview. He was counting on having it as a backup for the top of the 11:00 p.m. newscast—in case there were any difficulties with the power company news conference. One of the cardinal rules of doing live television was to anticipate the worst and make contingency plans accordingly.

"I need this piece cued up in Playback in less than fifteen minutes, Dean," he said.

"Yeah, yeah. I know," the editor responded. "Don't worry. It'll be ready." Dean picked up the can of soda and took a healthy swig. He then raised the condensation-fogged container and rubbed it against his brow.

"Is that *cold?*" Mitch asked, suddenly conscious of a Sahara-like dryness in his mouth. This dryness was in direct and unpleasant contrast to the dampness he felt under his arms and at the base of his spine.

Dean grinned and pressed the can to one side of his neck. "Icy."

"Where the hell did you get—" Mitch broke off, realizing there was only one logical answer. "Let me guess. Engineering."

"Yep. The department's refrigerator just happens to be hooked in to the backup generator." The editor extended the soda. "You want some?"

Despite the fact that he loathed grape soda, Mitch didn't hesitate. He accepted the offer and drank deeply.

The editor waved off his effort to hand back the can. "Keep it."

"Thanks."

"You're welcome." Dean returned his attention to the editing machines. "And like I said before, Mitch, don't worry. Christy's package will be where you want it, when you want it."

Mitch resumed his quick step down the dimly lit corridor. He'd just about reached the door to the control room when he heard the *click-click* of a woman's high heels behind him.

He stopped.

He turned.

Christy was approaching at a rapid pace, shuffling through a sheaf of script pages as she walked. She was so engrossed in her task, she almost bumped into him. She stopped a few inches short of a collision, her head coming up. Her gaze met his. Mitch swore the temperature in the hallway soared several degrees in the space of a single heartbeat.

"Oh . . . Mitch."

He heard a husky uncertainty in her voice. He also saw a sudden flush of color stain her cheeks. Her brown eyes, artfully enhanced with liner and mascara, were wide and watchful.

She took a step back. Despite this small retreat, she was close enough that Mitch could gauge the accelerated rhythm of her pulse by watching the vein that throbbed at the base of her throat. She was close enough that he could smell the elementally feminine fragrance of her body as well as the overlying scent of perfume, cosmetics and hairspray.

"Christy." He swallowed hard. "How are you holding up?"

"Fine," she answered, her voice still a bit breathless. Her gaze flicked downward for an instant then bounced back up to his face. "Grape soda?" she asked with a tinge of disbelief.

It took him a second to make sense of this inquiry. "Oh, yeah," he affirmed, gesturing with the can he'd forgotten he was holding.

"But you *hate* grape soda."

The observation was a punch-to-the-gut reminder of how thoroughly Christy knew his tastes. "It's cold," he said after a moment.

"Where in the world did you get cold—" Christy broke off, the corners of her mouth quirking. "Oh. Engineering, right?"

Mitch nodded. He held out the can. It wasn't much of an olive branch. Christy liked grape soda only marginally better than he did. But maybe, just maybe...

She hesitated, an odd expression flickering through the depths of her dark eyes. Then she murmured a word of thanks and accepted the proffered can. Their fingers brushed as she did so. Mitch caught his breath.

She took a long drink. Her lips were sheened with moisture when she finally lowered the can. She licked them with a curling stroke of her tongue.

Mitch felt the muscles of his belly clench.

"Christy," he began, his voice low and less than steady. "I know this is a lousy time. But I need to, I mean, *we* have to—"

Just then, the door to the control room burst open and Eye Chart came dashing out. He checked himself when he saw Mitch and Christy.

"Oh. You're here," he said, his gaze darting back and forth between them. "Dave, uh, sent me to, uh, find you. For the, uh, broadcast."

Mitch clamped down on a sudden surge of temper, realizing there was no point in getting angry with the production assistant. He glanced at his watch. Nine minutes to air. He looked at Christy. "Later?" he questioned.

She gazed at him silently for several seconds, then nodded.

10:59 p.m.

Mitch took a deep breath and scanned the bank of television monitors in front of him. Exactly one minute until air. Christy's overview package had arrived in Playback, as promised, thirty seconds earlier.

He was sitting in the swivel chair usually occupied by Dave Bauman. Dave was seated directly to his left, in the swivel chair normally occupied by director Bob Nichols. Nichols, unfortunately, was one of WEZE's elevator strandees. Dave had assumed his responsibilities. Mitch, in turn, had taken over Dave's producing duties.

"Opening preset?" Dave queried.

"Preset," came the crisp reply.

"Audio?"

"Check," Phil, the audio engineer, answered.

Mitch's gaze flicked back and forth between the two monitors that showed Christy sitting on the news set. She was peering into a compact and powdering her forehead, nose and chin. He saw her grimace with displeasure.

Leaning forward, he thumbed the switch that allowed him to speak to her through the small "IFB" device she wore in her left ear. "Don't sweat it," he said into the goosenecked microphone that sprouted out of the console in front of him. "You look beautiful."

10:59:30 p.m.

"Stand by. Thirty seconds," Dave Bauman announced. "Coming to Christy on One. Set the split for the toss to Evan."

Mitch thumbed another switch. This one allowed him to speak to Evan Tyler, the WEZE reporter who was standing by at the site of the impending power company news conference.

"Heads up, Evan," Mitch said, shifting his gaze to another monitor. "We're coming to you in about a minute."

The craggily handsome reporter whose image filled a screen nodded his head and gave a thumbs-up signal.

"Open Christy's mike. Stand by effects and animation."

"Ready Playback."

10:59:55 p.m.

"Five seconds!"

Mitch watched Christy straighten her script pages, square her shoulders and stare directly into the lens of Camera One. She exuded assurance and authority.

"Stand by Video Tape Recorder One."

The center of the control room's bank of monitors was dominated by two screens. One was labelled Program. The other was labelled Preset.

"Roll VTR One."

A promo slide advising viewers that WEZE's award-winning 11:00 p.m. newscast was coming up next appeared on the screen of the program monitor.

A three-two-one countdown on the top of the tape that would open the newscast sprang to life on the preset monitor.

11:00:00 p.m.

"Take VTR One. Take logo," Dave commanded.

A close-up of the governor of the state appeared on the program monitor. The WEZE logo was superimposed on the lower right-hand corner of the screen.

"I have just declared a state of emergency," the governor said. "I'm asking people to stay calm and pull together in this very difficult time."

The governor's face was replaced by aerial shots taken by WEZE's eye-in-the-sky camera at the exact moment the blackout had begun.

"Go, Christy," Dave cued. "Stand by VTR Two."

"An unprecedented power failure strikes the southeastern United States," Christy read. "Millions of lives have been disrupted. There is—"

"Roll VTR Two."

"—no word on when the electricity will go back on."

"Take VTR Two!"

WEZE's news theme began pouring out of the control-room speakers. A fast-paced montage filled the screen of the program monitor.

"Take Two," Dave ordered. "Go, Christy."

"Good evening," Christy said. "I'm Christine Kavanaugh. It's been a little more than five and a half hours since the lights went out. A massive power failure, reportedly triggered by one of the largest solar flares ever recorded, has left most of the southeastern United States without electricity. So far, there's no word of any blackout-related deaths. But there have been scores of injuries and accidents. Damage to property is impossible to calculate at this time. The question millions of angry and anxious people want answered: When will power be restored? The state power company is scheduled to hold a news conference at this hour. WEZE's Evan Taylor is standing by, live. Evan?"

A sudden, ear-piercing wail of feedback filled the control room.

"Hey, what the—"

"Turn it off!"

"Kill it!" Mitch commanded, his gaze sweeping the bank of monitors. Evan Tyler looked as though he'd been jabbed with an electric cattle prod.

The shrilling stopped.

"Cue Evan," Dave instructed.

Evan, evidently cued, started speaking. Mitch could see his mouth moving. But there was no audio accompanying the reporter's flapping lips.

"Open his mike, Phil," Dave ordered the audio engineer sitting two seats to his left.

"I did!" the sound man answered. "I've got him potted all the way up. I told you before, the heat's making this equipment—"

At that moment, what sounded like the audio track of an X-rated film erupted from the control room's speaker system.

"Oh . . . oh . . . baby . . ."

"Brent. Oh, Brent . . ."

"Oh, yes, Linda. Mr. Salami likes that. Yes, baby. Mr. Salam—"

Mr. Salami was abruptly cut off.

"—power company's president, is now coming to the microphone," Evan Tyler's voice boomed. "Let's listen."

"Did that go out on the air, Phil?" Mitch asked.

"Man, I sure hope not," the audio engineer replied fervently.

Mitch exchanged glances with Dave Bauman.

"Maybe we should've let Brent do a live report on the trauma of being trapped in an elevator after all," the producer observed.

11:13 p.m.

"All right, Dave," Mitch said, discarding a handful of script pages. "Out of this package, we're going to go to Wally."

"Got it," Dave confirmed.

Flicking the console switch that allowed him to talk to everyone in the studio, Mitch spoke into the goosenecked microphone in front of him once again. "We're going to do the explainer on solar flares next. SueBee, I need Christy's toss up on prompter. Wally, we'll probably have time for some Q-and-A after your piece."

He glanced up at the bank of monitors, frowning as he focused on the screen marked Camera Three. The picture was jumping and rolling.

Mitch switched around. "Sam," he said, addressing the young man seated at a computer terminal behind him. "What's wrong with Robo-Cam Three?"

Like many television stations, WEZE had switched to so-called robo-cams—robotically operated cameras. When they worked, they worked superbly. But on those relatively rare occasions when they didn't...

"I've got an orientation error," Sam reported, pecking at his computer keyboard. "This heat is really—okay, okay. Everything's fine."

Mitch swiveled back to face the monitors. The picture from Camera Three did, indeed, look fine.

"Coming to you on Two in ten, Christy," Dave said. "Playback, I need to see the top of Wally's solar-flare tape, please. Sam, move One to the right. No. The *other* right. Open Christy's mike. Take Two. Cue her."

Christy's face appeared on the program monitor.

"It may be difficult to believe this current blackout could have been caused by something that happened millions of miles from earth," she said. "But as we've told you, experts are blaming this huge power failure on a solar flare. Joining us to explain exactly what solar flares are and why they can cause so much trouble is our very own meteorologist, Wally Parker. Wally?"

"Take Three," Dave said.

There was, Mitch later learned, a very technical way to describe what happened next. He, however, preferred a more direct summation of the event.

To put it bluntly, Robo-Cam Three went berserk.

Mitch came halfway out of his chair, unable to believe what he was seeing on the monitor. The robo-cam was...*attacking*...Wally the weatherman.

"What the—!" Sam, the robo-cam operator, exclaimed.

"Take Two," Dave ordered sharply.

"I can't!" yelled a technician.

"What do you mean, *you can't?*"

"I mean, the switcher's locked up! I can't get off the shot!"

Mitch swung away from the monitors. "Sam—"

"This shouldn't be happening!" Sam gasped, hammering at the keyboard.

"Shut it down. Shut it down, *now!*"

"I can't, Mitch! It won't listen to me!"

Mitch glanced back at the monitors. "Dammit—"

"Hey! The switcher's unfrozen!"

"Take Two," Dave responded instantly. "Cue Christy."

Mitch hit the IFB as Christy's face popped up on the program monitor. "You've got Wally's copy," he said. "Go with it."

Christy did just that. Almost as soon as she started reading, there was the sound of something crashing, off-camera.

"I think robo-cam just went through the weather set!" Sam cried.

"Roll the solar-flare video," Dave ordered.

A bellow of pain. Again, off-camera.

"Ohmigod! I think robo-cam just ran over Wally Parker!"

Mitch lifted his gaze to the monitor for Camera Three. It was impossible to tell what was going on. The image on the screen was wildly blurred, as though the robotic camera was spinning around in circles.

"—magnetic energy is stored in the sun's corona," Christy declared calmly. "Sometimes, this energy is released in a spectacular-looking discharge like the one you're now watching. This is a solar—"

Suddenly, Camera Three's monitor went black.

"Oh, no..." moaned Sam.

"I think the robo-cam just committed suicide," Mitch said, massaging his temples. "Somebody go check on Wally."

11:20 p.m.

"Thank you, Jeanne Simpson, for the update from city hall," Christy said. "Now, we have a few additions to that list of emergency numbers we—"

Kuh-POP!

Mitch leapt to his feet as he saw one of the studio lights explode. He watched, horrified, as several of the white-hot shards ignited a small fire to Christy's left. "Omigod."

"Oh, sh—!" somebody else cried.

Floor director Wayne Jackson charged onto the news set, brandishing a fire extinguisher. The flames were put out in a matter of moments.

Christy never missed a beat, not even when the smoke from the fire set off one of the studio smoke detectors. She simply raised her voice to compete with the high-pitched alarm.

Mitch hit the IFB switch. His hand was shaking. "Wrap and throw to break, Christy."

"Break?" Dave Bauman echoed incredulously. "What break? We've blown out all the commercials!"

"Any break you can find, Dave," Mitch replied through gritted teeth. "Maybe that public service announcement about coping with job stress. And let's get that damned smoke detector switched off!''

11:25 p.m.

The program monitor showed WEZE's Delia Reynolds reporting live from what was billed as a Blackout Block Party.

"—of course," she was saying in a breathy voice, "there's one question everyone here is asking."

"Have *you* met Mr. Salami?" someone in the control room called out.

"And that question is: Where were you when the lights went out?" Delia turned and thrust the microphone she was holding into the grinning face of an obviously inebriated young man. "Sir, why don't you tell our WEZE audience where *you* were when the lights went out."

"Well," the young man drawled, "when the lights went out I was—"

Two decades' worth of broadcasting experience warned Mitch what was coming and told him what to do about it.

"Bleep it!" he barked.

11:26 p.m.

"—apologize to any of our viewers who were offended by that last comment," Christy ad-libbed a few moments later. "Live television can be unpredictable, as you've probably noticed during this evening's broadcast. And for those of you who may be concerned, our weatherman—Wally Parker—was *not* seriously injured by his unfortunate encounter with one of our cameras a short time ago. Now, summing up what we know about the blackout at this hour—"

"Man, Christy is good," Dave Bauman said admiringly.

"She's one of a kind," Mitch responded.

11:28 p.m.

"Roll close credits."

Mitch switched his gaze from the program monitor to the two small screens that showed Christy sitting at the anchor desk. She was staring at something—or someone. He saw her lips shape the question *"You what?"* Then he saw her reach beneath the desk and bring out a red phone.

There was an identical red telephone sitting to his right. Mitch snatched it up as soon as it rang.

"Are you all right, Christy?" he asked, still watching the monitor.

"I'm just fine," she answered with a weary laugh. "But SueBee Hawkins says she thinks she's in labor."

"She what?"

At that moment, the door to the control room swung open and Gus Mulroney marched in. "Hey, Mitch," he said. "You know those minor disturbances over on the South Side? Well, they may be turning into a riot."

Chapter Seven

Christy caught up with Mitch just as he was opening the door to the stairwell. "Mitch!" she called, dashing down the hallway. "Wait!"

She saw him stiffen. Then he took his hand off the doorknob and turned to face her.

Thank God, she thought.

The last time she and Mitch had met in this corridor, she'd nearly collided with him. This time, there was no nearly about it. She slipped as she tried to check her forward momentum. If Mitch hadn't caught her, she would have fallen.

"Hey, slow down," he advised.

Christy drew a shuddery breath, trying to steady herself emotionally as well as physically. Only a few scant inches separated her from Mitch. She could feel the heat of his body. Smell the scent of his skin. She knew that if she closed her eyes, she would still be aware of his proximity.

"Mitch," she finally whispered, gazing up at him. Despite the dimness of the corridor, she could read the signs of stress in his face.

He opened his hands and took a step back. "How's SueBee?"

Christy blinked, surprised by the question. "She's lying down in the conference room," she said. "Somebody's trying to get in touch with her husband. But never mind about that right now. Gus just told me you're going out to cover the disturbances on the South Side."

"That's right. Eye Chart's going to drive me over."

"But you're a news director! Why are *you*—"

"Because there's nobody else to do it. Evan's sticking with the power company, Jeanne's dogging the developments around city hall and Bill Hernandez is at police headquarters. We can't send anybody up with the heli-cam because the FAA's grounded all civilian air traffic in the region. The only reporter we've got in the field is Delia and I can't trust her with this kind of story."

As much as she wanted to, Christy couldn't argue Mitch's reasoning. "Were you just going to leave?" she questioned. "I mean, if I hadn't spoken to Gus—?"

"Hey." Mitch smiled crookedly. "I'll be back before you know it."

"We may be talking about a *riot*, Mitch!" Christy had had some experience with riots. She'd covered about a half dozen of them. "This is a—a—"

"Major journalistic opportunity?"

Deep down, Christy understood that Mitch was trying to ease her anxieties—and very probably his own—by playing it cool and casual. She'd adopted the same nonchalant attitude at various times during the course of her career. But to hear him utter *that* particular phrase—

She saw his expression change. Radically.

"I didn't mean that the way it came out," he said urgently. "Please. Christy. I'm sorry. I didn't mean it."

Christy suddenly realized she was very close to tears. Coping with the seemingly nonstop insanity of the 11:00 p.m. broadcast had drained her stores of self-discipline. She blinked her eyes, struggling not to cry. Then, unable to bottle up her feelings completely, she confessed, "I don't want anything to happen to you."

Mitch made an inarticulate sound, deep in his chest. "I don't want anything to happen to me, either, sweet—"

"Hey, Mitch!"

The voice, slightly adenoidal, supremely enthusiastic, was unmistakable.

No, Christy thought despairingly. Not *again!*

She heard Mitch curse under his breath.

"Hey, wait up!"

Exerting every shred of willpower she had left, Christy composed herself and pivoted. Eye Chart was loping down the corridor, laden with equipment. He was grinning, like a kid heading off to camp.

"Boy, I thought you'd be halfway down the stairs by now, Mitch," he declared once he reached them. "I got held up because Andy Castle had to put together some stuff for the field crew."

"Let me give you a hand," Mitch offered without inflection.

"Oh, sure. Thanks a lot." Eye Chart glanced at Christy. "You were *incredible* on the eleven," he told her. "The best."

There was only one polite response. Christy made it.

"You're welcome," the young production assistant replied, then suddenly furrowed his brow. "Oh, uh, look. You know before—when I, uh, saw you and Mitch? Right after you'd finished climbing the stairs? Well, uh, I'm really sorry about what I said. About you being together, I mean. I guess I was being insensitive, huh? Gus keeps telling me I've got a problem with that. So, uh, I'm sorry."

Christy managed a smile. "That's all right, Eye Chart."

Eye Chart peered anxiously at Mitch. "Uh—"

"It's forgotten, Eye Chart." Mitch yanked the stairwell door open with more force than was necessary. "I think we'd better get going."

The younger man brightened. "Great!" He entered the stairwell.

Mitch looked at Christy. "Christy—"

She forestalled him with a shake of her head. He had a job to do. She had to let him do it. "I understand. You've got to go. Just tell me one thing. When's 'later'?"

One corner of Mitch's mouth kicked up into the start of a rueful smile. "Not soon enough."

And then he left.

Christy waited until the stairwell door slammed shut before she slumped against the corridor wall. She exhaled on a shaky sigh. She found her mind drifting back to another parting. A parting that had followed a reunion she'd never dared dream would really occur....

"Christy? Christy Kavanaugh?"

Even before she'd turned, she'd known who the speaker was. The thrill of response she'd experienced when she'd heard the resonant male voice had been more than enough to inform her of his identity.

"Mitch," she'd breathed. "Mitch Nelson."

It had been shortly after 7:00 p.m. on August 18, 1988. George Herbert Walker Bush's formal acceptance of his party's presidential nomination had been just a short while away.

She'd never been able to calculate how long she and Mitch had stood, staring at each other, just inside one of the press entrances to New Orleans's massive Superdome. Conventional measures of quantifying time hadn't seemed applicable to the situation.

"I think one of us is supposed to say something like: 'My God, how long has it been?'" Mitch had finally declared.

"I don't need to ask, Mitch," she'd told him simply. "I know."

For a second, he'd looked stunned. And then he'd smiled. She'd seen an admission to match her own in the slow curving of his lips. "So do I," he'd responded huskily. "Ten years—"

"—two months—"

"—two weeks—"

"—and a couple of days. But who's counting?"

They'd both laughed. She'd suddenly felt giddy.

"You've changed your hair," Mitch had commented after a moment.

She'd patted self-consciously at the feathery coiffure that had replaced the casual cascade of hair she'd sported when they'd been together.

"I like it," he'd added, his gaze moving over her. The expression in his gray-green eyes had been both assessing and intimate.

"Thank you." She'd lowered her hand, wondering whether her cheeks looked as hot as they felt. "You—your hair is different, too."

Mitch had shrugged, the easy movement underscoring the broadness of his shoulders. "Shorter and grayer."

"It's very...adult."

He'd seemed startled by her adjective. She'd been a bit startled by it herself, too, until she'd realised that "adult" was precisely the right word. Despite the early maturity forced on him by his parents' untimely deaths, the Mitch Nelson she'd known in New York had still had a touch of boyishness about him. The Mitch Nelson who'd stood before her in the Superdome had been utterly, absolutely, a man.

He'd given her a quick, crook-cornered grin. "Thanks, I think."

There'd been a short silence. She'd spent it trying to absorb—and accept—the changes time had wrought in both of them.

"So, Christy." Mitch had cleared his throat and, in an achingly familiar gesture, thrust a hand back through his hair. "You're here doing a political documentary for public television, right."

It hadn't really been a question. Still, she'd nodded a confirmation. Then she'd countered, "And you're here because you're the executive producer of New Orleans's top-rated local news show."

"I guess we both still read *Broadcasting* magazine, huh?"

Another silence.

"I heard about your two Emmys, Mitch."

"I heard about your three."

"I heard about your winning a Peabody Award, too."

"And I heard about your getting a Nieman Fellowship at Harvard."

A third silence.

She'd swallowed hard and looked directly up into his eyes. "I also heard you got married."

Mitch's lean features had tightened. "That's right," he'd said. "And before too long, you'll hear I've gotten divorced."

She'd suddenly found it very difficult to breath. Virtually impossible to speak. "I...I'm sorry," she'd finally managed to get out.

"Don't be," he'd replied. "It was a mistake. For both of us."

"But—"

"Yo, Christy! Over here!"

"Someone you know?" Mitch had asked, looking over her shoulder.

She'd turned away for a moment, waving an acknowledgment at the man who'd hailed her. He'd responded by making a great show of checking his watch. She'd turned back to face Mitch. "My field producer," she'd explained.

"Time for you to go to work, I gather."

"I'm afraid so." She'd gestured. "You know how it is."

"Oh, yeah. I know exactly how it is. Look, what are you doing after the convention?"

Her pulse had performed a hop-skip-jump. "You mean tonight?"

He'd nodded.

"Well, uh, nothing, really."

"Will you meet me for a drink?"

"I—I'm not sure when—"

"I know a place." He'd reeled off an address. "I'll wait for you."

Mitch's "place" had turned out to be a small, out-of-the-way bar. Christy had joined him there shortly after midnight.

They'd touched, gently, on their shared history. Inevitably, they'd spoken about the quarrel that had split them apart.

"I said some awful things that day," she'd told him. "When I think back . . ."

"I didn't exactly distinguish myself in the sensitivity sweepstakes," he'd responded flatly. "I know I hurt you. I'm sorry."

"I'm sorry, too. I just wish—"

"Don't, Christy."

"But—"

He'd reached across the table and taken her hand. "We can't get the past back and we sure as hell can't change it. Let it go."

Her fingers had intertwined with his before she'd fully realized what was happening. "All right," she'd acquiesced.

Their conversation had ranged over many different subjects after that. In an odd way, she'd been reminded of the freewheeling exchanges she and Mitch had had in the weeks before they'd become lovers.

They'd evaded—avoided—the very personal for several hours. And then, sometime around 4:00 a.m., Mitch had reached across the table and taken her hand once again.

"Is there anybody?" he'd asked abruptly.

She'd shifted in her seat, suddenly realizing Mitch wasn't entirely sober. The signs of his inebriation had been subtle—his diction had been a little too precise, his gaze a little less than focused—but unmistakable.

"There's my work," she'd answered honestly, withdrawing her fingers from his.

He'd said nothing, made no effort to reclaim her hand.

"I have a good life, Mitch."

"I'm glad for you, Christy." He'd sounded as though he meant it.

She'd remained silent for several moments. Finally, she'd taken a quick sip of the wine spritzer she'd been nursing for more than an hour and asked, "Were you...serious...before? About getting a divorce?"

Mitch had broken eye contact, staring down into the glass he'd emptied a few minutes before. For a second, she'd thought he might signal for a refill. Instead, he'd pushed the glass aside.

"Yeah," he'd said, looking up at her again. "I was serious."

"I *am* sorry, Mitch. Really."

"She—Amanda—has somebody else."

"Is that why—?" She'd stopped, warning herself that the reasons for the breakup of her former lover's marriage were none of her business.

"Partly," Mitch had affirmed, answering the question she'd failed to finish. "She says I was unfaithful first."

Her reaction had been unequivocal. "I don't believe that."

"What? That she says I was unfaithful or that I was?"

"I don't believe you were unfaithful."

"Well, maybe not physically."

There'd been a tense pause. She'd endured it as long as she could, then she'd spoken Mitch's name.

He'd given her a very direct look. "You're the one she thinks I was unfaithful with, Christy."

"*What?*" She'd whispered the word.

"I called out your name when she and I were making love."

"Didn't you explain?"

"That made things worse."

Mitch had walked her back to her hotel a short time later. He'd seemed to have sobered up. She, however, had felt more than a little woozy.

He'd insisted on escorting her to her room. She hadn't argued. They'd ridden the elevator up to her floor and walked down the hallway in silence.

"Well," she'd finally said as they'd stood outside her door.

"Well," he'd responded.

And then Mitch had bent his head and brushed his mouth over hers.

She'd closed her eyes. She'd opened her lips.

A lighted match tossed on a pile of kerosene-soaked tinder would have caused less of a conflagration.

Mitch's arms had gone around her, pulling her tight against him. She'd felt his hands curve to fit her bottom, his fingers splay to cup and caress. He'd shifted her slightly, seeking the ineffable fit of hard to soft, male to female.

She'd brought her own arms up, twining them about his neck, threading her fingers through his hair. She'd moved her hips, dizzyingly aware of the potent thrust of his arousal. She'd heard him groan, felt him shudder.

His tongue had slid over hers. She'd tasted the savory bite of the black coffee he'd downed before they'd left the club to walk back to her hotel. She'd surged up on tiptoe, wanting to deepen the kiss still more.

Eventually, they'd broken apart. They'd both been trembling and breathing hard. Her entire body had been throbbing with need. Her blood had been thundering in her ears.

If he'd pushed her then, she would have succumbed. She'd never had any illusions about that. But pushing had never been Mitch's way, except on the disastrous day he'd flung an offer of marriage at her.

"Christy?" he'd finally asked, his voice low.

Ten years, she'd thought. It had been ten years, two months, two weeks and a couple of days since they'd seen or spoken to each other.

A long time. Maybe too long.

"No," she'd said after a few moments. "I want to, Mitch. But no."

"Is it because I'm still married? Because of the way you feel about husbands and wives who cheat?"

She'd flushed, recalling she'd once confided to Mitch that infidelity had been a hallmark of her parents' hollow marriage. She hadn't realized her revulsion about their behavior had been so obvious. "I...I wasn't even thinking about that," she'd answered with a twinge of shame.

"Then why?"

"Do you...do you remember the first time you phoned me? After the blackout?"

His brows had come together. He'd nodded.

"You tried to explain why you'd waited a week to call."

"I said what had happened between us had been pretty intense and that I'd thought we both needed a little time to step back from it."

"What's happened between us tonight has been pretty intense, too."

"And you think we both need a little time to step back from it?"

"Yes."

"I see."

"It's been more than ten years, Mitch. And even if everything seems the same when we kiss—"

"It's not."

"No. It's not." She'd gestured, searching for the right words. "There's a part of me that feels I know you better than I know anyone else in the world. But there's another part that feels I don't know you at all. You're not the same person you were in New York. And neither am I."

"True," Mitch had agreed after a few seconds. He'd stroked her cheek gently with his knuckles. She'd quivered at the contact. "Would you be willing to get reacquainted, Christy? To find out who we are—*what* we are—after ten years, two months, two weeks and a couple of days?"

She hadn't answered right away. She hadn't trusted her voice. "Yes," she finally replied. "Oh, yes. But—"

"There's always one of those, isn't there," he'd observed, lowering his hand. "What is it?"

"I have to leave New Orleans tomorrow—ah, well, today, actually. And I'm going to be on the road through November."

A smile had ghosted around the corners of Mitch's mouth. "You've never heard of telephone calls? Faxes? Postcards?"

She'd felt her own lips start to curve. "I'll give you my number if you'll give me yours."

A few moments later, Mitch had kissed her again.

A few moments after that, he'd been—

July 21, 1993
11:59 p.m.

"—gone?"

The sound of Andy Castle's molasses-rich voice brought Christy out of the past and back into the present. She pushed herself away from the corridor wall and turned to face WEZE's chief engineer. He was toting several pieces of equipment, including a battery pack and some cable.

"Sorry, Andy," she apologized. "I was, uh, uh—"

"Zoning out," he supplied. "No prob. This heat has everybody close to comatose. I just asked whether you knew if Mitch and Eye Chart were gone."

"Ah, yes. They are." She fluffed her hair, grimacing at the stiff and sticky texture created by the industrial-strength setting spray SueBee had used earlier. "They left, um, a little while ago."

"Damn. I thought of a couple more things the field crew might be able to use." The chief engineer frowned, then shrugged philosophically. "Oh, well. None of this stuff is vital."

"Can I help you carry something back to the shop?"

Andy grinned. "Thanks, but no thanks. Save your strength. If that 11:00 p.m. newscast was any indication, you're going to need it."

July 22, 1993
3:05 a.m.

Christy stared at the news-desk monitor, trying to concentrate on what Evan Tyler was saying. It wasn't easy. Dave Bauman had decided to continue broadcasting from the regular set rather than return to the announcer's booth they'd used prior to the 11:00 p.m. show. The heat generated by the studio lights had left her feeling as wilted as stir-fried lettuce.

"—and so," her colleague concluded, "power company officials are not offering *any* estimates about when electricity will be restored. The line they keep repeating is, 'We're working on it.' This is Evan Tyler, reporting live for WEZE news. Back to you in the studio, Christy."

"Thanks for that update, Evan." Responding to hand signals from the floor director, Christy shifted her gaze to Camera Two. She no longer had any scripted copy to read. Everything she said was ad-libbed. "Continuing with our special blackout coverage, we turn to—"

"Beeper with Lieutenant Dwyer," Dave Bauman announced through her IFB earpiece. "We just got new video from the South Side."

"We have a police department spokesman on the phone with us now," Christy said. "As we talk with him, we're going to show you new pictures from the south side of the city. I want to emphasize that this video is just in from the field. It is raw and unedited. Lieutenant Dwyer?"

"Yes, ma'am."

"What's the latest from the South Side?"

"Well, ma'am, the situation appears to be fluid at this time..."

Christy let the officer speak for about thirty seconds, scrutinizing the dramatic images appearing in her desk monitor. The pictures would have been unsettling under any circumstance. But to know that *Mitch* was somewhere in the middle of the chaos she was watching was disturbing in the extreme.

"Lieutenant Dwyer?" she interrupted, disciplining herself not to reveal the anxiety she was feeling. "I'm looking at video shot on the South Side just a short time ago. There are several fires—"

"Ah, yes, ma'am. We've had about a dozen arson incidents in the area. So far, there's no reports of any major injuries. As I was saying..."

The interview went on for another three minutes or so. Then Dave Bauman's voice came through her earpiece.

"Wrap him," the producer ordered. "Mitch is on the other line."

Christy complied, swiftly summing up the main points the police spokesman had made and thanking him for his information. She saw the small red tally light on Camera One wink on and turned to face it.

"WEZE's Mitchell Nelson has been reporting live from the South Side," she said. "He's on the phone with us once again. Mitch?"

There was a hum of static. "Christy?"

"Yes. You're on the air, Mitch. We were just speaking with Lieutenant Dwyer of the police department. He describes the situation on the South Side as 'fluid.' What's your assessment?"

"Well, if 'fluid' means it's changing from moment to moment, I'd use that word, too. Less than five minutes ago, someone started shooting from the top of a building about a block from where I am now. Police are attempting to cordon off—" there was loud crackling sound on the line "—moment."

"Mitch?" Christy said, raising her voice. "We're having a problem with this connection. Would you please repeat that last sentence?"

"I said there are no reports of anyone being injured by this apparent sniper. Police say—" The transmission broke up for several seconds, then Mitch's voice returned, cool and calm. "—vandalism and looting. We've also seen— *Hey!*"

"Mitch?"

Nothing. Not even a hum.

"Mitch?" Christy repeated, going cold inside. "Are you there?"

"We've lost him, Christy," Dave Bauman said through her IFB.

Chapter Eight

3:43 a.m.

"Dammit!" Gus Mulroney slammed the telephone receiver he'd been holding back into its cradle. "Dammit to hell!"

"Nothing?" Christy questioned, struggling to keep her voice steady. She'd come into the control room from the news set a few moments before, following the completion of yet another blackout update.

"Less than nothing," the assignment editor responded, his expression sour. "It's not enough that the power goes off. Oh, no. Now the freaking phone system has to start screwing up, as well!"

Christy looked at Andy Castle. He was in the control room supervising efforts to repair the robo-cam operating terminal. "Any luck reaching our crew, Andy?"

The chief engineer glanced up and shook his head. "Not yet."

Christy transferred her attention back to Gus. "What about the other local stations?" she asked. "Maybe one of them—"

"I've been in touch with everybody," the assignment editor cut in. "If anyone finds out anything, we'll hear. Believe me, we'll hear."

Christy gnawed her lower lip and rubbed her anxiety-dampened palms against the skirt of her dress. She felt so helpless!

"We're concerned, too, Christy."

The statement came from Dave Bauman. While plainly meant to reassure, it carried a hint of reproach.

"I know you are," Christy said quickly, looking at the producer. "I'm sorry if I sounded critical. It's just that...that..." She broke off as her voice began to wobble.

"Not knowing is hard to take," Gus finished.

Her eyes slewed back toward the assignment editor. Despite his gruff tone, the expression on his jowly face was very gentle. "Y-yes," she agreed, the word catching in her throat. "It is."

There was an unsettling pause. Christy had the feeling everyone in the control room was staring at her.

"How's SueBee doing?" she asked after a few moments.

"Better since we got hold of her husband," Dave Bauman answered. He seemed relieved by the change of subject. "He should be here pretty soon. Wally's keeping an eye on her right now. He says she's got a long way to go."

"You think Wally's any better at making obstetrical predictions than he is at forecasting the weather?" Gus inquired, reverting to his usual sardonic mode.

"He's the closest thing to an expert we've got," Dave responded. "He's coached his wife through four deliveries. Including twins."

There was another pause. This one was broken by floor director Wayne Jackson. He'd trailed Christy into the control room following the cut-in.

"Yo, Phil," he said. "What's the latest from the honeymoon suite?"

The sound engineer swiveled away from the audio board. "Well, I think Linda's pretty much lost her appetite for salami."

"A lovers' quarrel, huh?"

"You got it, man. As a matter of fact—"

"How are things in the other elevator car?" Christy interrupted. She didn't want to hear about lovers' quarrels. "Is everybody all right?"

"Oh, uh, yeah. They're fine," Phil replied. "Just listen." He leaned over and thumbed a switch. A split second later, an off-key chorus of male voices issued from the control-room speakers. The sound engineer let the audio continue for a few moments, then shut it off and explained, "The guys started singing when Linda and Brent started yelling at each other."

"What are they fighting about?" Gus asked. "Did she finally figure out that Mr. Salami is really—"

The assignment editor broke off as the door to the control room swung open and Eye Chart entered. He was shirtless and sweating. He was also smiling. Christy's heart leapt.

"The guard from the lobby just called," the production assistant announced. "SueBee's husband finally got here. He's on his way up."

Christy sagged, physically and emotionally.

"Thanks, Eye Chart," Dave Bauman said after a moment.

"No problem. I told SueBee. Boy, after seeing her in the conference room, I understand why they call it *labor*. I mean, she's really working. It makes me feel bad I forgot Mother's Day again this year, you know? Because my mom did natural childbirth when she had me. I always figured she was kind of exaggerating when she talked about how awful it was. Not anymore. But, uh, anyway. Is there any word on Mitch?"

"Not yet."

"Oh." Eye Chart heaved a sigh. "Well, you know what they say. No news is good news, right?"

"No, kid," Gus disputed sharply. "In this case, no news is hell."

Christy looked at the older man. He looked back at her. His gaze was steady and full of sympathy.

Suddenly, she understood the reason for the compassionate expression she'd seen on his face. He *knew*. Somehow, Gus Mulroney knew about her and Mitch. She was absolutely certain of it.

"I—I'll be back in a couple of minutes," she said abruptly, her throat tight, her eyes stinging. She headed for the exit.

"Mitch'll be okay," she heard someone declare as she pushed open the control-room door. "You know how he is."

Oh, yes. Christy knew. She knew because Mitchell Thomas Nelson was more than her lover. He was also her best friend.

* * *

Mitch hadn't waited a week to make use of the telephone number she'd given him in New Orleans. He'd dialed it the very next day.

Two days later, *she'd* called *him*.

It had been early January before they'd managed to see each other again. In the interim, she'd racked up a series of long-distance phone charges that had rivaled the foreign debt of several small nations. She'd also written Mitch more than two dozen multipage letters and received at least as many in return. One of these letters had informed her of the official dissolution of Mitch's marriage.

They'd arranged a rendezvous—or, more precisely, taken advantage of the fact that their busy schedules were going to put them in the same city on the same day—in Washington, D.C.

They'd embraced when they'd met at Dulles Airport.

They'd flirted during a long, leisurely dinner.

They'd kissed outside her hotel room.

They'd done more than that once they'd gotten inside.

And yet...

Beneath the ardor, she'd sensed awkwardness. Uncertainty. Instead of bringing them closer together, the impulse to physical intimacy had seemed to push them further and further apart with each passing moment.

She'd wanted to recapture what they'd had together more than a decade before in New York City. She'd wanted to be swept up by untrammeled passion, to be carried away by unthinking pleasure. But that hadn't happened. As profoundly as Mitch's touch had excited her, as powerfully as she'd known hers had aroused him, that simply hadn't happened.

"Hurry," she'd pleaded, urging Mitch on with fevered kisses and frantic caresses. "Please. Hurry."

"I'm trying," he'd said hoarsely, fumbling with the back of her dress. "But I can't get...this damned zipper..."

She'd squirmed, goaded by an impatience that had bordered on desperation.

Mitch had yanked at the zipper, cursing under his breath.

"Tear it," she'd demanded wildly.

"What?" He'd sounded genuinely shocked.

"Just tear it, Mitch!"

"You want me to rip your—"

Knock! Knock!

They'd both gone as still as statues.

Knock! Knock! Knock!

"Y-Yes?" she'd finally managed to stammer.

"Housekeepin'!" a lilting female voice had announced through the door. "You wan' me to turn down your bed?"

She'd felt Mitch let go of the zipper.

"Ma'am?" the voice had prompted.

"Ah, no," she'd called. "No, thank you."

"Okay. Have a good nigh', ma'am."

There'd been an odd silence. After a few seconds, she'd turned and looked up at Mitch. In a curious way, she'd felt as though she were seeing him for the first time since they'd entered the hotel room. She'd had the sense he was viewing her in exactly the same fashion.

Frustration—undeniable, unmistakable—had been the dominant emotion she'd read in Mitch's changeable gray-green eyes. Yet she'd glimpsed a flash of relief, as well. That's when she'd known they weren't going to make love. Not that night. Not in that hotel room.

And she'd known Mitch knew it, too.

There'd been no need to speak. They'd moved away from each other and begun straightening their clothes.

"Darn this thing," she'd muttered through gritted teeth, struggling with the zipper on the back of her dress.

"Let me do that," Mitch had said quietly, easing her hands aside.

All it had taken was a gentle tug. The previously jammed zipper had glided up the line of her spine in the space of a single heartbeat. She'd trembled when she'd felt the brush of Mitch's faintly callused fingertips against the nape of her neck.

"All done," he'd murmured.

After a moment, she'd turned to face him once again. "Mitch, I—"

He'd forestalled her with a shake of his head. "I know, Christy. Believe me, I know."

She'd gestured, searching for a way to articulate what she was feeling. "I...I wanted it to be the way it was before."

"So did I, sweetheart."

It had been the first time in more than a decade she'd heard this endearment. Her heart had skipped a beat. She'd flushed from breast to brow. "What's happened to us, Mitch?" she'd whispered.

He'd taken a step back, forking his fingers through his already disordered hair. "What's happened to us?" he'd echoed. His mouth had curved into a ruefully tender smile. "I think what's happened to us is that sometime during the past few months we became friends."

"F-friends?" The shock of his words and the shape of his smile had made it difficult for her to speak. "But we were friends—"

"Were we, Christy?" The smile had disappeared. "Would friends have split up the way we did ten years ago?"

She hadn't known what to say.

"Think about it," he'd urged.

She had. And in doing so, she'd recognized the truth of his words. As intimate as she and Mitch had been a decade before, she'd never shared herself with him the way she had since their unanticipated reunion in New Orleans—except, perhaps, during the hours they'd spent trapped in the subway.

"You don't believe friends can be lovers?" she'd finally asked.

"I don't believe friends can go to bed with each other for one night then head off in opposite directions the next morning," he'd answered frankly. "And we both know that's what was going to happen here."

An emotion she hadn't been able to identify had lanced through her. What had she expected? she'd wondered. That a renewal of their physical relationship would lead to declarations of undying love? Perhaps even another proposal of marriage?

No, she'd told herself firmly. Of course not. Marriage was not—had never been—for her. Or rather, she was not—had never been—for marriage.

She'd lifted her chin and gazed up at the man who'd been her first lover. "It felt good, Mitch," she'd said honestly. "Having you touch me again. Being able to touch you back. It felt good."

He'd nodded, making no effort to hide how her admission moved him. "It felt better than good."

"But it didn't feel . . ." she'd hesitated ". . . right."

"I know."

They'd stood there, staring at each other for what had seemed like a very long time.

"Friends?" she'd eventually asked, offering him her hand.

"Friends," he'd agreed and accepted it.

More than four years of friendship later, Mitch had offered her a job as the co-anchor of WEZE's 6:00 and 11:00 p.m. newscast. Accepting the job had felt better than good. It had also felt utterly right.

"I've wanted to work with you for a long time," he'd told her, his voice warm with admiration.

"And I've wanted to work with you, too," she'd responded, meaning it.

"Any misgivings?"

She'd smiled, contemplating some of her colleagues-to-be. "Professional?"

His mouth had quirked. He'd clearly divined the direction of her thoughts. "Or personal."

She'd been conscious of a tug of physical attraction. She'd seen Mitch's eyes glint green and known he was experiencing the same pull. The passage of time had done little to transmute their sexual chemistry. It had, however, transformed their ability to deal with it.

Or so she'd told herself.

"No," she'd answered. "You?"

"Absolutely not."

They'd shaken hands then, as though sealing a bargain. And they'd kept that unspoken bargain until a warm night in early June when her car had refused to start and Mitch had ended up driving her home to her apartment.

She'd invited him to come in for a cup of coffee— the kind of strong, chicory-flavored brew she knew he'd developed a taste for during his time in New Orleans. He'd assented with an easy grin.

They'd talked late, as they'd done so many times before.

They'd touched lightly, something they'd done before, as well.

Yet this night, they'd touched again.

And again.

And then they'd kissed. Teasing. Testing. Relearning tastes. Rediscovering textures. And they'd gone on kissing, lips demanding, tongues delving....

They'd made love. Once. Twice. They'd made love and it had been beyond anything she'd ever experienced or imagined.

Whispered words and the sensual search of Mitch's fingers had awakened her the next morning. She'd stirred languidly, feeling completely at peace with herself and the world for the first time in her adult life.

This is the way it's supposed to be, she'd decided.

Twenty-seven days later, Mitch had told her that what they had together—what she'd believed to be so perfect—wasn't enough for him. Her lover and friend had told her he wanted more. He'd told her he wanted—

July 22, 1993
3:50 a.m.

"Christy?"

The voice was Gus Mulroney's. It punched through Christy's reverie like a gravel-encrusted fist.

She realized she was sitting in one of the edit bays. She had no recollection of how she'd gotten there. It didn't matter. Only one thing mattered to her anymore.

"Is there word on Mitch?" she asked.

"No," Gus said, stepping into the workspace. "I'm sorry."

Christy dipped her chin. A sob welled up inside her throat. Struggling to suppress it, she bit down hard on her lower lip. A split second later, she tasted the copper-salt tang of her own blood.

Please, she prayed. Please let him be safe. Please let him come back to me.

"Uh, Christy, look—"

She lifted her head. "How long have you known, Gus?"

The assignment editor shifted his weight, but didn't shy from the question. "About you and Mitch, you mean?"

"Yes."

"I didn't know anything for sure until today. Uh, no. Make that yesterday. Mitch and I had a talk after the meeting in the conference room. I asked. He answered."

She moistened her lips. "And before that?"

"You don't have to catch two people making whoopie in an elevator to know there's something going on between them," Gus replied. "I had a strong hunch about the two of you from the start."

"Along with almost everybody else at WEZE."

Gus frowned. "Are you worried people think you got your job the way Delia got hers?"

"Do they?"

"Does it matter?"

Christy opened her mouth to give the obvious answer then shut it when she realized the obvious answer no longer applied. Had the revelation that her involvement with Mitch was common knowledge among her colleagues come twenty-four hours earlier, she would have been desperately concerned about the implications for her professional reputation. But now...

"No," she said. "It doesn't. Because Mitch and I know the truth."

The assignment editor eyed her consideringly. "He wouldn't let it slide if people *did* think that, you know. Not that they do. But if they did, Mitch would be the first one to set the record straight. He's damned proud of your work, Christy. He understands how much your career means to you. Maybe—maybe there was a time when he didn't seem to. But not anymore."

It took Christy a moment to absorb the implications of Gus's last few sentences. "Mitch told you what happened between us fifteen years ago, didn't he?" she asked slowly. "He told you how we broke up."

"He gave me the bottom line, yeah."

"And did he give you the bottom line about yesterday?"

"He said you were supposed to get married but didn't."

"Did he—" she swallowed convulsively "—tell you it was my fault?"

"Actually, I got the impression he thought it was his."

"*His* fault?" She shook her head, a sense of guilt bearing down on her. "How could it be? *I'm* the one who...who..."

"Loves him?"

There was a silence. "Yes," Christy finally whispered. "Oh, yes."

"But?"

She flinched from the question as though it were a knife.

"Mitch did that, too," Gus observed after a few moments.

"Did what?"

"Got all bent out of shape when I asked about the 'but' that's lousing things up for the two of you."

Christy averted her gaze, remembering the confrontation in the stairwell. "Mitch says I use 'but' as an escape clause."

"Do you?"

She'd never thought of the word as such until Mitch had made his accusation. In point of fact, she'd never really thought of the word—or her use of it—at all until the past eight hours or so. And now that she had . . .

She looked at the assignment editor once again.

Gus didn't wait for her to verbalize the admission she knew must be written on her face. "What are you trying to escape from?" he asked. "Mitch?"

"*No!*" The denial erupted out of her. She clenched her hands and leaned forward. Her heart was beating very rapidly. "Is that what Mitch thinks, Gus? Is that what he told you?"

The assignment editor didn't answer. He seemed bent on pursuing his own agenda. "Are you afraid he's going to want you to put his career before yours?"

The question startled Christy. After a moment, she shook her head.

"Are you sure?"

She thought back over the professional support Mitch had given her since the night they'd agreed to be friends instead of lovers. He'd been her sounding board—her closest confidant and most perceptive critic—for more than four years. She liked to think she'd been the same for him.

"There was a time when I wouldn't have been," she replied truthfully, paraphrasing something Gus had said earlier. "Not anymore."

"So the problem is marriage."

Christy drew a ragged breath. "Marriage scares me, Gus," she confessed. "I know Mitch wants—"

"What he wants is not to lose you."

"L-lose me?" The notion made no sense to her.

"Mitch needs to be sure of you."

"After sixteen years, how can he not be sure—?" Christy broke off, her memory suddenly replaying the words her friend and lover had flung at her in the stairwell.

"You can't stop saying it, can you?" he'd demanded.

"Wh-what?" she'd questioned.

"But," he'd answered. *"It's always there. Your little escape clause. You love me... but. You'll marry me... but."*

Her memory flashed back nearly a month, to the Sunday afternoon she'd agreed to become Mitch's wife.

"Are you... are you sure?" he'd asked.

She'd evaded the question. *"It's what you want, isn't it?"*

And a few moments after that: *"I've gone along with your wanting to keep our involvement a secret because I know the kind of gossip there'd be if people at the station found out we were having an affair. But our getting married is something else. If you're hoping to hide—*

"*Oh, no,*" she'd interrupted. "*Never. If I marry you—*"

If.

But.

No wonder Mitch felt he couldn't be sure about her. Every commitment she'd ever made to him had come with conditions!

Dear God, Christy thought, appalled. *What have I been doing?*

To say her problem was with marriage was far too simplistic, she realized. Her anxiety about saying "I do" was only a symptom of something much more serious.

She'd discovered, very young, that loving hurt. That committing to another person with a whole and open heart meant inviting rejection, or worse. So she'd learned to hold back, to hedge her emotional bets at all times, with all people. Even her devotion to her career had been a defense mechanism. Being courageous professionally had enabled her to be a coward in her personal—

"Christy? Gus?"

Christy stiffened. It was Dave Bauman calling. He sounded upset.

"In here," Gus yelled.

A moment later, Dave materialized in the doorway of the edit bay. "We just got word from the hospital," he said. "Nikki Martin's been brought into the emergency room."

Christy felt the blood drain out of her face. Nikki Martin was a member of the WEZE field crew that had been assigned to cover the trouble on the city's South Side. "Is she all right?"

"She got hit in the head by a bottle."

"Oh, no."

"Details are real sketchy," the producer went on. "But it doesn't sound like she's too badly hurt. Apparently somebody else on the crew went after the guy who threw the bottle and Mitch weighed in to cool things off."

"And then?" Gus asked.

"I'm not sure. Nikki's the only one at the hospital, so I guess that's a good sign. We still can't reach the mobile unit. We're trying to get another beeper with the police department right now." Dave paused, his gaze shifting from Gus to Christy. He studied her silently for several moments. Finally, he cleared his throat and said, "Look, Christy, I know you're shook up about this. If you want to take a break—"

"No."

"It's okay," Dave assured her. "We can slap a little extra cover-up on Wally's black eye and—"

"No," Christy repeated firmly. She lifted her chin. "I don't want a break, Dave. I'll do the next cut-in. And the next one. And the one after that. Because when Mitch comes back on-line—and that's when, not if—I'm going to be there for him."

"But—"

"No 'buts.' Not anymore."

4:18 a.m.

"Out of this soundbite in ten, Christy," Dave Bauman informed her through her IFB. "Then recap and wrap."

Christy nodded her understanding. She scanned the notes she'd taken during the past few minutes, reviewing the points she needed to make.

"Stand by," Wayne Jackson instructed, wiping his brow with the back of his hand. "Coming out on Two."

She squared her shoulders and gazed into the lens of Camera Two. The red tally light winked on. The floor director pointed at her.

"Go," said Dave.

"That was police spokesman Lieutenant Leo Dwyer," Christy declared, referring to the clip of videotape that had just finished airing. "To sum up: A tense standoff between authorities and an apparent sniper continues. So far, the unknown gunman has not injured anyone. However, at least two dozen people have been hurt in the ongoing disturbances on the South Side. Among them, WEZE sound technician Nikki Martin, who has been hospitalized with a mild concussion. As you may be aware, we lost contact with our South Side field crew, including special correspondent Mitch Nelson, a little more than an hour ago. We're still trying to link up with them again. Unfortunately, the blackout has disrupted communications systems throughout the area. The power failure that's plunged most of the southeastern United States into darkness is nearly eleven hours old. A state of emergency remains in effect. Power company officials are unable to estimate when—"

"We've got Mitch!" Dave Bauman suddenly announced in her ear.

Christy froze. She couldn't speak. She couldn't move. She couldn't think.

"It's Mitch!" the producer repeated, his voice soaring nearly an octave above normal. "We're patching him through!"

Christy pulled herself together. "I've just been told that we've reestablished contact with Mitch Nelson," she said, wondering whether the microphone she'd clipped to the lapel of her blazer was picking up the pounding of her heart. "Mitch? Can you hear me?"

"Yes, Christy," Mitch responded, coming through loud and clear. "I can hear you. The sniper incident on the South Side is now over. Just moments ago, the gunman put down his weapon and surrendered peacefully to police...."

Mitch's report lasted about a minute. Christy followed up with a series of questions. Mitch's answers were crisp and concise.

Christy hadn't planned to do what she did when Dave Bauman finally instructed her to wrap the beeper. She just did it. It wasn't professional, but that wasn't important.

"Mitch, one last thing before you go."

"Yeah?"

"I love you."

There was a shaky exhalation followed by a long silence on the other end of the line. Then, quietly, a question.

"Is that . . . all, Christy?" Mitch's voice was half wary, half wondering.

"No," she answered. "That's *everything*."

4:29 a.m.

Christy came off the set after the cut-in, feeling as light as a helium balloon. Dave Bauman had offered his congratulations, along with the information that her colleagues in the control room were applauding, through her IFB. Floor director Wayne Jackson had given her a thumbs-up in addition to an "all clear" hand signal at the end of the update.

The only person who seemed troubled by her unorthodox on-air announcement was Eye Chart. He'd materialized in the studio as she'd been unplugging her earpiece and plucking off her lapel microphone.

"Uh, Christy?" he began, sidling up to her. "Can I ask you something, uh, personal?"

"You can always ask," she responded, fluffing her hair.

"Well, uh—" he took a step closer and lowered his voice "—was that a 'This Just In'? What you said about loving Mitch, I mean."

Christy smiled. "Actually, Eye Chart," she said, "it's a developing story. After a whole lot of years, I finally got the lead right."

The production assistant took a few seconds to digest this statement. "So, you and Mitch have been, uh—"

At that moment, the door to the studio swung open. A young man Christy had never seen before staggered in. His face was flushed, his clothes were rumpled and drenched with sweat.

"My name is...Bobby Lee...Hawkins," he gasped. "And I'm tryin' to find...my wife, SueBee. She's...havin'...our baby."

Chapter Nine

Christy found Wally Parker slumped against the hallway a few yards from the door to the conference room. He looked utterly exhausted.

"Aren't you supposed to be on the air?" he asked, eyeing her blearily.

"I just finished an update," she answered. "I wanted to check on SueBee."

The weatherman straightened. "Everything seems to be okay." He yawned and gestured toward the conference room. "Bobby Lee's in with her. She's getting a little cranky, but that's—"

"Don't you dare *go tellin' me you love me!"* SueBee's voice suddenly rang out. *"That's how you got me into this mess in the first place!"*

The angry yowl sent a jolt of adrenaline rushing through Christy's veins. Her gaze slewed from Wally to the conference room door and back again. "Wh-what in heaven's n-name?" she stammered.

The weatherman smothered a yawn. "Par for the course."

"And don't you go sayin' you know what I'm goin' through, either, Bobby Lee!" the makeup artist ranted on. *"There isn't a single, solitary member of your en-*

*tire sperminatin' sex who has the faintest notion of
what I'm goin' through! But if you'd like a hint—"*

"Sue-BEE!" Bobby Lee's voice went from indignant to anguished, soaring about three octaves in the process.

Christy clutched at the weatherman's arm, genuinely appalled.

"The old grab the groin ploy," Wally explained, wincing. "My wife did it to me during the delivery of our youngest."

"I...I see." Christy released her grip on her colleague and drew a steadying breath. She waited tensely, wondering what she might hear next. After several long seconds of silence she asked, "What did you, uh, do?"

The weatherman looked puzzled. "What did I do?"

"After your wife grabbed your, er..."

"Oh." Wally chuckled. "I got a vasectomy a couple of weeks later."

Christy wasn't certain what to say to this, so she decided to say nothing at all.

After a few moments, the weatherman yawned once again. Christy followed suit. Emotionally, she was still as "up" as she'd ever been in her life. But physically...

"Speaking about people telling other people they love them," Wally commented. "I heard about you and Mitch. Congratulations. I think it's great."

Christy smiled, her sense of weariness slipping away. "So do I."

8:05 a.m.

"—Evan Tyler, reporting live."

"One quick question, Evan," Christy said, pumping as much energy as she could into her voice. Her throat was dry and scratchy. The sockets of her eyes felt as though they'd been lined with sandpaper. Beneath her navy blazer, her cream silk top was soaked with perspiration. "A short time ago, Jeanne Simpson reported that officials at city hall are accusing the power company of negligence in connection with this continuing blackout. Any reaction?"

"Well, Christy, that kind of finger pointing is to be expected," the reporter returned solemnly. "Publicly, the power company is denying there's anything it could have done to prevent this blackout. However, our sources *do* indicate an internal investigation is already under way into the possibility that human error might have been a factor. Still, the first priority remains getting the electricity back on."

Christy nodded. "Thanks, Evan. We'll be back to you later."

"Toss to Mitch," Dave Bauman prompted through her IFB.

Responding to a hand signal from Wayne Jackson, Christy shifted her gaze toward Camera Two. "Ah—as we've been reporting, the blackout triggered a series of disturbances late last night on the city's South Side," she ad-libbed. "A WEZE mobile unit is now on the scene. Mitch Nelson is standing by, live. Mitch?"

A rush of heat that had nothing to do with the ungodly temperature in the studio surged through Christy's veins as Mitch's face appeared on the newsset monitor.

"Christy, authorities are describing the situation on the South Side as 'completely under control,'" he declared, raking a hand back through his dark, dishevelled hair. The gesture called attention to a small, flesh-colored bandage on his left temple. It also underscored the fact that his wrinkled white shirt was unbuttoned halfway down his chest. "We haven't seen anything to contradict that assessment. Things began calming down around dawn...."

The live image in the monitor dissolved to videotaped scenes of arson and looting. Mitch's voice, slightly roughened by exhaustion, detailed the events depicted. The tape ended with the surrender of the suspected sniper.

Mitch's angularly attractive face popped up in the monitor once again. There was a fractional pause, then he resumed speaking.

"The alleged sniper is due to be arraigned later today," he stated. "As we've reported, no one was hit by any of the shots he fired. However, at least twenty-six people were injured during the disturbances in this area, including WEZE technician, Nikki Martin. Nikki remains hospitalized in satisfactory condition. Meantime, the preliminary estimate of property damage caused by last night's trouble is upward of several million dollars. Right now, residents are out and about, trying to clean up...and to figure out how to cope with the continuing lack of electricity. Given that the temperature is already above ninety degrees, the main priority for many people is keeping cool. This is Mitch Nelson—''

''Give me a quick wrap and a 'bye,'' Dave Bauman instructed through the IFB.

''—reporting live from the South Side. Back to you in the studio, Christy.''

''Thanks, Mitch,'' Christy responded. ''And now, recapping the latest on the blackout...''

10:11 a.m.

''...after nearly eighteen hours, there's still no word on when we can expect power to be restored. We'll be back at half past the hour with another update. For the WEZE news team, I'm Christine Kavanaugh.''

''All clear,'' Wayne Jackson announced after a few moments.

The studio lights faded. Christy slumped forward. Resting her elbows on the news-set desk, she pressed her face into her palms.

Lord! She was at the point where she'd sell her soul for a shower and eight hours of sleep.

No. Her current state was even sorrier than that. She was at the point where she'd kill for an ice cube and a catnap!

''Christy?'' It was Dave Bauman, speaking through her earpiece.

She made a grunting sound. She wanted to be left alone. She wanted to be left alone so she could fantasize about cool breezes and chilled fruit juice.

And Mitch. She wanted to fantasize about Mitch, too.

His mouth. Kissing her...everywhere.

His hands. Caressing her...everywhere.

His—

Christy shifted suddenly, feeling herself flush. She decided she'd better defer the fantasizing about Mitch. A few more seconds of it and the sweat on her body would start turning to steam!

"I've got some good news and some better news," Dave told her.

Something in his tone made Christy lift her head. "What?"

"The good news is, we've got food and cold drinks on the way up."

Christy licked her lips. Her stomach growled. The engineering department's supply of soda had run out hours ago. So had the contents of the studio's two snack machines. Her breakfast had consisted of a cup of lukewarm water and a handful of stale corn chips.

"And the better news?" she asked after a moment or two.

"Mitch is helping to deliver them."

10:59 a.m.

"One minute to air," Wayne Jackson said.

Christy closed her eyes and inhaled deeply, trying to focus on the task at hand. It was well nigh impossible. The only thoughts in her head revolved around Mitch.

Where was he? she wondered anxiously. And why was it taking him so long to complete the climb to the twenty-fourth floor?

"Thirty seconds to air," the floor director announced. "Out on One."

Christy opened her eyes, blinking against the prick of impending tears. Swallowing hard, she drew herself up. Get a grip, she told herself.

"You okay?" Wayne Jackson queried.

She nodded. She had to be strong. She had to be!

But what if—oh, God, what if the stress of all those stairs—

"Fifteen seconds, sweetheart," an out-of-breath but unmistakable male voice suddenly murmured through her IFB. "Do a good job...and you can share...my grape soda."

"Mitch!" Christy gasped.

"In five," Wayne sang out. He extended his right hand, fingers and thumb splayed for the countdown.

Four. Three. Two...

11:00 a.m.

The lights went back on. All of them. Everywhere.

The air-conditioning kicked in.

Phones started ringing.

Dozens of pieces of previously moribund equipment returned to life.

"We're back in business!" someone in the control room yelled.

Mitch jumped to his feet, his gaze raking the bank of monitors before him. Three live shots were up. Each one showed a WEZE field reporter gesturing wildly, clearly signaling that he or she had something very, very important to say.

"Track the announcer's cart!" Dave Bauman hollered.

A split second later, a deep male voice issued from the control room's speakers. "This—" the prerecorded voice intoned "—is a WEZE special report."

Mitch hit the switch that allowed him to speak to the woman he loved. "Power's on," he said, checking the monitors that showed Christy's face. Her smile illuminated the screen. Her dark eyes were dancing. He felt as though she was looking directly at him—into his heart and soul. "Toss to Evan."

"Cue, Christy," Dave Bauman ordered. "Ready."

"Good morning," Christy said, her voice cool and crisp. "I'm Christine Kavanaugh. And the news at this moment is . . . terrific."

11:03 a.m.

Wally Parker came careening into the control room with the announcement that SueBee Hawkins had just given birth to a bouncing baby boy.

11:04 a.m.

Brent Harper came stumbling into the studio with the announcement that he had everything under control.

11:29 a.m.

Christine Marie Kavanaugh received an "all clear" from Wayne Jackson, then walked off the WEZE news set and into the arms of Mitchell Thomas Nelson.

Chapter Ten

11:30 a.m.

Kisses. Swift and sizzling.

"Mitch. Oh, Mitch."

"Christy. Oh, Christy."

More kisses. These, slow and sweet.

"I love you." Christy wanted to repeat the words over and over and over again. "I love you so much."

"Oh, God." Mitch hugged her. "You don't know how it makes me feel to hear you say that."

Christy went up on tiptoe, locking her arms around Mitch's neck. She shifted her body against his, relishing the hard proof of his response to her. "I think I've got a pretty good idea," she whispered provocatively.

Mitch groaned deep in his throat and claimed her mouth once again. She opened her lips to him, welcoming the possessive sweep of his tongue over hers.

Many breathlessly beautiful moments later, they eased apart. Christy gazed up into Mitch's face. The tenderness she saw in his expression made her tremble to the very core of her soul.

"Will you marry me?" she asked.

Mitch's lean features tightened. His eyes glinted with emerald fire. Slowly, ever so slowly, he lifted his left hand and caressed her cheek. His fingers were shaking. "Are you sure?"

"Surer than I've ever been of anything in my life." She inhaled on a shuddery breath, then repeated her question. "Will you marry me?"

"Yes," Mitch replied, his voice as unsteady as his fingers had been. "Oh, yes, my love. I'll marry you."

The insight Gus had offered many hours earlier came back to Christy. "Are *you* sure, Mitch?"

The look he gave her then was beyond words. Christy knew it would live in her heart forever. "Absolutely," he said.

They kissed again. Christy emerged from this embrace in a teasing mood. Leaning back against the secure circle of Mitch's arms, she tilted her chin and asked, "When?"

"When, what?"

"When will you marry me?"

Mitch's mouth quirked. He stroked his thumbs against the base of her spine. "How about later?"

Christy shook her head, struggling to keep the corners of her lips from curling up. "Not soon enough."

A frown, obviously feigned. "Well, what about—"

Just then, the studio door swung open. Christy felt Mitch stiffen. She deduced the reason even before she heard the distinctive voice of WEZE's ubiquitous production assistant.

"Hey, uh, Mitch," Eye Chart began. "Are you going to—oh. *Oh*. Uh, I didn't . . . I mean, uh, uh, never mind. This can, uh, wait."

A moment later, the studio door swung shut.

"What do you know," Mitch murmured, nuzzling the lips of his very willing wife-to-be. "There may be hope for the kid after all."

6:54 p.m.

Christy bit the inside of her cheek, trying not to laugh.

"Ah, thank you, Linda," Brent Harper said stiffly, doing everything he could to avoid making eye contact with the attractive redhead seated to his right. "That was a very, er, *interesting* report on the, er, trauma of being trapped in an elevator by a power failure."

"My pleasure, Brent," Linda responded with a smile. The curve of her perfectly glossed lips was like sugarcoated cyanide—sweet but lethal.

Brent turned scarlet beneath his bronze-toned pancake makeup. The effect was striking. After an extremely awkward moment of silence, he swiveled left. "So, ah, Christy, what do you think?" he inquired, his voice almost as high as the color in his face.

Christy thought a number of things, including that her co-anchor looked a lot like a sunburned radish. Fortunately, she was too professional to say so.

"I thought it was a very interesting report, too, Brent," she assured him. She paused a beat, checking to see which tally light was on, then transferred her gaze from her red-cheeked colleague to the correct camera.

"That just about wraps up this special edition of the six o'clock news," she read off the TelePrompTer machine. "But before we go, we have some happy news about one of the members of our WEZE family. Our makeup artist, SueBee Hawkins, gave birth to a little boy this morning. Mother and child are doing well. And SueBee and her husband, Bobby Lee, have decided to name their new son Wallace, in honor of WEZE's weatherman, Wally Parker."

"Isn't that wonderful?" Brent ad-libbed, flashing his teeth at the camera. Although he was still flushed, his voice had returned to something approaching his normal register. "And there's more. Just a few hours ago, my co-anchor snuck off and married WEZE's news director, Mitch Nelson. The ceremony was performed by that very distinguished occupant of the bench, Judge Josiah Patterson Burnside. Congratulations, Christy. We're all very happy for you."

Christy lowered her eyes, savoring the sight of the simple gold band that circled the ring finger of her left hand. "Thank you," she said softly. "I'm very happy for me, too."

"I understand our assignment editor, Gus Mulroney, and our producer, Dave Bauman, were the witnesses?"

"Yes, that's right."

"Well, I'm just sorry *I* wasn't able to be there, too. I could have—" Brent gestured evocatively "—given you away."

Christy almost choked.

"Wrap it up," Dave Bauman instructed through her earpiece.

"Oh, I'd never *dream* of imposing on you like that, Brent," she said after a moment, then turned her attention back to the appropriate camera. She took a deep breath and launched into the scripted good-bye. "We're going to leave you with some of the sights and sounds of Blackout '93. What you're about to see and hear was put together by our ace editor, Dean Yaeger. For the entire WEZE news team, I'm Christine Kavanaugh—"

"—and I'm Brent Harper. Thanks for watching."

"Great show, Mrs. Nelson," a resonant male voice murmured through Christy's IFB. "Mr. Nelson would like to see you in his office as soon as you get off the set."

7:01 p.m.

Christy raised her hand to knock on the door to Mitch's office.

My husband's office, she thought as she rapped her knuckles against the wood.

Husband. Mmm. Her appreciation of that word— and all it implied—was increasing with each passing moment.

"Come in," Mitch called.

Christy did as she was bidden. "You wanted to see me, Mr. Nelson?" she inquired demurely as she shut and locked the door.

Mitch stood up and stepped out from behind his desk. "Among other things, Mrs. Nelson."

"Other things?"

"I intend to do more than look."

"Ah."

"*Much* more."

Mitch crossed the room in a few swift strides, obliterating nearly all the space between them. Although he came to a halt well within touching distance, he made no effort to reach out for her.

There was a pause. Christy felt her cheeks grow warm and her knees go wobbly. Her blood began to heat, her brain began to hum. After a few moments she lifted her left hand and stroked Mitch's cheek. He turned his face into the caress, pressing his mouth against her palm.

"So many years," Christy murmured. "If I'd said yes to you in New York—"

Mitch sealed her lips with his fingers and shook his head. "If you'd said yes to me in New York, it probably would have been a disaster," he told her frankly. "Neither one of us was ready for marriage back then. You did the right thing, for both of us. Don't ever regret the past, sweetheart. It's made us who we are and gotten us to where we want to be. Sure, it's taken a long time. But since 'later' is finally now..."

"I love you."

"I love you, too."

Christy gave her husband, friend and lover a tremulous smile. "No *buts?*"

Mitch drew her to him. "No buts," he answered steadily, then maneuvered her back a step. "No ifs." A second step. "No ands." A third step.

"Mitch, what are you—"

He reached behind her. A switch clicked. The office went dark.

"My favorite kind of blackout," Christy declared, melting into Mitch's embrace with a blissful sigh. "No lights…mmm…but plenty of…*ohhhh*…electricity."

What happened next was not interrupted by Elmo "Eye Chart" Tsitsiliavoglou. Nor was it reported on WEZE's 11:00 p.m. news.

CAROLE BUCK

I was born in Kansas City on the Fourth of July. This circumstance may help explain my fondness for fireworks and my passionate belief in personal independence.

One of my most vivid memories centers on a primary school essay in which I asserted that I must be somebody important because my birthday was celebrated by the entire U.S. of A. "Very imaginative!" my teacher enthused.

Well, no. Not really. Because until I reached the age of eight or so, I genuinely was convinced that all the Independence Day parades and pyrotechnics were just for me!

I started "telling tales" very young. My initial efforts were only moderately successful. For some reason, my mother didn't believe our house had been invaded by invisible cookie-stealing monsters.

I co-authored my first book in the fourth grade. It was titled *Gunther's Gorilla*. Writing it persuaded me that whatever else I did with my life, I wanted to find time to scribble down stuff I'd made up.

There were a lot of "whatever elses" to consider before I finally settled on a career. I wound up in the television news business, originally based in New York, now in Atlanta. For more than fifteen years, I've had a frontrow seat on history in the making. The view is astonishing, and I wouldn't want to give it up.

I hope you'll enjoy my contribution to this "blackout" collection. A note to my newsroom colleagues, past and present: No, this story was NOT inspired by any of you.

One final observation about the day I was born. It was a real . . . summer sizzler.

Carole Buck

STEAM BATH

Suzanne Carey

Chapter One

"Get a load of *him*," Janet Rhys whispered, nudging fellow middle-school teacher Melisande Taylor in the ribs. "Now that's what I call a man worth bidding on."

Glancing up from her copy of the annual La Palma Hospital Bachelor Auction's roster of eligibles, thirty-year-old Mel squinted at the man in question. Dark-haired, expensively dressed, in his late thirties or thereabouts, he'd taken his place a few minutes late.

Without her glasses, Mel couldn't see three feet past the end of her nose. The stage in Plant High School's auditorium was definitely beyond her range. Or at least it was when it came to details. But she could pick up clues. She had a general impression the newcomer was ruggedly built. Good-looking. At home in his own skin. Yet as he took a chair at the far end of the row near the wings and surveyed the audience, something about his manner suggested he wasn't keen to participate.

I'll bet he's afraid the woman he draws will be too fat, too old, too something for his taste, she thought. If Janet, at forty-seven, wants a serious prospect and not just a glossy weekend getaway...

"I thought you liked the distinguished-looking banker with gray at his temples," she said.

Janet shook her head impatiently. "Too old."

Putting on her glasses for a better look at the man Janet *was* interested in, Mel did a double take. "Jan, you can't bid on him," she exclaimed. "That's my boss, Joe Carbone!"

Mel's friend shot her a surprised look. "You mean...at the office?"

Mel nodded.

"You're kidding. He's gorgeous! And certifiably single, or he wouldn't be on the block. The committee makes darn sure of that. How come you never mentioned..."

As a part-time salesperson who supplemented her modest teaching salary by selling pricey condos for Ricci & Carbone, a Tampa, Florida-based construction and development firm, Mel was at the bottom of its pecking order. She'd been introduced to its personable chief executive. And he'd smiled at her on several occasions as he'd strolled through his first-floor sales offices. But she doubted he'd remember her.

"I don't really know him," she confessed. "I'm just a lowly peon around there. Our paths seldom cross."

Succumbing to curiosity at the same moment, she and Janet checked their programs. Joe Carbone's name and thumbnail biography hadn't been included. Apparently he was a last-minute addition to the program—maybe as a substitute for one of the announced candidates. Mel's hunch that he'd been pressured into taking part against his will only intensified.

"I can't believe you haven't wangled an introduction," Janet said. "Or made a point of bumping into him. From where I sit, he looks like the perfect antidote to a lingering case of Doug Jameson-itis."

The daughter of a brilliant, strong-willed physics professor and a gentle, if unsuccessful, concert pianist, Mel had been brought up to feel intellectually confident. But she wasn't terribly outgoing in social situations. Attracted to strong, self-sufficient men like her father, she felt safer with the Doug Jamesons of this world. At least they didn't try to dominate her.

"Maybe he's not my type," she countered.

Janet laughed. "Holding out for a Woody Allen look-alike, huh?"

At the podium, Cary LeBuff, a popular Bay Area TV newscaster who'd volunteered to conduct the bidding, was elaborating on the various bachelors' attributes, and adding a few choice comments of her own. Pretending to listen, Mel didn't answer. Though she hated to admit it, she had to agree with her friend's implicit comment. It was high time she gave Doug his walking papers.

There'd been a time when she'd thought herself in love with him. Now she knew better. Yet, though she'd relegated him to the fringes of her life, she continued to let him hang around. So? What does it hurt? She shrugged mentally. He can be fun. He's smart. And sensitive.

He was also selfish, irresponsible and tied to his mother's apron strings. Fired in a wave of cutbacks from his deejay job at a local radio station, Doug was taking his time about looking for another one. Two weeks earlier, he'd given up his apartment and moved in with his parents. The switch made it more convenient for his mother to wash and iron his shirts.

Though they'd made love a few times early in their relationship, for the past eight months or so, she and Doug had been strictly "friends." Weary of his unreliability and seemingly open-ended adolescence, Mel had insisted they give each other some space. Unfortunately, at the moment, he was the only man in her life. They talked on the phone every couple of days. Or rather Doug talked, usually about his problems. Mel's function was to listen and sympathize. On the rare occasions when she let him con her into going out for dinner, she usually ended up paying the check.

She liked being independent. A generous woman. It was just that, with Doug, it was all give and no take. She needed a little TLC sometimes, too. A shoulder to lean on. She yearned to settle down, get her life in order. Now that I'm thirty, she thought, I'd like to marry a nurturing, responsible guy and have a couple of kids with him.

She'd been forced to admit Doug Jameson didn't fill the bill. Meanwhile, the non-Doug horizon looked bleak. Despite the perils of promiscuity in the nineties, reluctance to commit was common among males in her age bracket. At least it was in her experience. Before Doug, there'd been a good-looking, seemingly stable and mature instructor at St. Petersburg Junior College. And it had been the same story.

Though Joe Carbone towered head and shoulders above both the instructor and Doug when it came to wealth, confidence and drive, Mel thought it likely he shared their dedication to bachelorhood. According to the office gossip, he was something of a ladies' man. Supposedly girlfriends came and went with the tides.

If and when he settles down, she decided, appraising his muscular physique, flirty dark eyes and mobile mouth, it'll be with someone who looks like Julia Roberts. Or Kim Basinger. Probably a combination of both. Well, it wasn't any skin off her nose. Rumor had it he was a high-school dropout. She preferred educated men.

Though he was careful not to show it, Joe picked up on Mel's scrutiny almost at once. He was intrigued by it. Sure, when he'd agreed to fill in for Bart Compton, a well-known defense attorney who'd come down with a case of chicken pox, he'd expected to be sized up like a leg of lamb in the butcher's case. Yet he felt he knew the rather pretty young woman who was giving him such a thorough once-over from her place in the second row.

He was positive he'd seen her before...maybe even on a semiregular basis. I've got it, he thought suddenly, resisting the urge to snap his fingers. She works for me, part-time in condo sales!

He couldn't remember her name. Since he'd seen her last, she'd done something different with her hair. A natural looking dark-blond shade, it was shorter. And lighter, as if she'd recently spent a fair amount of time in the sun. With those studious-looking glasses perched on her nose, he hadn't recognized her.

She's kind of cute, he thought. And shy. Definitely a lady. He remembered thinking when they were introduced that he might ask her out. But he'd hesitated. He was her boss and he hadn't wanted her to feel it would be a career decision if she didn't say yes. With interest, he contemplated the possibility that she might bid on him. If that was the plan, things were looking up. Relaxing despite the uncomfortable folding chair that was too minuscule for his tall frame, he gave her an encouraging look.

Oh, no! Mel thought, averting her gaze. He caught me staring at him. Hoping to God he hadn't recognized her, she was abjectly grateful when Cary Le-Buff chose that moment to introduce him and explain about the substitution.

"You've all heard of Ricci & Carbone, the firm that just finished the huge Bahia Towers condominium development on Harbor Island, and has been going great guns on both sides of the bay despite the current sag in building starts," Cary advised the audience in her upbeat way. "Maybe you're even aware that it's won a number of environmental awards.

"What you may *not* know is that it was founded in 1945 by our twelfth bachelor's grandfather, Gennaro Ricci, an Italian immigrant who came to America as an eight-year-old and fought on the U.S. side during the Second World War. For many years, it was a small firm exclusively devoted to building single-family houses.

"Joe's father, Mike Carbone, was the son of immigrants and a master sergeant in the U.S. Army. Married to Ricci's daughter and only child, he hoped to retire from military service when he hit the twenty-year mark and join his father-in-law in the family business. Instead, he was killed in Vietnam when Joe was twelve years old. Following his death, Joe's mother went to work as her father's secretary, leaving Joe to care for his three younger sisters after school.

"When Joe's grandfather had a serious heart attack in 1973, it looked as if the business would have to close. Just seventeen, Joe refused to let that happen. Dropping out of high school six months before graduation, he took over the company's reins and made it what it is today. In the process, he sent his three sisters to college at his expense."

A buzz of approval arose from the nearly all-female audience. Embarrassed by what he considered an invasion of privacy and a sentimental summation of him as a person, Joe longed to head straight for the exit. He and Cary had dated a few times. When he'd answered her questions about his past, he'd assumed they were just talking. He hadn't expected her to regurgitate every shred of information she'd gleaned in public that way. Why had she felt it necessary to lionize him?

As if in answer to his unspoken question, Cary tossed back her shoulder-length blond hair the way she did each night on the six o'clock news. "I can see you're squirming, Joe," she acknowledged with no visible hint of regret. "Sorry, doll. I thought the ladies in our audience might like to know they'd be getting a genuinely nice guy for their money, not just another pretty face."

Before he could object or toss off an astringent one-liner to counteract her syrupy praise, Cary had moved on to a description of the dream date he was offering. In a moment of madness, he'd agreed to transport the winning bidder via his personal yacht to Captiva Island for a weekend of sun, swimming in the Gulf of Mexico, gourmet dining and after-dark entertainment. On Monday morning, he'd fly her back by charter plane at his expense.

However, if the pretty blonde in the second row decided to bid on him...

"Sounds perfectly glorious," Janet commented to Mel under her breath. "Don't you think so?"

"Heaven on earth," Mel quipped facetiously.

So he was good to his mother and sisters. He was probably kind to animals, too. No doubt he paid his parking tickets. That didn't make him dream-date material. He wasn't remotely the sort of man that interested her. *What's the matter with you?* an inner voice protested. *The man can't help it if he's pure catnip. Besides the fact that he's your boss and it wouldn't be wise to get involved, what do you have against him?*

Pretending to study the program, she cast another surreptitious glance in his direction. He had humorous dark eyes. A mouth that looked as if it might run to passion. The kind of body that engendered amorous thoughts. Like it or not, she was forced to concede that whoever "won" him once the bidding started would be getting herself quite a confection.

Apparently that's what Janet had in mind. Since winning fifty thousand dollars in Florida's scratch-off lottery a month earlier, she could afford it. But did it make sense? Was Joe Carbone really worth the upward of one thousand dollars it would cost her for a weekend date with him?

With just a dozen bachelors up for grabs, the bidding quickly got under way. Rolling her program into a businesslike tubular shape, Janet tapped it lightly against her knee but didn't raise it when the banker Mel thought was perfect for her came up for consideration.

After some brisk and good-naturedly competitive bidding, a blond computer programmer they knew slightly snagged him. A minor-league baseball player was up next. Then came the toothy, elegantly manicured and overdressed owner of two BMW dealerships.

At last it was Joe's turn. Janet leaned forward in anticipation. If she prevails, Mel vowed, I'm outta here. She had no intention of hanging around like a fifth wheel while her friend and Joe Carbone worked out the details.

"Okay, ladies," Cary LeBuff was saying. "This is the moment I know many of you have been waiting for... the chance to bid on Bachelor Number 11...a prime example of American manhood on the hoof. And, as I said, a nice guy. Exceedingly generous. Picture yourself cruising down to Captiva with your hair blowing in the breeze and Joe's arm around your shoulders. Sunning next to him on a sugary sand beach. And dancing in the moonlight. I'll leave the rest to your imagination!"

A titter swept the audience, making Joe long to throttle the perky newscaster for unduly raising the bidders' expectations. He'd agreed to wine and dine his date. Be attentive and gracious to her for the sake of charity. But he'd be damned if he personally was on the menu.

Appearing to realize she'd overstepped, Cary cooled it. "Okay, ladies," she announced in a more matter-of-fact tone. "Let's start the bidding. Don't forget . . . for this particular date there's a five hundred dollar minimum."

"I'll give you five hundred dollars," a tall brunette volunteered.

"Make that five hundred and fifty dollars," a chubby redhead chimed in.

Before long, the bidding had escalated to fifteen hundred dollars. Silent if visibly impatient until then, Janet raised her program. "Two thousand five hundred," she said in her husky, authoritative voice.

There were several audible gasps. Coming as it did from an unexpected quarter, the thousand-dollar jump silenced the other bidders.

"Twenty-six hundred anyone?" Cary inquired, her tone one of surprise mingled with amusement. "Or are the stakes too high? I give you fair warning . . . you're about to throw away a once-in-a-lifetime opportunity. Joe Carbone and a fabulous weekend with him on Captiva Island are going once . . . going twice . . . *sold* to the lady in red in the second row!"

The applause was punctuated with a few sighs. With just one bachelor to go, Joe had undoubtedly fetched the highest price of the evening. Flashing his wry, brilliant smile in response to Cary's effusive congratulations, he did his best to hide the disappointment he felt. His date for the Fourth of July weekend looked like a very nice woman. They'd probably have fun together. It was just that he'd been hoping the little blonde...

Based on the earnings from her part-time sales job, he guessed, she probably couldn't afford it.

Roses of embarrassment blooming in her cheeks, Mel scrunched down in her seat. Thanks to Janet's winning bid, Joe Carbone's interest in them had deepened. It was too much to hope he'd miss Mel's discomfort over the way things had worked out, or the bright, triumphant glance Janet had flung in her direction, as if in response to active discouragement on her part.

"Do you really think he's *worth* two thousand five hundred dollars?" Mel whispered, gathering up her possessions as a first step toward beating a hasty retreat.

Janet grinned. "Why don't you tell me? You're the one who's going to Captiva with him."

Mel stared. A flock of butterflies flitted in her stomach. "You must be out of your mind!"

"Aren't you the friend who took care of me after my auto accident last year? Brought me groceries and cooked dinner? Cheered me up when I was down? And helped with my physical therapy?"

"Well, yes. I suppose I am. But I don't see..."

"If I remember correctly, you even slept on my lumpy old couch for the first couple of weeks I was out of the hospital. You were on call so much that, with your teaching job and part-time sales position, you hardly had any time to yourself."

Mel had to admit everything Janet enumerated was true. She just didn't see how it had any bearing on the situation. To let Janet spend two thousand five hundred dollars on a thank-you gift —*especially when that gift was a date with Mel's boss*—was completely out of the question.

"So what? We're friends," Mel retorted. "I didn't do any of those things in hopes of getting a reward."

"I know you didn't."

"Then don't talk foolishness!"

"Mel, please . . . let me do this for you."

Without meaning to, they'd begun to raise their voices. Heads were turning—Joe's among them, unless Mel missed her guess. She made a point of not looking at him.

"I appreciate the thought, Jan," she said, barely mouthing the words though she tried to make them emphatic. "It's very generous. But you're stuck with him, I'm afraid. Joe Carbone isn't my type. And besides, it would make things awkward for me at work. I absolutely, positively can't accept."

For the first time ever, she and Janet were at an impasse. Falling silent, they waited for the auction to draw to a close. Her perkiness undimmed, Cary announced the auction's proceeds and advised successful bidders to make out their checks to the La Palma Hospital Foundation.

"My friend Donna Pesci, here, will collect them and give each of you a receipt," she concluded. "Once you're square with her, you and the man of your dreams are free to discuss arrangements."

Chapter Two

Joe watched Mel walk out into the muggy late June evening as the woman who'd paid through the nose for a weekend with him stood in line at the podium to make out her check. In his opinion, Mel had a nice walk. Just the right amount of hip action.

Funny, he thought. I could have sworn they were together. He'd been hoping for a word with both of them. Maybe once the Fourth of July weekend and a quick overseas business trip he'd committed to several months earlier were history, he'd amble down to condo sales and test the waters. It was against his policy to date employees, but he'd make an exception for the little blonde. If she seemed the least bit interested, he'd ask her out to dinner or something.

"You mean...you're not planning to go on the date *yourself?*" Donna Pesci was asking Janet in disbelief. "You spent two thousand five hundred with the idea of passing it on to someone else?"

"That's right." With a flourish of her pen, Janet scribbled Mel's name and phone number on the Rolodex card provided. "If you'll just tell Mr. Carbone...."

"Why not tell him yourself?"

Having filed Mel away for future reference, Joe had come over to the podium to join them. Smiling his wry, engaging smile, he lifted the Rolodex card gently from Janet's fingertips and scanned what she had written.

"Pleased to meet you, Melisande Taylor," he said, making the natural mistake as he held out his hand to her. For some reason, her name rang a bell. But he couldn't place it. "You paid too much for it," he added. "But that doesn't prevent me from looking forward to our date. Care to stop off for a drink somewhere so we can discuss arrangements?"

A thoughtful look came over Janet's face. She didn't set him straight. "I'd love to," she said. "Unfortunately I live across the bay, in St. Petersburg, and I caught a ride over here with a friend. She's probably tapping her toe in the parking lot at this very moment. Would you mind just giving me a call?"

Joe's brown eyes lit with pleasure. Ten to one, the "friend" who drove Melisande Taylor to Tampa this evening is my little blonde, he thought. Meanwhile, something about the cool, self-possessed manner of the older woman who stood looking up at him hinted she didn't have personal designs. He guessed she just wanted a lark. And could afford to pay for it. If that was the case, maybe she wouldn't mind answering a few questions.

"No problem," he said. "I'd be happy to."

Mel's eyes widened above the rim of her pilsner glass half an hour later as, seated at a table for two at a restaurant on Fourth Street North in St. Petersburg, she and Janet waited for their nachos to arrive.

"You did *what?*" she burbled as a mouthful of beer threatened to go down the wrong way.

Janet didn't bat an eyelash. "You heard me.... I gave Joe Carbone your name and phone number. The fact is, he thought I was you. He'll be phoning you tomorrow at the office to work out the details."

Mel was aghast. She was being railroaded against her will. It also irked her that, though they'd been introduced when she went to work for him, Joe Carbone didn't remember her name. Apparently she hadn't made much of an impression.

"Well, you can just call him first thing in the morning and set him straight," she said. "I'm not going! And that's *that!*"

"I thought you were tired of being single. That you wanted to settle down...."

"Not with somebody like Joe Carbone!"

"What have you got against him?"

Mel pursed her lips. "For one thing, he's too flamboyant. A smooth operator. And a ladies' man, if the office scuttlebutt is to be believed. Besides, you heard what Cary said. He didn't graduate from high school. I happen to go for brainy, well-educated men. I'd as soon pick somebody out of the personals."

"Isn't that how you met Doug?"

Coloring slightly, Mel had to admit it was. She hadn't scanned the personal ads since. These days, she stuck to reading her horoscope.

Janet appeared to regard her moment of weakness as a strategic opening. "Look," she said earnestly. "You're my best friend and I'd give a great deal to see you happy. But it's never going to happen unless you're willing to take a chance when one falls into your lap. You know the old saying about making lemonade when life gives you lemons? Well, a weekend with Joe Carbone is like being handed a bouquet!''

Mel had the grace to look abashed. ''Jan, I know it is. And I appreciate what you're trying to do. You're being very generous. The fact that I don't want to go...''

''Spending a few days on Captiva wouldn't be a lifetime commitment, for God's sake. It sure beats sitting home, watching reruns on television. No matter how much you might wish it, Mr. Right isn't going to fall through the roof!''

''You never know,'' Mel retorted, dimpling despite herself.

''Not unless he turns out to be a roofer. Joe Carbone—''

''Is my boss. Like I said...''

There was a break in the conversation as their waiter set a steaming platter of nachos in front of them and inquired if they wanted anything else. They didn't. When they were alone again, Janet leaned back in her chair. A master tactician when it came to handling her seventh- and eighth-grade math students, she'd obviously concluded a softer sell was in order.

''What do you say we call a truce and eat these dietbusters while they're hot?'' she suggested mildly. ''All I ask is that you'll *think* about what I'm proposing. Your luck with men the past few years has been the pits. For once, I'd like you to see how it feels to get the royal treatment.''

* * *

Determined not to fall in with Janet's plans, Mel couldn't get Joe Carbone out of her thoughts. As she lay in bed that night, punching her pillow into a more accommodating shape and listening to the drone of her apartment building's central air-conditioning, she kept imagining herself aboard his private yacht, with the breeze rippling through her hair and his arm around about her shoulders the way Cary LeBuff had described.

In the mental picture she couldn't seem to eradicate, his dark eyes glinted with mischief and desire. Damn him, but he was a movie-star *manqué*—the quintessential dream boat. At last, desperate for sleep and with another workday facing her less than eight hours hence, she went into the kitchen for a glass of milk and plopped a CD recording of a gentle rain shower on the stereo.

She was wavering a good bit more than she'd have thought possible the following morning as she pulled into the employee parking garage behind the concrete-and-glass tower that, among other businesses, housed Ricci & Carbone's main office on Tampa's Harbor Island. Look at it this way, the risk-taker in her suggested. You have three basic choices. You can spend the Fourth of July at a cook-out on your parents' patio in Gainesville. Home alone unless Doug decides to come over and cry on your shoulder. Or generating your own fireworks with Joe Carbone.

Put like that...

Keyed up over the prospect of Joe's call and the need to decide whether or not to reject Janet's gift,

Mel found herself swamped with work. She'd managed to put the whole "Dream Date Weekend" mess on the back burner by the time her phone rang shortly before lunch.

"Condo sales," she said distractedly. "Mel Taylor speaking."

In the office he maintained on the building's top floor next door to his penthouse apartment, Joe frowned. Did the gray-haired, forty-something woman who'd won him in the date auction work for him, too? Or a competitor? Reading from the Rolodex card she'd filled out, he'd dialed a complete number, not an extension. But it was a local exchange.

Whatever the case, this morning she sounded like a different person. "Joe Carbone, as promised," he said. "How's it going today?"

His voice was deep and pleasantly rough, like velvet stroked against the grain. The impetus to turn down Janet's grand gesture eroded a little further.

"Okay, I guess," Mel temporized.

Where's the smooth, take-things-in-stride manner she displayed last night? Joe wondered. Maybe she regrets her two-thousand-five-hundred-dollar expenditure. If so, he couldn't blame her. Unfortunately it was too late to change her mind. The hospital's renovation effort was desperately short of cash. No doubt her check had already been deposited in the bank.

"Well, uh, thanks again for bidding on me," he said, hoping she wouldn't feel cheated when she heard what he was about to say. "I hate to throw a monkey wrench into the works. But my secretary reminded me when I came in this morning that the vice president plans to stop over in Tampa the afternoon of Friday, July 2. That's when we were supposed to leave for Captiva, if you recall. It seems I got my dates mixed up. Anyway, the mayor's holding a reception and cocktail party for him a stone's throw from my office, here on Harbor Island. I've agreed to act as cohost."

Mel felt as if the proverbial cat had got her tongue. "You mean...the vice president of the United States?" she asked, sorting out her impressions.

"That's the one."

To think she'd almost talked herself into going out with him! Less than twenty-four hours after the auction, he was trying to wriggle out of his commitment. At the very least, attempting to postpone it to some unspecified date. Though she hadn't really approved of the bachelor-auction concept to begin with, she regarded a successful bid as a contract. Jan had every right to expect value given for value received.

"If you have to cancel, you have to cancel," she said disparagingly, the disillusionment she felt plainly audible in her voice. "Naturally Janet...that is, *I*...will expect a full refund."

Who the heck was Janet?

"You don't understand."

Quickly, in the rough velvet tones she found so difficult to resist, he explained he was inviting her to attend the party with him.

"There are mooring poles outside the Columbia," he pointed out, referring to the waterfront restaurant that was scheduled to provide hors d'oeuvres and drinks. "I know...it's bound to be ninety degrees in the shade. But, unless we're smack in the midst of a late-afternoon thunderstorm, the reception will be held alfresco, on the steps overlooking the river and the convention center. My yacht will be tied up there, waiting for us. At most, we'll lose a couple of hours.''

Concluding the weekend date Janet had purchased for her was a lost cause only to find it still available to her posed something of a quandary for Mel. Contrary to her strong protestations of the night before and completely against her better judgment, she found herself wanting to go.

''The way I see it, there's just one problem,'' Joe added when she didn't speak. ''As the mayor's co-host, I'm supposed to help greet the vice president at the airport. That means I won't be able to pick you up in person. Would you mind terribly if I sent a limousine instead?''

Putting down the phone a minute or so later, Mel was dazed and slightly incredulous at the way things were working out. As if listening to someone else talk, she'd heard herself say a limousine would be fine and give him her address. Though he seemed to have no idea who she was, or guess that she worked for him, she'd tacitly agreed to accompany her boss on a romantic weekend.

In due course, he'd find out. What if I don't measure up to his standards? she asked herself, overcome with apprehension. And if he considers the weekend a bore? I don't think I could stand to go on working for him.

* * *

Declaring herself delighted at Mel's change of heart, Janet did everything she could to shore up her shaky resolve and persuade her to buy some new clothes. Reluctant to spend the money, as she was saving for the down payment on a condo in Indian Rocks Beach, Mel let her friend talk her into several frivolous purchases. If she'd balked, she guessed, Janet would simply have offered to pay for them. She'd already done too much.

Yet as she modeled her choices before her bedroom mirror, Mel was glad she'd splurged. Her new yellow bikini and white piqué sundress piped in red with a nearly bare, crisscross back and midthigh-length pouf of skirt made her look like a million bucks.

Inevitably Friday, July 2 rolled around—a day that quite possibly would "live in infamy," if the weather report from Mel's gut was to be believed. With her immediate supervisor's permission and a distinctly light-headed feeling, she left work early to bathe, change and finish packing her things. As the appointed hour neared, her nervousness increased at a geometric rate. I shouldn't have agreed to go, she told herself firmly. This isn't my kind of thing at all. Maybe if I call Joe Carbone and explain I made a mistake...

She jumped when, just as the chiming clock in her living room struck the half hour, the chauffeur he'd hired rang her doorbell.

As the uniformed, middle-aged driver escorted her downstairs and helped her into the limo's back seat, his admiring glances gave her confidence a boost. So did the state of her hair, which looked its absolute best, and the unaccustomed three-inch height of the heels she was wearing. Though she wasn't the type to make a fuss over her assets, she knew she had better-than-average legs. The flirty, designer pumps she'd bought to go with her dress were enormously flattering.

As the limo sped up Fourth Street and onto the Howard Frankland bridge, a pearl-gray metallic streak expertly slicing through traffic as it crossed the bay's milky blue sheen, she let her penchant for fantasy take hold. Far from honoring his commitment out of duty, the dream-weaver in her whispered, Joe Carbone would fall madly in love with her. If she refused to go on seeing him after their weekend date was over, his heart would break.

She didn't really believe it, of course. Handsome *and* rich, a man like Joe would have his pick of the available talent. As they negotiated the modest canyons that ran between Tampa's tallest buildings, swung past the convention center and swept up the little hump of a bridge she crossed daily during the summer months on her way to work, Mel began to get butterflies in her stomach. She hoped she hadn't laid herself open for trauma and rejection.

Security was tight in deference to the vice president's visit. Just past the bridge, a policeman stopped them and asked to see her invitation. As he scanned it and let them pass, she could see through the limo's right rear passenger window that the reception was already in full sway.

On the terraced concrete steps that led from the island development's shops and restaurants to the river, men in lightweight dinner jackets and women in colorful party dresses that bared the smooth tan of their shoulders were laughing, talking, availing themselves of free drinks. A few were dancing to the fizzy, sophisticated beat provided by a group of musicians who'd set up shop with their backs to the water. A large red-and-white striped tent extending from the Columbia probably housed the outdoor bar and a buffet. Yachts by the dozen and a host of smaller boats had tied up at the landing's heavy mooring poles.

A wraith in contrast to the party din, the limo glided soundlessly to a halt. Now what? Mel wondered, her confidence plummeting as the driver got out, walked around and opened the door for her. Am I supposed to grab my luggage, such as it is, and pick my way through a crowd of strangers while I try to locate my escort?

He found her first, materializing before she'd taken a half-dozen steps.

"You!" he exclaimed, his rough, sweet voice overflowing with surprise and pleasure as he relieved her of the canvas duffel. "I don't believe it! What are you doing here? I thought..."

Mel hadn't realized he could look so debonair. Sticky and stifling in its intensity after the limousine's frigid, air-conditioned interior, the late-afternoon heat didn't seem to faze him. In his formal bow tie and exquisitely tailored dinner jacket, with his dark eyes radiating what appeared to be a genuine welcome, he looked cool and unruffled. Yet he was hotter than hot when it came to sex appeal. All man and then some, she thought. Like Sean Connery in *Thunderball*.

Despite her misgivings, the stone of her intransigence began to melt. Okay, she conceded, keeping the admission strictly private property. On a physical level, I'm attracted to him. But that doesn't mean . . .

"The date was a thank-you gift from a friend," she explained, wilting a little in the merciless sunlight and hoping she wouldn't start to sweat. "She was the one who bid on you. I . . . almost didn't accept."

The way Joe looked at life, there were no coincidences. He'd always believed in a grand design. That afternoon, he was convinced, he'd been offered a glimpse of it. A weekend with the little blonde he'd been wanting to date was wish fulfillment at its most gratifying.

"I'm glad you did," he murmured, sounding as if he meant every word.

Shifting her duffel out of the way, he raised her hand to his mouth. Mel's eyes widened. She didn't move. The warm, infinitely gentle brush of his lips against her skin had her mesmerized.

Well, well, Joe thought, gazing down at her in fascination as he let her fingers slip from his grasp. What have we here? The kind of woman who can make a man yearn for paradise?

When they'd been introduced just after she'd joined his firm, and again when he'd spotted her at the date auction the previous week, he'd categorized her as sexy but principled—the sort of attractive, old-fashioned girl a guy wanted to cuddle and kiss but felt perfectly comfortable bringing home to meet his mother. He hadn't expected to be singed by such high-voltage sparks. Or fall prey to smoky-green eyes that didn't waver as they blurred helplessly into his.

Yet she was reserved. Even a little shy. He'd bet his third-quarter earnings on it.

"You work for Ricci & Carbone, don't you?" he asked. "I know we've met. Is your name Melisande Taylor? Or am I mixing you up with the woman I met the other night? I'm embarrassed to say I don't remember it."

He didn't seem to mind that she was his employee. Or that she wasn't the date he'd been expecting.

"Actually, that *is* my name," she acknowledged. "My friend Janet Rhys, who paid for this weekend, gave it to you instead of hers . . . probably in hopes of getting me to go along with her plan. Most people call me 'Mel.' In answer to your second question, I work for you part-time in condo sales . . . evenings, weekends and summers. The rest of the time, I teach."

She had a straight, slender nose, lightly dusted with freckles. Long lashes. A knockout figure. And a decided air of innocence.

"I want to hear all about your teaching career," he said. "And anything else you care to tell me. Luckily we have all weekend to get acquainted. What d'you say we put your bag on board the yacht and get ourselves some drinks? Maybe even dance a couple of numbers? Naturally, before he goes, I'd like you to meet the vice president. He's in that knot of people over there. At the moment, I'd say it's about ten bodies deep."

Mel slid into a state of enchantment despite her best intentions. "Whatever you like," she agreed. "You're the impressario..."

"C'mon, then." Slipping a proprietary arm around her waist, he led her down the steps.

His yacht, the *Sorrento,* was big, sleek and powerful-looking, with hand-rubbed mahogany trim and the kind of superstructure Doug had once told her was a "tuna tower" for deep-sea fishing attached to its flying bridge. Stowing her bag in its luxuriously appointed cabin while she waited on the dock, he pulled the mooring rope taut and returned to her side, lithe, poised and confident.

"What'll it be?" he asked, tilting her chin upward with one finger. "Something cold to drink? Or a dance?"

He was invading her personal space—bombarding her with scent and sound and images. Though it plunged her into sensual overload, she didn't object. She was keenly aware of his coiled, muscular strength and laughing brown eyes. His clean, spicy after-shave. The typically Italian way he used his hands. Until now, she'd only known him at a remove. The primitive excitement of having him focus on her with such mastery was almost more than she could take.

"Both," she decided, throwing caution overboard. "In reverse order, if that's all right."

"My preference exactly."

She thought he'd lead her to that part of the landing where a number of couples were dancing. But he didn't. Instead he simply enfolded her on the spot. Simultaneously the musicians ranged at the water's edge switched over to a slow number. With a smooth tug she imagined had been perfected via years of practice, he gathered her close and tucked her right hand against his chest in a protective little gesture.

To the right and left of them, people were chatting and sipping at cocktails. Smiling indulgently, they made way so that, almost before Mel realized what was happening, she and Joe were dancing in a little carved-out space. To her consternation, he grinned and nodded his thanks to their audience. The smiles broadened. Never a willing exhibitionist, Mel nestled closer—in search of refuge, she tried to tell herself. Joe responded with a little growl of satisfaction and rested his cheek against her hair.

How long they danced, insulated by a cocoon of party chatter and silhouetted against the frieze of downtown Tampa beneath a brassy sky, Mel couldn't have said. Just a few minutes, she supposed. Part of her wanted it to go on forever. It was utterly insane. An illusion that would send her crashing. Yet as they moved together to the music, she had the strangest sense of being exactly where she belonged.

At the end of the number, the musicians took a break. Somebody switched over to recorded music with a faster beat. A beeper went off, shattering the spell they'd begun to weave together.

"Damn," Joe said.

Reaching into his jacket pocket, he withdrew the offending device and punched a button. *Call 555-3496*, his message service requested.

The number was that of his chief construction supervisor's mobile phone. A trusted employee and well aware of Joe's commitments for the evening, not to mention the entire weekend, the man wouldn't have bothered him unless it was necessary. Joe hoped nobody had been hurt.

"I'd better go inside and phone," he said regretfully, thrusting the beeper back into his pocket and lacing his fingers through Mel's. "May I get you something from the bar first?"

She was still bemused, a little floaty. "I am rather thirsty," she admitted.

Walking her to the red-and-white striped tent, he ordered her a gin and tonic with a twist of lime. When the bartender produced it, Joe handed it to her and gave her a little squeeze. "I'll be right back," he promised. "Don't turn into a pumpkin."

A moment later, his tall frame was disappearing through the Columbia Restaurant's open sliding-glass doors. Glancing around at the other guests, Mel didn't recognize anyone. Unfortunately, however, it looked as if a sunburned, bleary-eyed, fiftyish man was bent on making her acquaintance.

"Haven't we met somewhere before?" he asked in a slurred voice before she could move out of reach. "Say the bar at Malio's?"

"Sorry. But you're mistaken."

Carefully balancing her drink to keep from spilling it, Mel turned her back on him and started down the steps. She'd wait for Joe by the yacht. To tell the truth, she was grateful for a moment to collect her wits. Despite the heat, the realization that, once the vice president and his entourage had departed, they'd board the *Sorrento* and head for Joe's getaway cottage on Captiva had her breaking out in goose bumps.

Joe Carbone may not have much formal education, she mused, letting the breeze off the water disarrange her hair and cool her cheeks. And he's probably a ladies' man, the way everyone says. But he certainly has nice manners. I've never dated anyone who could eclipse him in that department.

Several minutes passed and he didn't return. I wonder if something's wrong? Mel thought as she watched a cigarette boat finished in fluorescent orange tie up next to the *Sorrento*. Maybe I should go inside... see what's keeping him.

The cigarette boat's occupants scrambled up on the pier, leaving the motor running.

"I know," said the fifty-something lush at her elbow. "It was the Marriott."

Oh, *no,* Mel thought. Not again!

Wincing at the powerful blast of alcohol that emanated from his breath, she took a backward step. "I told you," she emphasized. "We don't know each other. If you wouldn't mind..."

Her unwelcome admirer clearly had no intention of giving up. Somewhat unsteady on his feet, he closed the gap between them and rested one pudgy hand on her arm. "No time like the present to get acquainted, then, is there?" he said cheerfully. "My name's George Allardyce. What's yours? I'll bet you're a Libra."

He was about to slosh his drink on her dress!

Horrified, Mel pushed him away and backed up a little farther. "If you don't stop bothering me," she warned, "I'm going to scream!"

Seconds later, she was doing just that. Catching on the edge of the concrete seawall, one of the three-inch heels she'd bought to flatter her legs and match her new dress had encountered empty space. With a sickening rush of what might have been adrenaline, she lost her balance and fell backward. His eyes popping out of his head, the drunk made a grab for her and missed.

I won't die, Mel affirmed wildly, expecting the Hillsborough River to close over her head at any moment. *I can swim.*

Instead of the river, she hit the cigarette boat. Pain slammed into her head and left knee like a freight train. Jarred loose by the impact of her fall, a gearshift lever gave way beneath her shoulder. There was a jerk of forward movement, followed by an earsplitting crash. Sagging against the cigarette boat's steering wheel, Mel lost consciousness.

Chapter Three

At the pay phone in the Columbia's bar, Joe heard the crash. He thought immediately of the vice president.

"Ted," he said urgently, "something's happened. No... I don't know what. I'll have to call you back."

Racing outside to the promenade atop the riverfront steps, he saw that most of the partygoers had gravitated to a spot on the seawall near the piling where he'd moored his yacht. People were murmuring and gesturing as if at a disaster site. He couldn't spot the vice president anywhere.

"For God's sake, get an ambulance!" somebody shouted.

Had there been an assassination attempt? Fear roiling the pit of his stomach, Joe pushed his way through the throng of spectators. And did a double take. Somebody had rammed a cigarette boat into his yacht, thoroughly damaging the smaller craft and tearing up the *Sorrento*'s rear decking.

As he stared at the tangled mess, pride of ownership was the last thing from his thoughts. There, draped over the cigarette boat's wheel, was his little blonde. Her face was pale and her eyes were shut. One of her pretty legs was arranged at an unnatural angle.

A thin trickle of blood oozed from a cut on her forehead.

How the hell had she . . . ?

Bending over her in the boat, one of the Secret Service men who'd accompanied the vice president was taking her pulse. He nodded with satisfaction.

"Out cold," he called to one of his partners on the seawall. "And probably in shock. But still breathing. Has anyone phoned the paramedics?"

It seemed someone had.

A dozen people offered to help pull her from the wreckage. Both Secret Service men shook their heads. Without knowing the full extent of her injuries, they advised against moving her.

Brushing aside a policeman who tried to bar his way, Joe scrambled down into the ruined cigarette boat.

"Mr. Carbone," the agent who'd taken Mel's pulse remonstrated. "This isn't your responsibility."

Anguished, Joe stared at Mel's inert form. How on earth did this happen? he taxed himself. She could have been killed. If only he hadn't gotten that phone call. Gazing at her pale, uncomprehending face, he felt angry and utterly helpless.

"She's my date," he explained after a moment, barely controlling his emotions. "If she's in shock, shouldn't we cover her?"

"Good idea." The agent nodded.

In the distance, a siren wailed, its volume increasing. Taking off his spotless white dinner jacket, Joe spread it over Mel's shoulders.

According to the paramedics, her injuries didn't appear to be as serious as they might have been. She had a dislocated left knee. Some scratches and bruises. And a concussion—the latter condition determined by lifting her eyelids and shining a tiny flashlight on her unseeing pupils.

For safety's sake, they carried her to the ambulance on a backboard. She hadn't regained consciousness.

One of the paramedics stood ready to shut the ambulance's back doors. "You comin' with us?" he asked Joe, obviously taking him for a husband or boyfriend. "We're gonna need some information."

Having learned Mel would be taken to Tampa General Hospital, Joe had planned to follow in his Mercedes. Abruptly he reconsidered. She might wake up on the way. In pain and disoriented from her head injury, she might very well panic—particularly if she found herself among strangers.

He didn't want that to happen.

"Yeah," he decided, getting in. "I don't know her well. I'm afraid I can't tell you much."

At Tampa General, an hour ticked by. Pacing back and forth in the emergency room's nondescript waiting area, Joe hadn't managed to find out very much about Mel's condition. To his knowledge, she was still being diagnosed. Forty minutes or so after they'd arrived, a nurse had come out to say the physician managing her case had ordered a brain scan. She was still unconscious.

With time on his hands and a welter of questions in his head, he'd wandered out to the pay phone in the hall and called one of his longtime employees who'd been present at the reception.

Within minutes, the employee, his top estimator, had called him back. From what she'd learned after questioning several witnesses, and related to him, he gathered a drunk had accosted Mel. In an effort to fend him off, apparently, she'd stepped off the pier and fallen into the cigarette boat. Its distraught and guilt-ridden owners had confessed to leaving the motor running.

About to return to the waiting room, Joe realized someone ought to be notified. He thought of Mel's duffel bag. Chances were, she'd stuffed her purse into it; he hadn't seen her carrying one. If so, maybe it contained the necessary phone numbers. They probably had something on file at the office as well. Punching out the number, he contacted the estimator again. Would she mind fetching the duffel bag from his yacht and the personnel information he needed, and bringing them to the hospital?

It's a damn shame the way things worked out, he thought a minute later, plopping down in one of the waiting room's molded plastic chairs and then getting back up to pace. None of this would have happened to Melisande Taylor if I'd been there at her side. He wanted to wring the neck of the drunk who'd pestered her. The careless boat owners. Not to mention the painting subcontractor who'd gotten into a fight with one of the electricians working a big Clearwater job, causing Joe's construction supervisor to phone him for permission to fire the man.

By now, the vice president would be airborne on his way to Miami, where he had a speaking engagement. If she hadn't fallen victim to circumstances, he and Melisande Taylor would be aboard his undamaged yacht, charting a course beneath the Sunshine Skyway bridge to the Gulf of Mexico and heading south, with the low, palm-studded coastline of Manatee and Sarasota counties to their left and, on their right, the sun flattening to a glowing copper disk as it sank slowly in the west.

At the date auction, he'd felt distinctly uncomfortable when Cary LeBuff had urged potential bidders to imagine themselves making the trip with his arm draped possessively around their shoulders. The implication had been that even more titillating clinches would be forthcoming.

Since then, assuming his companion would be the potentially likable, fortyish woman who'd written out the check, he'd given a lot of thought to striking the right balance between intimacy and friendliness. He wasn't into faking the former, or sleeping with someone based solely on opportunity. Though she'd seemed nice, the woman Mel had called Janet hadn't struck any sparks.

His outlook had changed dramatically when Mel had stepped from the limousine. The need to preserve his emotional privacy—maintain a certain amount of distance because of the artificial nature of the situation—had melted like an ice cube in the Florida sun. No doubt that was because he'd already been inter-

ested in dating her. Auction or no auction, when he
returned from his business trip to Italy the following
week, he'd planned to ask if she'd go out with him.

Now she was injured. He had no idea how seriously. Or what her prognosis was. It wouldn't surprise him if, when she was on her feet again, she'd be
so annoyed with him for leaving her alone in a crowd
of strangers that he wouldn't stand a chance.

Joe's estimator, Carole Kinley, arrived with Mel's
duffel bag, purse and a photocopy of her personnel
record just as the emergency-room doctor who'd been
treating her summoned him to a quick conference.
According to the brain scan, Mel's concussion wasn't
serious. Her dislocated left knee had been success-
fully reduced. There was a hairline fracture of the
corresponding patella, or kneecap. A new type of cast
with Velcro fasteners, which could be removed for
bathing, had been applied. She should continue to
wear it until the swelling had gone down and the joint
functioned normally, a minimum of two to three
weeks. A set of crutches had been ordered.

"Has she regained consciousness?" Joe asked,
hoping for a chance to speak with her.

The doctor shook his head. "Not yet. There was
some bruising of the right front lobe . . . relatively minor considering what happened, but traumatic none-
theless. She should wake up in a couple of hours.
When she does, she'll probably have a splitting head-
ache."

Following a brief interruption in which he answered a lab technician's question, the harried physician added that Mel was being moved upstairs to a

patient room. "You her boyfriend? Or a relative?" he asked.

Joe shook his head. "I don't know her well."

"Her people ought to be notified."

"I've already thought of that. I'll do my best."

Joe found numbers for Mel's parents and Janet Rhys in Mel's small, neat purse. The latter listing was a local one. Trying them both, he found Janet at home and explained what had happened. He could tell immediately she was devastated. Demanding to know the full extent of Mel's injuries and making little sounds of distress as he enumerated them, she informed him she was on her way to the hospital.

Feeling a measure of relief, he tried Mel's parents again. Apparently they'd gone out for the evening. By now, he guessed, their daughter had been transported to her room. Still carrying her purse and duffel bag, and with the photocopy from her personnel file tucked in the inside pocket of his rumpled dinner jacket, he bought three dozen long-stemmed red roses at the hospital flower kiosk and headed for the elevators.

Motionless and pale in her hospital bed, Mel looked considerably younger and far more defenseless than she had when she'd arrived at the riverfront landing outside the Columbia a few hours earlier. Like a hurt child, Joe thought. The dark smudges beneath her eyes and the large, painful-looking knot on her forehead tore at his heart.

As he stood looking down at her, a nurse came in to take her pulse. Commenting on Joe's roses, she found a vase for them. She also stowed Mel's belongings in the locker provided and removed her billfold to the hospital safe.

After she'd gone, Joe pulled up a chair and sat down beside Mel's bed. Her breathing was light and even, as if she were asleep. In her hospital gown, without a trace of makeup and despite the bumps and bruises she'd suffered, she was delicately pretty. Yet he had a distinct impression of strength.

I'm sorry things got so messed up for us, he told her silently. Very, very sorry that you got hurt. More than you can possibly know, I was looking forward to making your acquaintance. Slicing through the waves with you aboard my yacht. The two of us walking barefoot on a moonlit beach and listening to the breakers...

Maybe when she recovered, they could do those things. He owed her the date, and anyway he wanted to spend time with her. When they'd danced, meshing as if his arms had always been empty of her, he'd sensed something extraordinary was taking place.

I shouldn't be here, taking advantage of your unconscious state to study you, he thought. We're strangers still. And, injured as you are, you deserve your privacy. Yet he couldn't bring himself to leave her... at least, not until her friend arrived.

His beeper went off as Janet, looking distraught, walked into the room.

"Is she still unconscious?" the woman who'd paid for Mel's date asked, anxiously scanning her friend's inert figure and transferring her worry to Joe's face.

He nodded. "The doctor said it might be a while. Supposedly she isn't in any danger. Would you excuse me for a moment while I phone my message service?''

Once again, the call was from Joe's construction supervisor. There'd been more trouble at the Clearwater site. Apparently the painting contractor had returned, plastered to the gills, and committed several acts of vandalism. Joe would have to drive across the bay and take a look.

He couldn't win for losing. "I'm terribly sorry," he told Janet, "but something's come up. I have to leave. When Miss Taylor wakes up, please tell her how badly I feel that she was hurt and ask if there's anything I can do. I'll phone later this evening to see how she is."

Mel's hospital room was dark, lit only by second-hand light from the hall when she opened her eyes shortly after 4:00 a.m. Blinking, she lay absolutely still. Where am I? she wondered, becoming aware of distant conversation, rubber-soled shoes squeaking against tile flooring. This isn't my bed. Or even my apartment. I don't *remember* this place.

There was something stiff and constraining attached to her left leg. Experimentally she tried to shift it and found that the slightest movement hurt. Her head hurt, too. In fact, she ached all over. She had the funny feeling that, if she tried to move too drastically or too soon, she'd shatter into a million fragments.

It was as if she'd smashed into an immovable object.

The cigarette boat, her brain prodded. *And it did move. There was some sort of crash . . .*

"Oh, my God!" she moaned aloud, remembering.

"Mel? Did you say something?" Getting up from the chair where'd she'd been dozing fitfully, Janet came over to the bed.

"Where are we?" Mel asked. "How did you . . . get here?"

"This is the hospital, hon. Joe Carbone called me. Neither of us were able to reach your parents."

That's because they're on their annual pilgrimage to cooler climes, Mel wanted to say. She didn't have the energy. "Is . . . he here, too?" she managed.

"Who? Joe Carbone?"

"Mmm."

Janet shook her head. "He left right after I came."

Making the best of a bad bargain, Mel thought. Some "Dream Date Weekend" this turned out to be. He probably considers me the klutz of the century. Yet, except for wearing the unfamiliar three-inch heels and letting a persistent drunk rattle her, what had happened hadn't been her fault.

"Talk to me," Janet prodded. "Tell me how you feel."

"Rotten, actually. Am I going to make it?"

"Of course you are. You suffered a concussion, that's all. A dislocated knee. And a hairline fracture of your kneecap. Considering the damage done to the boats involved, you got off lightly. Now that you're awake, everything should be okay."

"You said . . . *boats?* You mean the one I fell into didn't hit the pier?"

"Uh-uh."

"Then, what?"

"Joe Carbone's yacht."

Mel wanted to roll over and die. I'll never be able to face him, she thought.

"I wouldn't worry," Janet added in an obvious attempt to soothe her. "He's certain to have insurance. Besides, it was clearly the cigarette boat people's fault."

The situation was just too awkward. When she was back on her feet, she'd have to look for alternative part-time employment. Meanwhile, several of her office friends might be willing to split commissions on her sales in progress in exchange for concluding them.

It would set her plan to acquire a downpayment on a place of her own back by several months.

Wearily Mel shut her eyes, then allowed them to flutter open again. "I hate hospitals," she said with conviction. "I'm out of here the moment I can get my act together."

By the time Mel regained consciousness, Joe had been asleep for approximately forty-five minutes. He'd had one hell of an evening. In addition to his worry about her and disappointment over their ruined weekend, the damage at his Clearwater project had been extensive. He'd been forced to swear out a criminal complaint.

Returning to his luxury apartment atop the building on Harbor Island that housed his sales and business offices, he'd changed to shorts and a T-shirt, turned up the air-conditioning and opened a beer. His next order of business had been to call the hospital.

According to the cool, impersonal voice he'd reached, Mel's condition had been guarded. The moment he'd hung up, the phone had rung again. What now? he'd thought apprehensively.

The caller had been his oldest sister, a recent divorcée and the mother of rambunctious thirteen-year-old male twins. "Thank God I reached you," she'd exclaimed. "I caught Tommy in his bedroom half an hour ago, smoking pot. He needs a man's influence, and you know how his father is. Could you come over and give him a talking to?"

A sucker for family, Joe had agreed to do as she asked. Home again after delivering the requested lecture, he hadn't been able to unwind. Continuing to brood about Mel and the destruction of their weekend, he'd watched the late show, then raided his nearly empty refrigerator and reread part of a favorite mystery novel. Though he'd once reveled in it, he'd decided bachelorhood was the pits. There were times when a man needed comfort.

When he awoke the next morning, he was still on the couch with his reading glasses perched on his nose. Sunlight flooded the room, eclipsing the wattage of his reading lamp. His first thought of Mel, he dialed the hospital again. A different voice said cautiously that her condition had improved. Visiting hours started at 1:00 p.m.

Elated, Joe showered and shaved, read the morning paper and ate a couple of stale doughnuts. Since he'd already brought Mel flowers, he'd pick up a box of candy. The circumstances weren't the best and he had to leave for Italy late Monday afternoon. Yet if she wasn't feeling too rocky, maybe she'd like some company.

To his surprise, when he approached the nursing station on her floor around 1:15 p.m., his roses were the first thing he saw. Resplendent in the vase the nurse had found for him, they decorated the counter. Was Mel allergic to them or something?

Striding down the hall, he found her room empty and her bed stripped. Had she switched rooms? Or taken a turn for the worse and been shifted to intensive care? Surely her doctor hadn't released her yet.

Back at the nursing station, the unit secretary was transcribing notes. "What happened to Miss Taylor in 407?" Joe demanded urgently.

Pausing, the woman gave his query a moment's thought. "I believe she checked herself out this morning over her doctor's objection," she murmured, thumbing through her pile of charts. "Yes, here it is. A friend drove her home. No...she didn't leave any message."

Chapter Four

Returning to his office July 16 after ten days in Italy, Joe found himself facing a mountain of work. Thanks to the success of his mission, namely cementing a limited joint partnership with the award-winning firm *Construczione Italia* to build single-family homes in the U.S., he was in an energetic mood.

Only one aspect of his life was bothering him.

When he'd tried to call Mel at home the day she'd checked herself out of the hospital, a recording had informed him the number listed in her personnel file was no longer in service. According to directory information, the new one was unpublished.

On Monday, about to leave for Italy, he'd requested her current number from her supervisor, only to be frustrated again. Hiding behind a message machine, Mel had declined to answer her phone in person. Damn it, she works for me, he'd thought. She can't avoid me indefinitely.

Now her resignation lay on his desk. Neatly typed, it made no claims in reference to her accident. Nor did it mention their planned weekend together.

There has to be a way to give the lady her comeuppance, Joe thought, leaning back in his bronze leather chair and contemplating the Tampa skyline. It's true.... I feel semiresponsible that she got hurt. But in truth, I'm not to blame. I went inside to answer a phone call, and she's acting as though I gave her a push.

Just then, the intercom buzzed. "Kevin Frazier to see you," his secretary said.

Joe's regular attorney was out of town. A junior associate at his law firm, Kevin was filling in for him.

"Send him on back," Joe said.

After consulting him about several unrelated matters, Kevin raised the topic of Joe's smashed-up yacht. Unaware of the circumstances behind the mishap, the inexperienced young attorney wanted to know if Joe planned to seek damages.

"You mean . . . sue the cigarette-boat owners?" Joe asked with a frown. "I don't see the need. Neither they nor their insurance company has disputed the validity of our claim."

Kevin shook his head. "I agree . . . they've been cooperative. But we have yet to determine whether their policy will cover the necessary repairs. Since Miss Taylor was at the controls without their permission, she shares primary liability with them."

Whatever the law said, Joe didn't agree that Mel was to blame. Yet the idea of sending her a threatening letter had a certain appeal. At least it would draw a response from her. Once he had her on the phone, he could apologize and say it was all a mistake. After they straightened things out, he'd suggest they reinstate their plan to visit Captiva together.

The yacht wouldn't be seaworthy for quite a while. But they could always drive. Or charter a plane.

"You're the expert," he said expansively. "D
whatever you think best."

Holed up in her boxlike rental apartment with he
crutches propped beside the couch and the air condi
tioner going full tilt, Mel was in a rotten mood. It wa
July 21 and, outside, the midsummer heat was suffo
cating. Unless she wanted to spend the day in her un
derwear, pouring sweat, she had to run up her electri
bill.

It wasn't the most inviting of prospects, consider
ing that, at the moment, she wasn't bringing home
paycheck. To her distress, it looked as if she'd be lai
up until September. If she couldn't navigate any be
ter than she'd managed to do so far, she might end u
missing the opening weeks of the fall term as well
Slowly but surely, the money she'd been saving for
down payment on a condo would disappear.

So what if you quit your job at Ricci & Carbone
she told herself irritably, ignoring the muted soa
opera that flickered on her television screen. You wer
on straight commission there. You didn't get sick time
It wasn't any great loss.

She'd look for another part-time position in rea
estate just as soon as she was back on her feet. I don'
want to work for a man who probably thinks I'm a
clumsy as a cow on roller skates, she thought, banish
ing all memory of the tender way she and Joe ha
danced together. Certainly not one who couldn't b
bothered to call for me in person after Janet pai
through the nose so I'd be treated right for a change.

One drink, one dance, and he'd abandoned her to her own devices. The next time Mel talked to her friend, she'd insist Janet demand a refund.

As she sat and fumed, the doorbell rang. Mel rolled her eyes. "If it's a package, leave it!" she yelled. "If you're selling something, go away. I'm on crutches..."

A man's voice she didn't recognize answered in a diffident tone. "Sorry, ma'am. But this is fairly important. If you need to take your time getting here, I can wait."

"Oh, all right..."

Struggling to her feet, she limped slowly across the room. When she opened the door, the slight, balding man who stood there thrust a folded-up paper into her hands.

"Greetings from the Hillsborough County Clerk," he said without any visible trace of irony. "Have a nice day."

Mel's stomach turned over. Someone was suing her! Bracing herself against the doorframe for support, she unfolded the document and scanned its contents. Her emotional temperature shot upward to the boiling point.

As the owner of the yacht *Sorrento,* negligently rear-ended by her as she unlawfully appropriated the cigarette boat during her July 2 fall from the Harbor Island seawall, Joe Carbone was seeking unspecified damages. As if the accident had been her doing!

By God, she'd have it out with him.

She hadn't been a passenger in a car for nearly three weeks except for the grueling, pain-filled morning Janet had brought her home from the hospital and several visits to her doctor, also courtesy of Janet's help, Mel pulled a cotton sundress over her head, ran a brush through her hair and summoned a taxi. As an afterthought, she added earrings, a chunky necklace and makeup. If she was going to give Joe Carbone holy hell and make it stick, she needed all the confidence boosters she could muster.

The fact that her building had an elevator made things a little easier. But it was still a gargantuan task, with one leg immobile as a board, to stuff herself into a taxi. The driver had to help.

As they drove across the bay, using the same bridge the limousine chauffeur had chosen to transport her to the party, the head of steam that had slackened a little as she put on her lipstick began to rise again. She was fairly worked up by the time she hoisted herself out of the cab, hobbled into the palm-decked lobby of the building where she'd worked until recently and took an elevator to Joe's twelfth-floor office.

His secretary glanced up as she limped off the elevator on her crutches. "Aren't you...?" she began.

"That's right. Melisande Taylor. Otherwise known as the injured party. I'm here to see Joe Carbone."

It was clear her icy-but-furious tone wasn't lost on his well-dressed, fiftyish assistant. "I'll ask if he has the time," the woman said dubiously, turning toward her intercom. "However, since you don't have an appointment..."

"That's all right, Edie." The rough-velvet voice Mel would have recognized anywhere came from a partly open doorway. "I've tried to reach Miss Taylor several times, without success. I'll be happy to talk with her.''

Some of the wind *poofed* out of Mel's sails, if only for a moment. In his salt-and-pepper raw silk sport coat, pale gray sharkskin trousers and Italian floral print tie, Joe looked like the quintessential trendy young executive, albeit with more panache and flair than most. For a hot second, she remembered what it had been like to smile up into his intense but humorous dark eyes, and forgot he was the opposing party in a lawsuit.

When she came to her senses, she wanted to wring his good-looking neck. The ephemeral, not-quite smile that tugged at the corners of his mouth, causing the little quote marks that framed it to deepen, infuriated her. So did the tacit assumption of power his relaxed manner suggested.

By contrast, she felt frumpy and awkward in her cast and print cotton sundress, with the hard rubber cushions of her twin supports throwing off her posture and digging into her armpits.

''Is there something inherently amusing about a woman on crutches?'' she snapped, causing the secretary to stifle an indrawn breath. ''Or is it me, personally, that you enjoy baiting? I want to know why you're suing me when I'm the victim in this scenario!''

Ol' Kev's letter must have been pretty strong if she mistook it for an actual lawsuit, Joe thought, belatedly adopting what he hoped was a neutral expression. Well, at least it did the trick. It got her here. Now it's up to me to smooth her ruffled feathers without capitulating too soon. We can't have her disappearing back into the woodwork.

"Won't you come into my office, Miss Taylor?" he asked, stepping aside so she could precede him. "I'm sure you'll be more comfortable there."

To Mel's ears, he only sounded solicitous. Searing him with a look that expressed doubt she could possibly be comfortable in his presence, she accepted his invitation. To her chagrin, as she attempted to brush past him, the tip of one of her crutches caught against the toe of a size ten loafer.

Its owner steadied her deftly by the shoulders. "Careful," he warned, flashing her his wry, bad-boy grin. "We don't want any more mishaps."

He *did* think she was a klutz. And that the accident had been all her fault. How dared he patronize her that way?

"Certainly not," she agreed, glaring until he dropped his hands. "I'd hate to think what kind of action you'd take if I happened to bump into your desk!"

Getting her to abandon her hostility would be a lot more difficult than he'd expected. Winking at his outraged secretary and reminding her it was time to go home, Joe gently closed his office door behind them. He was the soul of courtesy as he indicated one of the cushy leather armchairs he'd placed in front of his desk for guests.

"Now, then," he said when Mel was seated. "Would you like coffee? Or something cold to drink?"

"What I'd like is for you to drop your ridiculous legal action against me. *And* refund my friend's two thousand five hundred dollars, since our 'date' never took place. If you agree to do both, I won't darken your door again."

It was the last thing Joe wanted her to promise him. Far from disparaging her for getting upset, he admired her spunk. This delicately featured, feisty female with a slender but curvaceous figure, was one he suspected could be both principled and passionate. She had the wholesome, educated air of the schoolteacher she was. Yet she definitely didn't lack sex appeal. Something about her made the words "best girl" drift through his head.

He could remember his father referring to his mother that way. Though in looks and age they were quite different, he had a feeling that, in essence, Mel Taylor and Rose Ricci Carbone were a lot alike. The little blonde he'd been scheduled to transport to Captiva on his yacht was exactly the sort of woman he'd pictured pledging to keep him in sickness and health, and having his babies someday.

Better back out while you still can if you want to preserve your bachelorhood, he cautioned himself. His inner man didn't seem disposed to cooperate.

"Sounds like we're dealing with two separate issues here," he said at last, deciding she was worth the risk and sitting down next to her instead of putting the barrier of his desk between them.

Their knees—hers imprisoned in its bulky cast, his lean and beautifully shaped beneath his pleated trouser leg—were almost touching. Behind him, the

Tampa skyline shimmered in the heat, framed by a sweeping wall of glass.

"I suppose you're right," Mel conceded.

He leaned forward slightly, so that she caught a whiff of his after-shave. "Let's take the last one first. I see no reason to refund the two thousand five hundred dollars. It's not my fault our plans couldn't go forward. As soon as you've recovered sufficiently, I stand ready to honor my obligation."

It wasn't the most fortuitous choice of words. Mel stared. "You really expect…me to go *out* with you?" she asked incredulously. "After filing a lawsuit against me?"

She'd made a similar assertion earlier. It was time he set her straight. "A letter from my attorney is hardly equivalent to a lawsuit, Miss Taylor," he said, noting the curve of her mouth and thinking how pleasant it would be to kiss it.

"Don't you think I know the difference?" Digging into her purse, Mel brought forth the document she'd been served that afternoon and held it out to him.

He accepted it with a frown. To his astonishment, a quick perusal of its wording proved her right. He was *indeed* suing her. Given a blanket authorization to do as he thought best, Kevin Frazier had gone overboard.

The decent thing would be to back off at once. Apologize and write out a check to her friend if that's what she wanted. After everything she'd been through, she deserved nothing less.

Right, Joe thought. And if you do, she'll flounce out of here a winner. You'll never see her again. His only possible course of action if he wanted to establish a relationship with her was to let her talk him out of it—slowly, reasonably, so she had time to check him out and take a liking to him.

"I hate to admit it," he acknowledged, deliberately brushing his fingers against hers as he returned the document, "but you're right. This *is* a lawsuit. I think I know how it came about. Three days after you got hurt, I had to leave for Italy on a business trip. When I got back and found out that you hadn't returned my calls, I tossed the matter in my attorney's lap. Apparently this is how he chose to handle it."

It's close enough to the truth, he thought, justifying the explanation to himself. I didn't specify what my purpose was.

Too upset and embarrassed to talk to Joe when he'd phoned her apartment the Monday after she'd checked herself out of the hospital, Mel had entertained herself by fantasizing about his concern over her injuries and remorse for leaving her side. She'd been forced to conclude both were short-lived when, on Tuesday, his calls had ceased.

Now she realized he'd been out of the country and unable to get in touch.

I should have picked up the phone when I heard his voice on the answering machine, she conceded. If I had, I might not be facing legal action.

"So," she said after a moment. "The suit was your attorney's idea. Do you think it's justified?"

This, Joe observed, is where it gets tricky. He shrugged. "Why not? The *Sorrento*'s pretty banged up. If my insurance company has to pay, it'll probably raise my premium."

Whatever your premium, you can afford it, Mel thought. Since the damage didn't result from negligence on my part, it's your responsibility anyway. "The condition of your boat and the terms of your insurance policy have no bearing on my liability or lack thereof," she answered.

She was as smart as a whip. His brown eyes warm enough to rival the steamy July weather, Joe lowered his gaze a fraction, then returned it to her face.

"I suppose we could talk about it," he suggested, loosening his tie. "What do you say we adjourn to my apartment? The workday's over and we could kick off our shoes. Get comfortable. Sort things out over drinks. . . ."

In Mel's experience, the words "get comfortable" meant a pass was in the offing. Far from feeling sympathy for her as she limped around in a cast, propelling herself with crutches, he was focused on his own needs and desires. She felt deeply offended.

"Sorry," she retorted, getting awkwardly to her feet. "But I wouldn't feel comfortable doing that. I was hoping if we talked you'd see reason . . . acknowledge the accident to your boat wasn't my fault. I didn't come here for a tête-à-tête."

Joe hastily followed suit. "Please believe me," he said. "I was just trying to be hospitable."

"Sure you were. Like the spider, inviting the fly into his parlor. Or the wolf, playing host to Little Red Riding-Hood after hours!"

For once, Joe was speechless.

Moving determinedly on her crutches, Mel walked out of his office and traversed the secretary's silent, empty domain to the twelfth-floor lobby. As she punched the elevator call button, she glanced at her watch. It was 5:23 p.m. On a typical workday, the building emptied out fast. By now, it would be all but deserted. If she was lucky, she wouldn't run into any of her former colleagues and be forced to discuss her accident with them.

In response to her summons, the elevator began its hushed ascent, causing a succession of numerals in a panel above its mirrored doors to light up. A moment later, its mechanical purr ceased. The overhead panel went dark. Maybe it was Mel's imagination, but the air-conditioning seemed to shut down simultaneously.

Not to worry, she assured herself, leaning a little more heavily on her crutches as she adopted a waiting stance. It's just the typical power glitch associated with a lightning strike. The Tampa Bay area was the lightning capital of the world and the fact that it had been sunny when she'd walked in didn't mean there wasn't a thunderstorm lurking around someplace. It was the right time of day for it. The electricity would come back on at any moment.

It didn't.

Two minutes passed. Three. No cooling breath of air issued from the ceiling vent. The elevator shaft was as silent as a tomb.

Maybe it's a rolling blackout, Mel speculated. During the summer with its daily ninety-five-degree heat and everyone's air conditioners going full blast, such blackouts were a real possibility. Sometimes the power company just couldn't cope. If that's what had happened, she knew, restoring electrical service could take as long as twenty minutes.

Meanwhile, the lobby didn't contain a bench. Access to a bathroom had been cut off when the double glass doors leading to the secretary's work area had closed and locked behind her and suddenly she wouldn't have minded using one. With her crutches and injured knee, she couldn't picture herself negotiating twelve flights of stairs.

I can ignore the call of nature and stand here until the power comes back on, Mel thought. Or I can throw myself on Joe Carbone's mercy. Considering the way she'd stormed out of his office, all but accusing him of dishonorable intentions, the latter option would necessitate a certain amount of bowing and scraping.

Chapter Five

In the luxury penthouse that adjoined his private office, Joe had kicked off his loafers, removed his jacket and tie and morosely fixed himself a martini. What a mess! he thought, flopping down onto one of his twin black leather couches without bothering to turn on the stereo. Thanks to your smart-aleck posturing, you don't stand a snowball's chance in hell of convincing Mel Taylor you're a decent sort.

Funny, he could have sworn they'd be good together.

Propping his feet on a free-form glass-and-teak coffee table and shutting his eyes, he decided to call Kevin Frazier in the morning and direct him to call off the lawsuit. He'd insist the attorney write Mel a letter of apology. With it would go a check for two thousand five hundred dollars she could sign over to her friend. It wouldn't get him anywhere with her. But it was the right thing to do.

A man who liked a breeze, liked the air to move, he became aware of a growing stuffiness in the room. Apparently his cleaning lady had switched off the ceiling fan. And the air-conditioning didn't seem to be working. He was about to investigate when he heard the muffled noise of someone pounding on the glass doors of his secretary's office.

Could it possibly be . . . ?

To his distinct pleasure, it was Mel. She looked embarrassed, rueful and a mite frustrated. "Listen, I'm sorry to bother you after the way our conversation went a few minutes ago," she confessed before he could say anything. " But there's been a power failure. The elevator isn't working. I wonder if I could use your bathroom. And wait here in one of the office chairs until . . ."

Never let it be said, Joe thought, that the only son of Mike and Rose Carbone can't think on his feet. Or reverse course when the situation warrants. Thanks to a glitch in the electrical service, he had another chance to work his wiles on Mel. He planned to make the most of it.

He'd have to do something fairly soon about the building's backup system, though.

Stepping aside, he held the door open with what he hoped was an engaging yet trustworthy smile. "My offer still stands," he said. "Strictly on a hands-off basis, of course. The guest bath in my apartment is all yours. And the seating in my living room is much more comfortable. What's more, I have soft drinks in my refrigerator as well as beer and mixers for cocktails. I'll be glad to fix you whatever you'd prefer."

Mel hesitated. But in truth she was in no position to argue. For her to insist on remaining in his secretary's work area unsupervised, or expect him to hang around and keep an eye on her until the power came on again, would be grudging in the extreme.

"Okay," she conceded, wishing he wasn't quite so handsome, loaded with sex appeal and the opposing party in a lawsuit. "I mean, thank you. Under the circumstances, you're being very generous."

By now, Joe's private office was familiar territory. And, though comfortably furnished, unremarkable. As a result, she was stunned when he opened the connecting door to his living room.

She wasn't sure what she'd expected. Mediocre taste, perhaps. An inelegant mishmash of styles and colors. Despite his money and expensively tailored clothes, he'd had a minimum of formal education. She'd simply assumed discernment when it came to art and a flair for personal decorating were beyond his ken.

You're a worse snob than your parents, she admitted with a little shake of her head as she took in his soft gray linen-covered walls, teak flooring and jewel-toned oriental rugs. Impressed, she recognized a sculpture by Gay Landrum, paintings by Tootsie Webb and Joe Testasecca.

"Your apartment...it's wonderful," she said softly, unable to hide her jumble of emotions as she turned to face him. "Did you have help from a decorator?"

"You're looking at him."

"Well, he did a fabulous job."

Joe's grin relaxed a little. That's one in my favor, he thought. "Thanks," he answered. "It's too close to the office sometimes. But it saves me from a commute. The bathroom's down the hall. Second door on your left."

With Mel safely closeted in his guest bath, Joe beat a hasty retreat to the circuit breakers that were mounted above the washer-dryer in his pantry and laundry area. Whether or not the power failure continued for a while, the building's electrical service and elevator would begin functioning again in a few minutes, courtesy of a gas-driven generator he'd installed more than a year earlier. When that happened, Mel would leave—unless she wasn't aware the power had been restored.

Because of something that had happened to his middle sister, Claudine, who was mildly claustrophobic about elevators, he'd had similar generators installed in every building he owned or built that had more than three stories. When they were working properly, the changeover to auxiliary power was automatic. At the moment, however, the generator in the building where he resided was having some problems. Its switch had to be thrown manually. His night maintenance man, who came on duty promptly at 6:00 p.m., would attend to it.

Suppressing a stab of guilt, Joe flipped the master circuit breaker on his control panel to the Off position. Until he flipped it back, the duration of the power failure in his apartment would be up to him.

By the time Mel emerged from his guest bath and poked her head into his teak, stainless-steel and cobalt-blue tile kitchen, he was innocently rummaging in the freezer for a handful of ice cubes.

"What'll it be?" he asked, clinking them into chunky, cut-crystal glasses. "Soda? I've got cola, lemon-lime and grape flavors. Or would you prefer a martini? I'm considered an expert at making them."

"Cola would be fine."

"You've got it."

Still leaning on her crutches, Mel glanced around the room. "I have to hand it to you," she mused. "This kitchen is perfect too. I could move in here without changing a thing and be perfectly content..."

A moment later, she was blushing to the roots of her dark-blond curls. You idiot! she castigated herself. You sound as if you're coming on to him!

In the interest of putting her at ease, Joe pretended not to notice. "C'mon," he said, balancing their drinks and some munchies he'd found in the cupboard. "Let's make ourselves comfortable in the living room."

It was heaven to get off her feet. And to sip something cold and carbonated. Leaning back on the sofa that stood at a right angle to one where he'd chosen to sit, Mel propped her injured, aching leg on a throw pillow atop Joe's coffee table. Beside it were several hard-cover volumes, one of them devoted to the lives and works of Italian operatic composers.

"You like opera, too?" she asked in surprise before she could bite her tongue.

"Yeah. I grew up with it. My old man used to whistle Puccini while he shaved."

He was so suave, so at home among cultural trappings and politicos, yet so down to earth. An everyday guy who was also one-in-a-million. Pensive, Mel didn't pursue the topic of his musical taste, and a small silence, fraught with curiosity and attraction on her part, lengthened between them.

We really ought to discuss the lawsuit, she thought. Maybe if I didn't try to lecture him and wasn't so ready to take offense at everything he said, I could convince him to drop it. Yet she didn't bring up the subject. A fragile, unexpected rapport born of off-beat circumstances had sprung up between them and, for reasons she sensed were unrelated to the original purpose of her visit, she was reluctant to shatter it.

It would be so easy to let herself dream about him. She couldn't seem to get enough of the way those little grooves beside his mouth deepened when he smiled. Or the lively humor that glinted in his deep brown eyes. There was something both charming and disarming about the way he looked in his stocking feet, with five o'clock shadow tracing his jaw and his shirt casually unbuttoned at the neck.

Too bad he was a ladies' man—one of whom it had been said he had a different girlfriend every month. She certainly wasn't the sophisticated, glamorous type he was known to prefer. Before she went gaga over him, she'd do well to remember he'd never paid her any special attention while she'd worked in his condo sales department. Face it, she thought. We'd never have shared even the *beginnings* of a date if Janet hadn't footed the bill. If he seems interested in you now, it's just proximity.

Meanwhile the air in his apartment was getting stuffier by the moment. Before long, if the power didn't come back on, it would be like a sauna. The living room's wall of sliding glass doors, which opened onto a balcony, directly faced the late-afternoon sun.

''Shouldn't we open the windows and see if we can catch a breeze?'' she suggested.

Joe shook his head. "I don't think that would be such a good idea. You could fry eggs on the pavement out there this afternoon. Any remaining cool air would get swallowed up in the heat. But we could shut the drapes."

It wouldn't be dusk until around 8:30 p.m. Still, closing his roughly woven drapes and their opaque liners plunged the area where they sat into shadow. Switching on a lamp wasn't an option. Surely the situation wouldn't drag on until they needed candles.

If it did...

"The power failure was at 5:23 p.m.," Mel observed with a frown. "I know because I glanced at my watch a few seconds before it hit. It's after 6:00 p.m. now. And there hasn't been a flicker. With rolling blackouts like the ones we had during that cold snap a couple of Christmases ago, the power usually comes back on within twenty minutes or so. Maybe there's something about what's happened on the news. You wouldn't happen to have a battery-operated radio?"

The last thing Joe wanted was a radio announcer informing Mel the power had been restored. She'd wonder why his *hadn't* been. He supposed if worse came to worst he could speculate that the master switch had flipped of its own accord.

"Actually, I do...in my bedroom," he volunteered after a moment. "I'll get it."

Returning with an oversize portable radio that boasted shortwave and public service bands as well as a full range of regular ones, Joe set it down on the coffee table. Switching it on, he tuned it and raised the antenna. Mel didn't object when he sat down beside her to listen, though once again their knees were almost touching. It struck her that they were like two kids, huddled in front of a television set.

The FM station Joe usually listened to in his car to keep abreast of current events was on the air—thanks to its own backup generator. Though he and Mel had tuned in somewhere in the middle of an unscheduled news broadcast, it didn't take them long to discover that the power failure was ongoing and unbelievably widespread.

Far from being limited to Tampa or even the Bay Area, apparently, it encompassed the entire state of Florida from Miami to the Panhandle. Reports of similar outages were flooding in from Atlanta, Mobile, Charleston and other cities throughout the southeast. Even parts of the Bahamas had been affected.

Locally the failure had caused stop-and-go signals to shut down, snarling rush-hour traffic and exasperating motorists. As a result, a rash of accidents and several fistfights had occurred, most of them at busy intersections. U.S. 19 in Pinellas County and Dale Mabry in Hillsborough were said to be in gridlock. Ditto Gulf-to-Bay in Clearwater and Route 60 as far east as Brandon. Though it too was backed up, authorities were urging homebound travelers, where possible, to use the Interstate.

"I don't get it," Mel said. "If the blackout extends from Miami to north Georgia and from Mobile to the Carolina coast, it can't be a problem with the individual electric companies. There must be dozens of them. It sounds more like sabotage. But who would or could carry out an attack of that nature on such a grand scale?''

"Hush, there's more," Joe answered, reaching over to squeeze her hand so he wouldn't be misunderstood.

According to the announcer, Civil Defense officials were warning persons with breathing problems who depended on electrically powered concentrators for auxiliary oxygen to check their reserves and go to a nearby hospital at once if those reserves were depleted. That night, the expected low temperature, which usually occurred an hour or so before sunrise, would be in the upper seventies to low eighties. Persons subject to heat prostration and related problems were advised to take similar action. Telephone service wasn't affected, and a toll-free number was aired for those who needed assistance.

Because of the breaking nature of the blackout story, the announcer's monologue had an ad-lib quality. Abruptly it ceased altogether for a moment. Papers rustled next to an open mike as he exchanged a few unintelligible words with someone.

Then, "Ladies and gentlemen, I have good news and bad news," he said. "The good news is that what you're experiencing doesn't represent the catastrophic first step in a hostile takeover by a foreign power. Or sabotage of any kind, even if it *has* messed up your dinner plans.

"We just received an announcement from the National Security Agency in Washington. From what government meteorologists and astronomers from several major observatories around the country have been able to determine, the unprecedented power failure that has blanketed the southeast is the result of solar flares ... some of the most violent disturbances of their kind to occur since records have been kept.''

Joe and Mel stared at each other. Was it possible such a bizarre natural event could have taken place? And that, because of it, they were marooned in his apartment together?

''The bad news,'' the announcer continued with thinly disguised relish, as if coming to the punch line of a joke, ''is that nobody seems to know how long the situation will last. Estimates range from several hours ... to several days!''

Chapter Six

"What am I going to do?" Mel groaned, fumbling for her crutches. "There's no telling when the power will come on again. I can't stay here."

"Who says you can't?" Joe argued. "The elevator still doesn't work. And you're not fit to tackle the stairs."

"Maybe I could make it."

"Let's say for the sake of argument you could. Then what? With the roads jammed in every direction, how long do you think the trip home would take?"

He was right, of course—about the stairs *and* the traffic. If she attempted the former, she might cause herself further injury. As for the latter, it was anybody's guess whether she could find a taxi driver willing to negotiate it. She had exactly forty dollars in her purse. Hillsborough County fares were high and, given the trauma of driving her back to St. Petersburg through a giant traffic jam, it might not be enough.

She had to try. Spending the night in Joe Carbone's apartment was out of the question. The man was suing her, for God's sake. Besides, in the absence of air-conditioning, it was already so hot and airless she felt like stripping. She didn't want him for an audience.

Self-consciously she wiped a little mustache of sweat from her upper lip. "I feel I really ought to give it a tumble," she said, then winced at the unfortunate choice of words. "Not literally, of course."

It was a free country. Aware that, by now, the maintenance man might be using the generator-powered elevator to make his rounds, Joe kept his fingers crossed. Maybe the man had arrived late because of the traffic foul-up. He could only hope.

Luckily the stairwell had ample natural lighting during daylight hours. Its nighttime illumination, activated by an automatic timer and currently set to go on around 7:00 p.m., would have been a dead giveaway.

Escorting Mel to the twelfth-floor lobby and standing at the head of the stairs as she gingerly lowered herself one step and then another, Joe felt like a parent watching a toddler flirt with danger. He was a louse, making things so difficult for her.

"I wish you'd reconsider," he said.

Rivulets of sweat were running down Mel's sides beneath her dress. Ignoring them, she shook her head, thrust her crutches forward and descended another step. She felt as if she were rappeling down a precipice on stilts.

"It's not so bad," she boasted. "I can handle it."

She was three-quarters of the way to the eleventh-floor landing when she slipped. *"Ohhhhh..."* she cried, instinctively shielding her injured knee from harm as, her crutches clattering from her grasp, she slid the rest of the way to the landing on her buttocks.

Joe was beside her in an instant. "Are you all right?" he asked.

Her reply was barely above a whisper. "Physically? I guess so." Mentally she felt like an idiot.

"You're coming back upstairs."

He hadn't made a question of it, and she didn't object. Retrieving her crutches, he hoisted her over his shoulder like a sack of seed corn or cement. Her rump in the air, one hipbone pressed against his cheek and her head hanging ignominiously upside down in the vicinity of his shoulder blades, she made the trip back to the twelfth-floor lobby and his living room.

By the time he deposited her on the couch, they were both sweating profusely. Mel's cheeks were pink with embarrassment.

"Do me a favor...*stay*," Joe growled, raking back wavy dark hair that had gone damp with perspiration in an effort to cool his forehead. He was exasperated with her. Yet he admired her spunk. If they could just get back the tender but potentially explosive rapport he'd sensed when they'd danced together...

Mel bit her lip. "You mean here in your apartment? Or specifically here on the couch?"

"In one piece, dammit!"

They both laughed, easing the tension between them a hundredfold.

"Funny," Mel said after a moment, propping up her foot. "Just as you closed your apartment door, I could have sworn I heard the elevator."

It took all the cool Joe possessed not to give himself away. He'd heard it start up, too, and knew she wasn't imagining things. "Impossible," he answered.

"The power's still off. It must have been wishful thinking on your part."

As a result of their burst of activity and the ballooning heat, the apartment felt like an oven. Or a steam bath, Mel thought. For maximum benefit, we should be sitting around in Turkish towels.

Picking up a magazine from the coffee table, she fanned herself while Joe raided the ice-cube tray and made them fresh soft drinks. When he returned, the glass he handed her was wondrously icy to the touch and she rubbed it against her cheeks, forehead and throat before taking a sip.

Joe did likewise, regretting the necessity of leaving his circuit breakers set to Off with the temperature climbing toward eighty-five degrees. Yet he sensed weathering a freak occurrence of nature together as virtual prisoners in his apartment was a matchless opportunity for them to get past the barriers fate had erected.

"Look, I'm sorry about all the trouble I caused, forcing you to haul me up the steps like a side of beef," Mel said, wishing she could read the thoughts behind his mesmerizing brown eyes. "It was just that, with you suing me..."

"Maybe we can lay that issue to rest."

"I wish we could."

"Do you play poker?"

It was a loaded question. Sensing risk, Mel evaluated the possibilities. He might be good, but she was probably a lot better. She'd placed first in her dorm's poker competition senior year and augmented a partial scholarship with her weekly winnings at the card table.

"I haven't for ages," she murmured innocently, pressing her iced drink against her cheek. "Not since college. Why do you ask?"

"I thought we might run through a couple of hands to pass the time and, simultaneously, put the lawsuit issue to bed. If you win, I drop it. Simple as that."

She had the strong feeling he wanted to put *her* to bed. Proximity, she supposed. And opportunity. The camaraderie of being marooned together. Yet she didn't consider his suddenly obvious sexual interest in her an affront. Instead she felt cajoled, flattered, exquisitely complimented.

With his jet-set life-style and flock of girlfriends, Joe Carbone wasn't the kind of man to whom a wise woman would give her heart. Yet Mel had to give him his due. He was gorgeous. Surprisingly easy to know. And obviously quite intelligent. Given the situation in which they found themselves, with the caveats that governed everyday behavior relaxed out of existence, she could picture herself making love to him.

"And if I lose?" she asked. Privately she didn't think it likely. Insofar as the outcome of their card game, she believed, her virtue would be safe.

Joe shrugged. "We can cross that bridge when we come to it. How about if I limit myself to a stake equivalent to the amount of cash you're carrying in your purse? Whichever one of us runs out of money first, loses. I guarantee that, if you're stranded without cab fare once the blackout ends, I'll see to it you get home . . . eventually."

His mouth curved at the implicit challenge he'd issued, and Mel smiled back. A little flirtation couldn't hurt. Despite the rising temperature and the fact that she was breaking out in prickly heat, she felt charged up, invigorated.

Still fanning herself, she watched benignly as Joe shuffled the deck and dealt them five cards each. It was only when he positioned the pack to one side and paused to lightly trace the sensitive sole of her left foot, which was resting atop its pillow on the coffee table, that she realized what a sensuous pastime poker could be. Little stabs of desire awoke in her deepest places.

"Pretty foot," he said casually, raising his eyes to hers before picking up his hand and studying it. "When we get bored with cards, I'll borrow some polish from my secretary's desk and paint your toenails."

The thought of Joe Carbone giving her a pedicure so flustered Mel that she bet more recklessly than usual and lost the first hand. *Five dollars down the drain when I could have folded for one,* she thought in disgust. *Instead of calculating the odds, I was picturing him with my bare feet in his hands, stroking on polish and kissing his way up my calves.*

Two could play at that game. Removing a tissue from her purse, she blotted her forehead and neck, then unbuttoned the top button of her placket-front sundress to dab at the perspiration between her breasts. From beneath lowered lashes, she saw with satisfaction that Joe was thoroughly focused on her cleavage.

"My deal, I believe," she said, scooping up the cards. "Since it's dealer's choice, let's try a little 'Spit in the Ocean.'"

The variation was a new one on Joe and she won that hand plus the next two. His balance sheet, scrawled on the back of a business envelope, showed her thirteen dollars to the good. Another twenty-seven dollars, she thought, and the lawsuit is history. It'll be like taking candy from a baby.

When it came to cards, overconfidence had always been her Achilles' heel. Abruptly, as if he'd been sandbagging all along, Joe started winning again. When she got lousy cards, he had good ones. Whenever she had a decent hand—usually during *her* deal, she noticed—his was better. Bankruptcy was fast approaching.

"I don't suppose you'd cheat to take advantage of me," she said with a frown when she hit the two-dollar mark.

Grinning, he whirred the deck. "I doubt it."

At that point, she realized, he didn't have to. All he had to do was raise a two-dollar bet.

"It strikes me that there's something inherently unfair about not stating what I stand to lose up-front," she argued. "Since I'm almost at the point of having to pay up, and you still haven't said, I think I deserve another chance."

Joe considered her request with narrowed eyes. "You're right," he admitted. "How about stipulating that, if you lose, you'll go through with our date despite the lawsuit?"

She was in no position to bargain. "Sounds fair," she agreed, "provided you're willing to begin again from scratch. The only problem is, what do I use for collateral? A promissory note?"

"Uh-uh." Firmly Joe shook his head. "We've already got too much paperwork gumming up the works between us."

"Then what?"

He appeared to ponder her question.

Oddly Mel had the feeling any solution he'd propose had been in his mind from the start. She was convinced of it when he opened his mouth.

"It's getting too hot and muggy in here to think straight," he said, stretching and working the day's kinks out of his shoulders. "Yet here we are, like a couple of Puritans, still sweating it out in our street clothes. Since your luck is bound to change and I'll probably lose, what would you say to a round of strip poker?"

It was an outrageous suggestion. Unbidden, an image of Joe in the altogether leapt into Mel's head. She had little doubt that, with his broad shoulders, lean hips and flat midsection, he'd be a stirring sight. Unfortunately, if the play continued in the same vein, she was the one likely to be conceding in her underwear.

With the temperature climbing out of sight, she decided the world wouldn't end if he saw her in her bra and panties. A second chance to quash the lawsuit was just too good to miss.

"All right," she said. "I'm game. How do we bet and raise, if not with money?"

The little quote marks deepened beside his mouth. "I have a box of poker chips in the dining room," he confessed, rising to fetch them. "Some of the guys and I meet here to play every other Friday evening."

Mel picked up her cards with mixed emotions. Damn him, but his skill probably equaled hers. Plus, she guessed, he didn't mind cheating, at least not in the present situation. A moment later, she did a double take. Three aces had miraculously presented themselves.

Maybe her luck really was about to change! When she drew a four of clubs from the pack to match the four of hearts in her hand, it was all she could do to keep from crowing. Discarding, she raised Joe into the stratosphere. He bit. With a puny two pair against her full house, he good-naturedly took off his shirt.

She'd been right about his shoulders and midsection. They were luscious. Well-developed muscles that hinted at regular exercise despite a full business and social schedule rippled beneath smooth, deeply tanned skin. With everything that was female in her, she wanted to run her hands over them. Shifting her attention to the inverted triangle of dark chest hair that narrowed to an irregular seam above his belt, she couldn't keep her gaze from traveling in the direction it pointed.

Just in time, she caught herself. Oh, no, she thought. You're not going to work that scam on me again. No matter how sexy you act, I plan to tend to my knitting. When she won the next two hands, her suspicions about his honesty abated and she began worrying about what to do when he was down to his shorts.

If she knew him, and she was beginning to think she did, he'd probably insist on playing out the last hand, even if removing his shorts in front of her was the result. In the interim, he'd pulled off his socks, one at a time, in order to delay defeat.

Mel supposed his watch would come next. But she hadn't bargained with Joe's card-playing skill. Or catlike ability to land on his feet. On the following deal, which happened to be hers, he came up with a straight flush. The odds against it happening were more than seventy-two thousand to one, if she remembered correctly. Since she'd shuffled and dealt, she had to conclude cheating hadn't been a factor.

"Your turn," he said with a grin.

A bit grudgingly, she removed an earring. Thank heaven she'd decided at the last minute to wear jewelry. It was turning out to be a lifesaver. "A temporary setback," she murmured. "Life is full of them."

"Tut, tut. Where's your humility? You speak as if the game's in the bag. Meanwhile, you look kind of lopsided with just one earring. Let's see if we can't get you to take off the other one."

To Mel's chagrin, he succeeded in doing just that. Her necklace followed and then her wristwatch, not his. If only she hadn't worn a one-piece dress! When the next two hands fell to her, she began to relax a little. But she was still wary, not to mention utterly flummoxed by the sight of Joe in his paisley-print boxer shorts.

In lieu of his watch, he'd taken off his belt and slacks—probably in the interest of cooling off but also to rattle her. She had to admit his ploy was having the desired effect. He had great legs, with slim but well-developed calves and lean, muscular thighs.

Far from acting embarrassed, he seemed actually to be enjoying himself. Mel guessed that was because he'd stripped for so many women, and enjoyed their adulation. She doubted if he'd had to resort to gambling to get most of them to reciprocate.

Though logic didn't back her up and she had no real evidence of it, she was convinced he was masterminding things. Either that, or they were very evenly matched. From the beginning of the strip portion of their game, they'd basically alternated winning and losing hands, with her at a slight disadvantage. Now that disadvantage had shifted. With him down to his shorts and wristwatch, she was willing to bet, she'd start losing again.

The cards confirmed her hunch almost immediately. Three of a kind looked good, until his full house deflated it. "Time to slip out of that dress," he prodded.

As steamy as she already felt, Mel was aware her cheeks were starting to burn. *Where's my bravado now when I need it most?* she thought.

"Can't I just lower the top half?" she coaxed. "Your shirt and trousers were separate items."

"Sorry. It doesn't work that way."

"Oh, all right..."

A little awkwardly because of her cast, Mel wriggled out of her striped sundress. As she did so, she tried to tell herself the strapless polka-dot bra and matching bikini panties she'd worn under it weren't any more risqué than the yellow swimming suit she'd planned to baptize on her Captiva trip with him. But she couldn't get the idea to wash. By its very nature, underwear was far more intimate.

Unabashed by her obvious shyness, Joe looked his fill. In his eyes, she was exquisite. Not voluptuous, but rounded and feminine. As smooth as silk in tone. She has skin like cream, he thought, his lips parting slightly as he caressed her with his eyes. I want to touch her. Taste her. Make love to her like an avalanche and continue pleasing her, far into the night.

They had a lawsuit to dispose of first. In the meantime, he'd better stop thinking about the pleasures they could share unless he wanted his body to trumpet its arousal. Instinct told him Mel was special. He had no intention of spoiling things by jumping her bones.

"I guess you know how appetizing you look in that outfit," he said. "Speaking of appetite, let's finish the game and hunt up some candles. The sun seems to be going down at last, and it might not be too unbearable to cook out on the balcony. I have a gas grill and a couple of T-bones in the refrigerator."

Mel appreciated the compliment. And the casual way he'd chosen to change the subject. He was more of a gentleman than she'd thought. Determined not to lose now that things were getting critical and convinced he was too accommodating to strip completely if she didn't want him to, she found herself coming up short again.

"What'll it be?" Joe asked. "Your bra? Or the bottom half?"

Perspiration stood out like dew drops on Mel's forehead. If she didn't meet his eyes, she'd be forced to focus on his torso. Every subtle nuance of his glistening musculature taunted her. A man could run around naked to the waist and no one thought anything of it.

"You . . . can't be serious," she whispered.

Joe crooked one brow. "What's fair is fair."

"Won't you settle for a substitute?"

He already had the perfect one in mind. "Maybe a kiss would do it," he speculated.

Relief flooded through her. He wouldn't demand she choose between conceding defeat or exposing her breasts. "A kiss it is," she said, leaning toward him and lightly bussing him on the lips.

He shook his head disparagingly, as if she'd tried to pay her debt to him with inferior merchandise. "You call that a kiss?" he asked. Letting go of her shoulders, he came over to sit beside her. "Let's try that again," he suggested. "For a kiss to be authentic, it has to ring my bell."

He was trying to prod her into giving him her best. Fine, thought Mel. You want bells? You're going to be hearing them for weeks! "Close your eyes and pucker up," she directed.

Though it was deceptively gentle, there was nothing hesitant about her kiss. Soft and seeking, her velvety inner lips caressed his as if she were savoring a bite of some sinfully delicious dessert.

Desire awoke in him in an instant. From passive participant, content to close his eyes as requested and be acted upon at her leisure, he became a thoroughly engaged and ardent aggressor.

"Not so fast," Mel warned. "You're forgetting who's in charge of this operation."

The quote marks she liked so much flashed beside his mouth. "Sorry...I forgot myself," he admitted. "Please proceed."

"Okay. Half a kiss to go."

Framing his face with both hands, she addressed herself to his mouth again, this time boldly inserting her tongue. She realized at once that, if retaining control of the situation was an objective, the joke was on her. The erogenous zones of her palms and the soles of her feet tingled with an intensity she'd never dreamed was possible as desire broke over her in waves and focused between her legs.

Later, she couldn't have said exactly how she came to be sitting on Joe's lap. She only knew she was there and that she liked the feeling. The incomparable luxury of letting his hands rove over her bare skin at will was inciting her sensuality to riot.

She was too far gone to protest when he forgot himself a second time and tasted her tongue with his. Or complain when he slipped his fingers beneath her bikini panties for a braille exploration of her buttocks.

To her surprise, he was the one to call a halt.

No way am I going to push her further than she's ready to go, Joe thought. That would be the surest way of losing her.

"Let's say you won the next two hands," he proposed, his voice rough and sweet as he traced her softly parted lips with one finger. "I'd be forced to take off my watch and then my shorts . . . or kiss you back. Twice. If you lost, you'd have the option of removing your bra and panties, or giving me the same two kisses. Why don't we just skip the cards and get to the good stuff?"

Mel's mouth still had the softly crushed look he'd given it. "You mean . . . strip?" she whispered.

"For openers, I was talking about those two kisses."

Thinking about the "good stuff" had her vibrating in places he hadn't touched. About to demand a rain check, she yielded up her mouth.

Good Lord, Joe thought, amazed at the swiftness of her surrender. I wonder if she realizes what a delicious armful she is. Or just how sexy she is in that little bra-and-panty outfit. It doesn't leave very damn much to the imagination.

Even the whisper-light sheen of sweat that glistened on her skin made him think of lovemaking. In fact, the whole steamy, narrowly focused ambience of being marooned with her in his apartment made him think of it—even if he'd engineered their own private power failure himself.

For Mel, rational thought dissolved in pure feeling as she blurred into their common universe of touch. Something reserved and separate in her gave way as he apportioned his kiss into little installments, depositing them at every conceivable angle of her mouth.

It was like being eaten alive and—gloriously—living to tell about it. Take me, everything in her that was female and receptive wanted to shout. I don't care if we don't really know each other. Or that you're suing me...

He could feel the change in her at once.

"What's wrong?" he asked.

"The lawsuit. I just remembered it."

"Ah, babe." Another kiss landed on the corner of her mouth. "You can't seriously think I'd come on to you this way if I planned to drag you into court. I'm not that kind of guy."

"Then..."

"That whole stupid thing was a mistake. When I tried to reach you after you checked out of the hospital and you wouldn't return my calls, I'll admit I was put out with you. I was worried about the state of your health, for one thing. And I was hoping we'd have another chance to get to know each other. I've been wanting to ask you out since we were introduced shortly after you joined Ricci & Carbone...despite the fact that I don't usually date employees. The coincidence of your friend buying you a date with me was the nicest surprise I'd had in months."

It *wasn't* just proximity and opportunity with him. Mel felt as if she'd been handed the earth on a silver platter.

"I have to confess I'm flattered," she said, her palms resting lightly against the hair-roughened surface of his chest and feeling more at home there than she'd have thought possible just a short time earlier. "But I don't see what that has to do..."

"With the lawsuit."

"Yes."

"When I got back, I found you hadn't left any messages on my answering machine. Or tried to contact my secretary. Then, before I had a chance to phone you again, a new attorney at the law firm that regularly handles our legal business suggested you shared liability with the cigarette boat's owners for the damage to my yacht. I didn't agree with him. But I thought you needed a wake-up call. So I told him to do whatever he thought best. I expected him to write you a threatening letter, not take you to court."

Like the one before it, Joe's next kiss landed on an unprotesting surface. Mmm, thought Mel, resonating to it. I'm developing a definite addiction to him.

"You did it so I'd call you," she said slowly when it was possible again to speak.

"You got it."

"Then you never had any intention of suing me."

"Uh-uh. Where you're concerned, my motives are amorous, not hostile."

She was beginning to feel the same way—beginning, in fact, to trust him. Yet he was still an unknown quantity, a one-way ticket to emotional disaster if a quick fling or a one-night stand was what he had in mind. She couldn't dismiss the revolving girlfriends her former co-workers had gossiped about. Or the fact that he was successful, good-looking and could probably have anyone he wanted.

I'd rather not jump off a cliff and find out nobody's waiting to catch me, she thought. I need a little breathing space.

He seemed instinctively to sense what would please her best. "What do you say we mark this spot and come back to it after supper?" he asked. "It might be cool enough by now to open the sliding-glass doors and cook out on the deck. As I said earlier, I have a gas grill, so we won't need electricity. And a couple of nice steaks in the refrigerator. Since the door's been shut, they're probably okay."

"Sounds terrific," Mel said.

Sliding off his lap somewhat awkwardly because of her cast, she tried to push down her regret. It was one thing to ignore the boundaries that existed between them as relative strangers if he was pressuring her to abandon them, and quite another if that's what she wanted to do. Charmed, aroused, already a considerable distance down the garden path of being utterly besotted with him, her inner woman had lodged a gut-wrenching complaint.

For the moment, she knew, it was a complaint that would go unsatisfied. Frustration only added to the tingle she felt just being in the same room with him.

Before firing up the grill, Joe decided to try his battery-operated radio again. He quickly found out that some stations weren't on the air. Those that were seemed to be focusing on musical "blackout requests" interspersed with news bulletins about the massive power failure that had blanketed the southeast. From network commentators to local deejays, everyone was scrambling for information about solar flares and their effect on the affairs of humankind.

They caught part of a telephone interview with a Palm Harbor astronomer.

"In laymen's terms, solar flares represent large electromagnetic disturbances on the surface of the sun," the quiet, soft-spoken student of the heavens explained. "Appearing on its coolest areas, namely the so-called sun spots, even relatively small flares can interrupt shortwave radio communication. Larger ones can bring about power line disruption and telephone failure by introducing stray electrical currents that cause fuses or circuits to blow. Depending on the individual circumstances, generators may or may not be affected."

Maybe by now the elevator was nonoperational. Joe could only hope. It would let his conscience off the hook.

"How long could something like this last?" the deejay was asking.

The astronomer's shrug was an almost audible thing. "Theoretically," he advised, "it could go on for days. By the way, in addition to power failures, solar flares can cause a veritable feast of lights. Since it may be the only chance at our southern latitude for quite some time, I'd like to suggest sky watchers and astronomy buffs try to spot the Aurora Borealis."

The so-called Northern Lights wouldn't be visible from Joe's south-facing apartment. However… "We can take a look from my office conference room," he proposed. "No need to bother with crutches if you'll let me carry you. Afterward, you can get the steaks out of the refrigerator while I fire up the grill."

Mel found being carried through Joe's office in her bra and panties titillating in the extreme. And, though it was still too light outside for them to see anything approaching a celestial display, the trip wasn't wasted. As they headed back toward his apartment, he paused to open one of his secretary's desk drawers and snatch up a bottle of pink nail enamel.

"For the promised pedicure," he said with a grin.

Back on her crutches and aided by the stub of a candle Joe had lighted for her, Mel went prospecting in her cast and her polka-dot lingerie for the steaks he'd mentioned.

Perhaps because it was so small, his kitchen seemed even more oppressive and sticky-hot than his living room. When she opened its door, the still-cool breath of the darkened refrigerator felt wonderful against her heated skin.

She didn't dare abuse the privilege. Exposing its contents to the hot, humid air of the apartment would soon cause them to spoil. With her candle as a guide, she took out a head of lettuce and a tomato in addition to the steaks Joe had mentioned. She was halfway to the counter beside the sink where she'd spotted a knife rack and a cutting board when her candle guttered out.

In the pitch-darkness, she fumbled and dropped the steaks as she tried to relight the candle with the matches Joe had dropped into the drip-catching saucer of the candleholder.

"Joe," she called, doing her best to hang on to the tomato and lettuce. "Could you come here, please?"

When she didn't receive an answer, she began to grope her way toward the door—or rather the spot where she thought the door should be. It wasn't.

Simultaneously Joe entered the room. "Careful," he warned. "We don't want you falling and getting hurt again."

A moment later, he stepped on one of the plastic-wrapped steaks she'd dropped and skidded into her, causing her to lose her balance. They went down together, with Mel landing on top of him.

"Are you all right?" he asked, tentatively checking her out from a prone position that allowed him to revel in the soft pressure of her breasts against his chest and indulge his rapidly escalating desire for her by subtly repositioning her lower body against his.

Unconcerned about having proven herself a klutz once again, Mel was running an erotic spot check of her own. "I...think so," she whispered. "What about you?"

"I'm outstanding with you in my arms."

It was a deliberate play on words. Pausing to confirm that she was fully aware of his meaning, he kissed her again. This time, neither of them made a point of defining who was kissing whom. Instead, overwhelmed by the pent-up force of their previous interchange, they simply enfolded each other.

As she lay there on Joe's kitchen floor, atop the hard length of his body with his tongue enticing hers, Mel thought she'd never known such bliss. She'd certainly never felt such a compelling need to merge with another person. From her mouth, her breasts, the unexpectedly sensitive and vulnerable nerve endings that made their presence known as he lightly stroked her back, helpless pathways of desire spread to the place where she craved him most.

I want him inside me, she thought, half-coherent with the strength of what she felt. On top of me. Surrounding me. Opening me like a well to him and claiming my depths. Nothing will satisfy me but the chance to give him everything. She couldn't suppress a moan as the hard outline of his arousal pressed ever more blatantly against her.

She felt disoriented, rejected, then, when he suddenly relinquished her mouth and drew her head against his shoulder.

"What's wrong?" she asked.

"Nothing."

"Then..."

"We're going to be lovers. You know that, don't you?"

She wouldn't have to do without him. "Yes," she admitted, burrowing hungrily against his neck.

A wave of satisfaction flowed through him. It was as he'd hoped; they wanted the same thing. "Making love in a kitchen can be stimulating as a change of pace," he said after a moment. "But I don't want us to get started here. What do you say we skip the steaks and grab a bottle of wine instead...drag my guest-room mattress out onto the balcony? The sun's almost down and there's a light breeze stirring off the water."

He was inviting her to go out on his deck and have sex with him. Never one to rush into intimate relationships, Mel was bowled over with the certainty of what her answer must be.

"I can't think of anything I'd like better," she acknowledged, desire draining all resistance from her body.

Joe's guest-room mattress, which was queen-size, took up most of the space on his living-room balcony not occupied by his gas grill and two patio chairs. Tucking her crutches alongside it next to the railing, Mel took a seat while he went back for the wine and some pillows.

None of the nearby buildings was tall enough to overlook their nesting place. Meanwhile, the temperature had dropped, though it was probably still in the upper eighties. The breeze Joe had mentioned was wafting its cooling effect. Without any man-made lights to pierce its wholeness, the night would be like velvet.

Joining her, Joe poured the wine, a light and piquant chardonnay that had stayed cool enough to be pleasant. "To us," he said, his dark eyes resting on her with the warmth of a touch. "And to the inscrutable wisdom of the universe, which has given us this power failure. May we make the most of it."

Engulfed in feeling, Mel raised her glass. From the moment she'd agreed to his proposal, it seemed, Joe's sexuality had been turned on full force. Just the hard, handsome shape of his knee, which was lightly brushing her thigh, made her crazy with anticipation.

Chapter Seven

In the abruptly functioning, wordless communication that had sprung up between them, sipping at the chardonnay Joe had poured became a metaphor for ravishing each other. I want you so much, Mel admitted silently, gazing at him above the rim of her tulip-shaped glass. I'm burning to kiss and touch you everywhere.

They barely knew each other. Yet it was a blatant physical fact—one she hadn't been able to ignore despite her best intentions—that no other man had ever exerted a similar pull on her. Just being in close proximity to him caused her to lose control. With all the recklessness she possessed, she longed to lick his flat male nipples and trace the irregular seam of body hair that divided his torso past the point where it disappeared beneath the waistband of his boxer shorts. Her every nerve ending quivered with the urge to bridge their separateness.

No beginner at the art of love, though lately he'd begun to despair of ever really loving someone, Joe could read her passion as if it were expressed in the language of his thoughts. Unless he was very much mistaken, like his, it was boundless. Setting his glass on the textured concrete decking and placing hers beside it, he put his hands on her breasts.

Involuntarily Mel's nipples tightened. She drew a shaky breath.

"Take off your bra for me," he whispered.

The simple, straightforward request sent stabs of desire winging to her most private places. It was clear that, unlike her ex-boyfriend, Doug Jameson, Joe wouldn't reach summarily for his own satisfaction and attempt to please her as an afterthought. Instead, they'd be partners in the deepest sense—scale the erotic heights without once objectifying or retreating from each other. Having him, if only until the power came on again, would be worth the cost.

Like one bewitched in a dream she'd lost all hope of dreaming, she unfastened her bra's front clasp and let its demi-cups fall open. Her fullness spilled into his hands.

"God, but you're lovely," he said with a soft little explosion of breath, his eyes going smoky with anticipation.

Currents of desire swept through her, causing the tingle of receptivity she felt to quicken in the soles of her feet and the wet, aroused entry to her womanhood to throb with longing for his presence there. No other man could fill her. Just Joe, with his hard, sunbrowned body, wickedly knowing smile and potent outpouring of sex appeal.

He might be all wrong for her—uneducated in a formal sense, too rich for his own good, a ladies' man who couldn't give her the profound lifetime commitment she hoped one day to share. Yet at the moment it didn't matter. She'd been empty of him for as long as she could remember.

Pleasure escalated another notch when he lowered his dark head to her breasts and took one nipple into his mouth. The thrill his tongue called forth as he flicked it over her swollen bud in an irregular, heart-stopping rhythm was almost unbearable in its intensity. Yet it was just the beginning, she discovered, when he began to tug at her with his mouth. Spilling over with need for him, she let a little moan escape her as her fingers luxuriated in the thick, coarse texture of his hair.

"Joe...oh, *Joe*..."

"Tell me what you want, sweetheart."

"Just you...touching me everywhere. Please, can't we take off..."

His features were blunted with passion, his voice raspy, a little nasal as he answered her. "I want all of you, too," he said. "Here, babe...let me help."

Her cast caused them only a moment's awkwardness. Stripped of their underwear and all inhibition, they lay down atop his queen-size mattress. Twelve stories above Harbor Island, they'd wrestle in their nakedness, exposed to the muggy but distinctly cooler night air and a sky that was like ink except for its early sprinkling of stars.

Still damp from the homage of his mouth, her nipples welcomed the renewed attentions of his fingertips as he trailed kisses down her torso and stomach to part her tuft of wiry, blond curls with his tongue. Her response was so strong and immediate it nearly blew her away. Huge ripples of sensation spread outward from its locus as he initiated a litany of adoration.

In tandem with her heartbeat, her breathing quickened. Little moans of defenselessness were wrung from her as she clutched at the sweet breadth of his shoulders. The soles of her feet rubbed frantically over his hairy, muscular calves.

From the first second of his foray into her most private place, she'd gone achingly open to receive him. With all the lust she was capable of, she wanted him to drive her relentlessly toward the release she craved—*and* to plunge deep inside her. Could she partake, simultaneously, of the twin raptures she craved?

Joe sensed her exquisite conflict at once when she reached for him. "Babe...if I get in you now, I'll go off like a rocket," he growled, lifting his head partway. "Let me take you...a little higher first...."

With the loving, expert way he was pleasing her, she had little choice but to accommodate him. The ripples of feeling he was evoking continued to widen, each overlapping the last until she was immersed in an expanding sea of bliss. Unable to resist even if she'd wanted to, she gasped with pleasure and vulnerability when her response escalated to a higher peak.

She wouldn't linger at that level long. Aware from the helpless sounds she made and her utter lack of restraint that she was hovering near the brink, Joe substituted the ministrations of his hand for those of his tongue and dragged himself up to cover her after quickly assuming protection.

Briefly she faltered. He was too far up, wasn't he? How could they...? When he entered her, she understood. Positioning her so her face was half buried against his chest, he was able to graze the length of her responsiveness with each downward stroke.

Grasping and releasing him with her strong interior muscles, she helped to heighten the exquisite perception of fullness that was contributing to her abandonment. She was back at the point of delirium as he started to lose control.

Nothing in Joe's experience had prepared him for the thrill of bedding a woman he could love. By themselves, the physical rewards of making love to Mel were staggering. Coupled with the spiritual ones, he guessed, they could be infinite. He wanted all of her—to fuse himself to her very essence.

They reached their summit just seconds apart. Moving past it, Mel shuddered and lifted her hips as the final barriers between her and culmination were swept away. Little cries of rapture were wrung from her as, incandescent and drenched in sweat, she let the fierce discharge of energy permeate her every cell.

A second arc of trembling shook her as Joe reached his own attainment. I'm his, she exulted, awash in shivers and a flood tide of heat. And he's mine, if only for this moment.

Quieting, they moved into lethargy in the shelter of each other's arms. Intermittent and until that moment dense with humidity, the breeze freshened. A band of cumulus clouds had blown up and, as if bent on imitating the gooseflesh that had prickled their skin, it discharged a sprinkle of rain. Light and cool, the moisture touched them like a blessing.

"Want to go in?" Joe asked, rolling onto his side and searching her face.

The way she felt, it would take a forklift to move her. "Not unless you do," she whispered.

"Then we won't." Relaxing, he drew her head against his shoulder. "I like being rained on with you," he said. "It's like taking a shower after what we were doing a moment ago."

There wasn't any thunder and, after a few minutes, the light patter ceased. Refreshed and comfortable in her nakedness, Mel yawned and stretched. She felt sated yet extremely sexy right down to her toes. It's crazy to wish he loved me, she thought, doing her best to act like a grown-up and not set too much store by what had transpired between them. The chances of him caring for me are nil. And I haven't known him long enough even to consider commitment with him.

From what she could tell, Joe had gone to sleep. She was surprised, then, by the low rumble of his voice beside her ear.

"Tell me about your family," he requested lazily. "Do you have any brothers and sisters? Have you ever been married? What's your heart's desire?"

They were the kind of questions a man asked when he was genuinely interested in a woman. A bit shakily because she sensed the ground had shifted, Mel described her status as the only child of a brilliant but autocratic physics professor and a would-be concert pianist who'd abandoned her dream of a career to bear a child.

"I'm my mother's only chick," she explained. "She was determined that, if she couldn't have a musical career, then I *would*. The fact that I didn't have a musical bone in my body had nothing to do with it."

Lightly Joe stroked her arm—a feather touch. "I take it you're not a musician," he said with a smile.

"Hardly. My degree's in English. I teach language arts to middle-school students when I'm not selling real estate."

"What about your father? What did he want for you?"

Mel shrugged. She'd never been able to please the redoubtable R. Cummings Taylor, though God knew, she'd tried. Or to match his supreme self-confidence.

"For me to marry," she admitted spontaneously. "Provided, of course, that I found someone as brilliant and well educated as himself."

As soon as the words were out, she could have bitten her tongue. In light of Joe's interrupted education, she was convinced, they'd translate to a slap in the face.

He didn't appear to take them that way. "Education's important," he acknowledged. "When I quit high school to take over my grandfather's construction business, I thought I'd go back in a year or so. But I never did. I guess you could say I got my degree in the school of practicality and hard knocks."

Mel found herself listening to what he hadn't said. "So it bothered you to quit," she said, making a statement of the question.

He threw her a look. "Sure it did. I'm no dummy. And I'd considered college. A career as an architect. I simply did what I had to do under the circumstances. Running Ricci & Carbone and building quality housing that doesn't damage the environment has been a damn good substitute."

"So... you're satisfied with your life."

"In most ways."

He didn't tell her about his dream of settling down with someone and raising a family that was as warm and loving as the one from which he'd sprung. Or that he'd almost despaired of ever realizing it. Since she'd come into his life, his sense of having missed a very important boat had eased a bit.

"Just the same," he added when she didn't speak, "if I have kids someday, I'll try to talk them out of being high-school dropouts like their old man. That is, I will unless they have a *very* good reason."

Forced by knowing him to admit she'd been raised as something of an academic snob, Mel couldn't bear to hear him describe himself in such disparaging terms. "You're the last person anyone would think of as a dropout, despite your lack of formal credentials," she countered, one palm resting on his taut midsection. "Anyone can tell you're smart. I know for a fact that people admire your success and commitment."

The glow that had filled Joe's heart in the wake of their lovemaking expanded a little. She approved of him, not just as a lover but as a man who'd overcome adversity and a lack of formal credentials to make his mark. The thought was reasssuring, given the powerful attraction he felt.

He didn't put his feelings into words. Instead, remarking that turnabout was fair play, he described his three sisters and his mother, who'd recently begun keeping company with a widower.

The warmth he felt toward the female members of his family was unmistakable. Yet when Mel murmured that his mother must be very proud of him, she sensed his slight disagreement.

"She is, of course," he acknowledged after a moment. "I've done very well for myself, and all of us. Not getting married and presenting her with grandchildren is the only way I've disappointed her, I suppose."

Was he telling her he was a confirmed bachelor who enjoyed playing the field? And that she should look elsewhere for a steady lover? Or a husband?

Before Mel could think of a way to find out without directly putting the question to him, thunder rolled. Another band of clouds had swept eastward from the Gulf of Mexico. Some had anvil shapes.

"I have a feeling we're really in for it this time," Joe said ruefully. "Maybe we should duck for cover."

To Mel, his willingness to be there for her once the power came on again had ceased to matter though conversely she knew that, if they parted, she'd miss him all her days.

"I don't want to," she said, framing his face with her hands as the first big squally raindrops began to fall, plastering their hair with wet. "I want to stay out here on the balcony no matter how hard it pours...and make love to you again."

Chapter Eight

Mel stirred as a ray of sunlight cleared the rooftops and newly planted palms to the southeast and slanted across her eyelids. She had no idea what time it was. The place beside her where Joe had slept was empty.

Beneath her, his guest-room mattress was damp with dew. But it wasn't soaked. They'd turned it over following the second subtropical shower of the night before and their second lovemaking. The dampness was actually rather pleasant, considering the strong promise of renewed heat and humidity that filled the air.

At some point, Joe had fetched one of his shirts and arranged it over her shoulders. Sitting up, she thrust her arms into its sleeves and rolled up the cuffs. I wonder how things will go between us this morning? she thought, meditatively buttoning several buttons. Is he glad I'm still around? And that we made love? Or does he wish the power would come back on so we can separate?

Maybe the power was already operating. But she didn't think so. The sliding-glass doors that led to the living room stood open and she didn't detect any electronically produced blast of air-conditioning.

She was still speculating about what Joe's mood would be when he appeared, clad once more in his boxer shorts and looking like a million bucks despite his rumpled hair and dark stubble of shadow beard. The lacquered tray he was carrying contained two glasses and a carafe of orange juice.

"Sorry," he said with a grin that hinted at friendship and continued sensual interest. "No coffee. We still don't have the wherewithal to heat it yet."

"Orange juice sounds great."

Thoroughly charmed if a bit reticent, Mel accepted the glass he poured for her with thanks. Having spent the night in Joe's refrigerator with the door closed, the juice was refreshing if a little tepid as it slid down her throat.

"We have a few items left over from last night's agenda," Joe reminded, sitting down beside her and sipping his juice in turn. "Want to tackle them?"

Surely he wasn't going to resurrect the lawsuit and suggest they finish their strip-poker game!

"Name one," she challenged.

"Your pedicure."

A little stab of prurience pierced her to the quick. "I didn't think you'd really..."

"Then you don't know me, babe."

Draining his juice and setting the glass aside, he produced the bottle of polish he'd pilfered from his secretary's desk. "Here," he added, holding out one beautifully shaped hand. "Let me have one of your feet."

By now, the flood of warmth he could provoke between her legs simply by being who he was had become achingly familiar to her. Abandoning herself to it, Mel complied. To her pleased, somewhat shaky discovery, placing her right foot in his palm was enough to send her arousal spiraling into the stratosphere. The fact that he lightly, almost absently massaged her sensitive sole as he prepared to stroke on the polish did nothing to alleviate her titillation.

Sheer determination allowed him to paint all ten of her toenails a rosy pink before tingling nerve endings and a pair of overactive imaginations got the best of them.

"Careful . . . my polish will smear," Mel warned as he pulled her onto his lap.

"So what?" Imperturbably Joe dropped a warm little kiss on her mouth. "We'll have the fun of repairing it."

"But it's daylight. People are bound to see us . . ."

"Let them. We're decently clothed. They'll think we're doing our morning exercises."

They were "decently clothed" if her half-buttoned shirt and his boxer shorts qualified. A closer look would have revealed that she wore no underpants. His hands were under the shirt. The fly of his shorts was hanging open.

Half out of her mind with wanting him though he'd amply satisfied her twice the night before, Mel ceased all protest. A moment later, he'd arranged them so her inner thighs were gripping the narrow span of his hips and they were making love again.

They were laughing and teasing, chasing each other around the apartment with Mel navigating on her crutches and Joe using his fireplace poker for a cane when, at 11:05 a.m., Mel suggested they turn on his battery-operated radio to see what was happening in the outside world. To their mutual astonishment, the blackout was over. Power had been restored just five minutes before.

"So why is everything still dead?" Mel asked with a frown, attempting without success to switch on one of the living-room lamps.

Joe tried not to look as guilty as he felt. "I don't know," he improvised, racking his brain for an excuse to disappear into the laundry area for a moment.

The radio announcer saved his bacon. "According to a power company spokesman," he said, "subscribers still experiencing a power interruption should check their fuse boxes. The energy surge that accompanied yesterday's solar-flare activity may have caused some circuit breakers to blow."

"That must be it," Joe said hastily. "If you'll excuse me a moment, I'll check it out."

At first the start-up hum of his reverse-cycle air conditioning and the mechanical groans his refrigerator emitted when it kicked on resembled the sound effects of an alien world. Mel wasn't able to suppress the sigh that fluttered from her lips. *I don't want the blackout to be over,* she thought. *I'll have to leave. And I'm afraid I won't see him again.*

Joe's musings were similarly directed. While they were immersed in it, their confinement in his apartment had seemed timeless. Or at least as if they'd had all the time in the world.

Yet, during the minutes he'd wasted chasing Mel from kitchen to living room and back again, he could have been proposing dinner that evening. Maybe even have convinced her to go through with their dream-date weekend. Now that the lawsuit wasn't hanging over her head, she might disappear.

"I suppose we ought to get dressed," he said distractedly, aware that, if she wasn't already on the job next door, his secretary would be arriving soon.

On the rare occasions when she arrived at work and he was still puttering around next door in his apartment, Edie Magnuson had been known to rap at his door for a word with him. It probably wouldn't happen. But it could.

Mel put a completely different construction on his words. In her opinion, it sounded as if Joe was going to dismiss her from his life. Just like that. With no promises. No regrets.

An uprush of tears stinging her eyelids, she turned away. The polish bottle was standing on the coffee table where Joe had transferred it and, desperate for an excuse to get away from him for a moment so she could compose herself, she snatched it up.

"I'll just put this back where we found it," she announced, heading for the door that connected the apartment to his office and thence to his secretary's quarters.

If the elevator had been working that morning, as Joe suspected it had, Edie had probably been on the job for several hours. There could be any number of people in the office waiting for him.

"Mel... *don't!*" he exclaimed.

Before he could stop her, she was entering his private sanctum and limping barefoot across its thick carpet with his shirttails swirling provocatively just below her buttocks. Seconds later, she was opening the outer office door.

She stopped short just inside the threshold. To her amazement and consternation, just minutes after the power had come on again, Joe's secretary was seated in front of her word processor, calmly keying in a letter. A man dressed like a construction foreman was waiting patiently in one of the visitor's chairs. To make matters worse, a marketing specialist Mel knew slightly from her days in condo sales had just brought up some sample brochures for Joe's inspection.

None of them looked as if they'd recently climbed twelve flights of stairs.

"W-what is everyone doing here?" she blurted. "Without an elevator..."

Their eyes widening, the three employees turned to stare at her. Joe's secretary was the first to find her voice. "Miss...er, Taylor, isn't it?" she asked in a shocked if perfectly modulated voice. "Perhaps you'll recall, since you used to work here...during a power failure, the electricity in this building is supplied by generator. The elevator's been working since approximately 6:00 p.m. yesterday evening."

It was Mel's turn to stare. Joe had lied to her, just as surely as if he'd told her in so many words that there wasn't any backup system. The *why* of his deception didn't bear thinking about.

Belatedly she became aware of her state of undress. Dear God...what must they think of me? she asked herself, color staining her cheeks as she clutched the front of Joe's shirt together.

There wasn't much doubt about it—Joe's secretary and her two companions had guessed how she and their boss had spent the blackout hours. The talebearing their knowledge would generate could be expected to travel through Ricci & Carbone like wildfire.

Convinced she'd been duped, manipulated, laid open to petty gossip that she was just another in Joe's long line of conquests, Mel had but a single thought. She wanted out. Immediately. To take refuge in her own life as fast as one good leg, an injured one and her crutches could carry her.

My clothes, she thought. My purse.

Awkwardly changing course, she barged back through Joe's private office, bumping into him. Before coming after her, he'd paused to put on a pair of trousers. For some reason, his unwillingness to let his staffers see him in his underwear further infuriated her.

"Get out of my way," she ordered.

Joe was humble. Apologetic. "You're right," he admitted. "I've behaved like an ass. But I had my reasons. If I hadn't..."

In response, Mel pointed one crutch at him like a weapon. "If you don't stand back and let me collect my things, I'm going to scream bloody murder," she threatened.

About to argue with her, Joe stepped aside. There wasn't anything to be gained by creating a scene. If he gave her time to cool down and evaluate what had taken place, maybe he could talk some sense into her.

After the way things had been between them, they had a lot to talk about.

Sensing he wouldn't try to stop her, Mel brushed past him and snatched up her things from the black leather couch where she'd sat on Joe's lap at the end of their poker game. Furiously she met her own eyes in his powder-room mirror as she put on her rumpled sundress and brushed the night's tangles from her curls. He used me, dammit, she thought. Made a pass at me to pass the time. The Windham-Harbor Island Hotel, which was situated next door to his building, would have a phone. She'd call a taxi from there.

Five days later, with the air-conditioning going full blast and the fierce summer heat baking the concrete steps of the riverlanding outside his windows, Joe sat brooding at his desk. Since Mel had stormed out of his apartment and his life the previous Thursday, he hadn't been able to work. Or sleep. None but the most trivial of business functions had been transacted.

He'd tried repeatedly. But he hadn't been able to get hold of her. Each time he dialed her number, he got her answering machine. By now, he knew its breezy, impersonal message by heart.

Doesn't she realize what happened between us is more than casual dalliance? he asked himself. That I want...I want...

What he wanted was both simple and earth-shattering: to marry her and build a life with her.

The thought rocked him back on his heels. Has it finally happened, then? he asked himself in wonderment. Am I really hooked? But he already knew the answer. It had begun filtering into his consciousness when she'd turned up instead of her friend at the vice president's riverfront reception. He'd seen it for what it was when she'd appeared at his office to confront him over the lawsuit. He just hadn't put the realization into so many words.

Now he did. They hadn't known each other long. However, thanks to a quirk of the universe and the blackout it had created, he knew Mel Taylor was the woman for him.

Tilting back in his sleek executive chair, Joe regaled himself with mental images of the life they'd have together. Visions of Mel loving him to distraction put a smile on his face. They'd have children, of course. Two, at least. He pictured picnics in the park, family Christmases. Chubby toddlers with his eyes and her honey-colored hair would fling their arms around his neck.

First he had to get in touch with her—convince her his dream was right for both of them.

It wouldn't be easy. He'd deceived her, no matter how benevolent his motives or how rapturous the result. And he didn't know her place of residence. Since the number her supervisor had given him after her accident was unlisted, obtaining her address from the phone company wasn't an option. Grasping at straws, he'd assigned Todd Algren, a computer-hacking summer intern from the University of South Florida, the task of ferreting it out.

As if summoned by his thoughts, Todd requested a moment of Joe's time via Edie Magnuson's intercom a short time later.

"Send him in," Joe said, hoping against hope.

The skinny, bespectacled intern was beaming as he walked in clutching a page torn from a continuous-form printout. "I found the address you wanted in the darnedest place, Mr. Carbone," he said elatedly. "Though she may not know it because the acquisition notices haven't gone out yet, Melisande Taylor is one of your tenants. She lives in 722-E, Hibiscus Towers, off Fourth Street North in St. Petersburg. That's the complex you bought last month with an eye to expansion and renovation."

Mel was renting from him! The possibilities for effecting a reconciliation were suddenly endless. Thanking Todd and instructing Edie to see that his next paycheck included a substantial bonus, Joe had taken the elevator downstairs and backed his Mercedes out of its customary parking space before picking up the receiver of his mobile phone.

The maintenance man he'd contacted met him by the Hibiscus Towers tennis courts. "Let me get this straight, Mr. Carbone," he said in puzzlement. "You want to test the E-building generator? We can if you want. But like I told you...it didn't give me no trouble during the blackout."

Focused though he was on the prospect of holding Mel in his arms, Joe was both patient and affable. "Humor me, Fred," he replied. "What I'd like you to do is give me sufficient time to get up to the seventh floor, and then pull the switch. Oh, and by the way... before you do, I want you to set the automatic timer on the generator to Pause for five minutes before it begins to operate."

He'd rather have allowed himself twenty. But there were other people in the building to think about.

Scratching his head though he expressed his basic understanding of what was required of him, Fred rode over to E building in Joe's Mercedes. If he wondered about the huge bouquet of yellow roses that lay between them on the elegant leather upholstery, he didn't mention it.

A few minutes later, Joe was rapping on Mel's door. After a slight delay, she opened it.

"*You!*" she exclaimed, attempting to shut it again in his face.

"Not so fast."

Wedging the door open with his foot, Joe managed to push past her into the apartment. It was charming and a trifle bookish, as he'd expected.

"These are for you," he said, thrusting the roses into her hands.

"I don't want them."

"Okay by me. Tell me what you want for an engagement present in addition to the magnificent ring you're going to get. The sky's the limit."

Mel stared. What did he mean, *engagement present?* Was this another strategy to get her to hop into bed with him?

"What I want is for you to leave," she insisted.

As she spoke, the air-conditioning shut off with a sigh. The lamp she'd been using to reread a Dick Francis mystery novel in hopes of suppressing the misery she felt went out. The blades of her ceiling fan drifted lazily to a standstill.

"Looks like another power failure," Joe said. "Solar flares again, do you suppose?"

The circuits in Mel's brain were trucking on overload. "I do not," she shot back. "You engineered this one completely, didn't you? I can't imagine how you got by with it. But I know you did."

He merely grinned at her.

Though it made no sense at all, Mel could feel herself weakening. He was so incorrigible. And he had such a wicked smile, with those little quote marks framing it. She'd been so hungry for the sight of him.

"I want to know how you arranged to strand yourself in my building," she reiterated.

Setting his bouquet aside on her front hall table, Joe gathered her into his arms. "I'm your landlord, babe," he revealed, planting a rapacious but tender kiss on her mouth. "Not to mention the man you're going to marry. Say *yes* and we'll have time to work up a sweat before the power's restored."

His words prompted an involuntary recollection of what they'd done on his balcony together. Like no other she'd experienced, their lovemaking had been both raunchy and spiritual, an amalgam of hunger and helplessness and delight. She also craved his company, as she'd learned to her sorrow the past five days. It's insane, she thought. But I love him. It was reason enough to cooperate.

"Are you . . . really serious about this?" she asked.

Sensing she was ready to capitulate, Joe relieved her of her crutches and swept her off her feet. They were formally engaged and hot in the middle of doing what pleased them best when the power came on again.

"That's the generator," Joe whispered, deepening his possession of her.

Each thrust of his hardness and heat against her most sensitive places caused paradise to expand a little. If she lived to be a hundred, she'd never get enough. "You mean ... there's one ... in this building, too?"

"Mmm-hmm. I had it installed ... two weeks ago. In case I forgot ... to mention it ... I love you."

Abruptly, tremulously, she was at the brink. "Oh, *Joe.* Surely you know ... I love you, too."

Further speech wasn't possible as she dissolved in a paroxym of shudders. Joe followed in seconds, defenseless in his ecstasy as gooseflesh spread over his back and thighs. Their separateness abandoned, they blurred and blended into each other.

The air-conditioning was chilly against their heated skin as Joe pulled up the top sheet on Mel's bed and drew her back into his arms. "Know something?" he said, satisfaction a warm undercurrent in his voice. "I'm glad our Captiva weekend was spoiled, though I'd never have wanted you hurt to bring it about."

As far back as she could remember, Mel had never felt happier. Or more secure. So this is what love is like, she thought. It's wonderful. "Why's that?" she answered contentedly, giving him the cue he wanted.

"Because if it hadn't been, and we'd gone through the motions, we might have taken months to reach this point. That steam bath we endured in my apartment was nothing short of a godsend."

You fashioned it to your own design, she told him silently. Amused and tolerant of his unconventional tactics since they'd resulted in so much bliss, Meg snuggled closer. "You're probably right," she said.

"I *know* I am." Complacently Joe feathered a kiss against her ear. "Do you think your friend would mind," he added, "if we applied her gift to a honeymoon?"

SUZANNE CAREY

I was born in Moline, Illinois, a medium-size town on the Mississippi River, and grew up just down the street from the Highland Theater. Every Saturday afternoon, the latest adventure-romance movies got my imagination going. Throughout the ensuing week, my playmates and I spun out the theme of the latest flick in a drama with our dolls.

I guess you could say I wrote my first novel in high school. The school was co-ed but strict. The librarian even censored *Seventeen* magazine. You can bet there weren't any romance novels on the shelves. I tried to fill the demand by writing (in longhand!) a romantic serial, complete with illustrations. I passed out a chapter per week. I thought it was pretty hot stuff, but what did I know? *Or* my friends? It became an underground sensation!

A year out of high school, I married and started raising a family. But my yearning to write never diminished. When my three children were in school full-time, I began college, majoring in English. I wanted to learn all I could, in order to be a journalist and write novels about man-woman relationships. I graduated Phi Beta Kappa, and loved every moment of my college days.

Because my husband didn't approve of me going back to school or working, ultimately my marriage failed. I was a single mother for a while, working as a newspaper reporter, columnist and magazine editor. I moved to Florida. My children grew up. I dated occasionally but stayed single. Finally, I met the love of my life, Bill Matson, at a Clearwater newspaper.

A retired Air Force colonel, Bill had a second career as a journalist. With him, I finally learned what the songwriter meant when he said, "Don't change a hair for me." Bill loved me exactly as I was, and that's how I loved him. We were independent, individual people, yet so much a part of each other that we were almost the same person. Sadly, he died of cancer three years ago. I still miss him terribly and love him with all my heart.

Four years before we met, I wrote my first novel for Silhouette, *Kiss and Tell*. I've been writing romance novels ever since. The plots come from anywhere and everywhere. I get swept up in them just as I hope you, my readers, do.

When I sit at my computer and write, I feel you and I are very close. Like you, I've known loss, disappointment and uncertainty. I've felt joy come flooding into my life. I can say with conviction—it's out there for every one of us!

Suzanne Carey

**Fifty red-blooded, white-hot, true-blue hunks from
every State in the Union!**

Beginning in May, look for MEN: MADE IN AMERICA!
Written by some of our most popular authors, these stories
feature fifty of the strongest, sexiest men, each from a
different state in the union! Favorite stories by such
bestsellers as Debbie Macomber, Jayne Ann Krentz, Mary
Lynn Baxter, Barbara Delinsky and many, many more!

Plus, you can receive a FREE gift, just for enjoying these
special stories!

You won't be able to resist MEN: MADE IN AMERICA!

Two titles available every other month at your favorite
retail outlet.

**Relive the romance...
Harlequin and Silhouette
are proud to present**

by Request

A program of collections of three complete novels by the most
requested authors with the most requested themes. Be sure to
look for one volume each month with three complete novels by
top name authors.

In June: **NINE MONTHS** Penny Jordan
           Stella Cameron
           Janice Kaiser

**Three women pregnant and alone. But a lot can
happen in nine months!**

In July: **DADDY'S**   Kristin James
           HOME   Naomi Horton
                         Mary Lynn Baxter

**Daddy's Home...and his presence is long
overdue!**

In August: **FORGOTTEN** Barbara Kaye
           PAST   Pamela Browning
                          Nancy Martin

**Do you dare to create a future if you've forgotten
the past?**

Available at your favorite retail outlet.

HARLEQUIN®   Silhouette

REQ-

If you've been looking for something a little bit different,
a little bit spooky, let Silhouette Books take you on
a journey to the dark side of love with

Every month, Silhouette will bring you two romantic,
spine-tingling Shadows novels, written by some of your
favorite authors, such as *New York Times* bestseller
Heather Graham Pozzessere, Anne Stuart, Helen R. Myer
and Rachel Lee—to name just a few.

In May, look for:
FLASHBACK by Terri Herrington
WAITING FOR THE WOLF MOON by Evelyn Vaughn

In June, look for:
BREAK THE NIGHT by Anne Stuart
IMMINENT THUNDER by Rachel Lee

Come into the world of Shadows and prepare
to tremble with fear—and passion....

SHA